When Jerry, an authoritarian professor, meets Cat, a fierce-  ly independent paraplegic woman, some turbulence must be expected, but Nature's excesses make that turbulence look trivial. After the devastating earthquake and amidst widespread hunger, their bid for love looks audacious.

Return to Paradise

Doctor Paul Bronski, pursued by the military counterintel-  ligence on suspicion of stealing an army's secret drug, finds refuge in the community of boaters drifting in the middle of the Pacific. The pretty harbormaster, Grace, has her own reasons to avoid the authorities. When she and Paul fall in love, their problems multiply. Can these determined individuals escape the strangling embrace of the state? It depends …

Woman on the Moon

Doctor Morrison is fired as a husband, father and  doctor. What's going to happen next? Quiet philosophy reading, alcoholism and—finally—suicide look like his future until a weird old man lures him into a dubious intrigue. The fountain of youth, an exotic woman and love for a child draw the doctor deeper and deeper into the Darien jungle, where his morals break one after another.

Demon of Darien

Shark of Waikiki

by

Alex Modzelewski

Vagabond Works
Kailua, Hawaii

Shark of Waikiki

This is a work of fiction. Names, characters, places and
events are the product of the author's imagination
 or are used fictiously.
Any resemblance to actual persons, living or dead,
events, or locales is entirely coincidental.

Vagabond Works
48 Kailua Road, Kailua, Hawaii
http://www.Vagabondworks.com

ISBN 978-0-9815183-5-0

For Ania,
who just wanted to laugh.

ACKNOWLEDGMENTS

This book has been reviewed by
Jean Nowak and Gene Parola, two friends
who offered many suggestions leading to its current form.
Their contribution is gratefully acknowledged.

Chapter 1

Doc trable. Shark busted. Come quik. FBI!!!

The message scribbled on a narrow scrap of paper, apparently torn off an envelope, was not getting any clearer as I rubbed my swollen eyes. I smoothed the paper, folded five times like an origami, to uncover some additional letters hiding in the wrinkles. But even pressed with an iron, the note remained cryptic.

A big red eyeball, magnified by a fishbowl, was glowing at me like a vat of molten metal, adding to my grumpy bewilderment. The pigeon's malevolent eye glared while his beak kept banging arrogantly onto the plywood. "Wake up, you God-damned-quack!" Caudillo seemed to yell at me across the aquarium, "ES URGENTE!"

The fog still lingering in the valleys of my brain started lifting under his assault. I threw a blanket over the cage and the glowing eyeballs lost their glare immediately. They shut down a moment later. Caudillo just could not help it; darkness sent him into deep catatonia within seconds.

I started to analyze the message delivered in a little

pouch attached to the pigeon's leg. I could guess its author. Certainly, Shark, who wrote eloquent but very up-to-the-point messages that never exceeded three words, did not write this note. It had to be Mele, Shark's woman of a few months standing. This six-foot-tall girl with the shoulders of a Bulgarian weightlifter stepped into my friend's life when, panicked by the horrifying consequences of his love life, he was trashing aimlessly around Keehi like a big muscle-bound tuna on a boat's deck. Mele brought a semblance of order—with a war club if necessary—where mindless anarchy reigned for so many years.

That Shark might be in a lawful custody did not shock me. His appearance alone could prompt a recent police academy graduate to draw his service weapon and put Kamekona under arrest on weapons charges. He looked more dangerous than the battleship Missouri meekly chained in Pearl Harbor like an aging junkyard dog.

At least, such had been my impression six months earlier when I met him for the first time on the Keehi Lagoon shore. I was just walking away from the Harbor Master's office, closed again due to some obscure Hawaiian holiday, where I wished to protest the eviction notice for non-payment of my boat slip fee. How do they find those deficiencies so efficiently, I wanted to ask, if they never seem to be open and working. Faced by a metal door, barred and secured with a big padlock, I could only relieve my frustration by spitting into the shimmering water and incanting a well-suited string of profanities.

As I was passing the M-dock, still a hundred yards short of *Magic Carpet's* berth, something unnatural registered in my peripheral vision, sending my heart in a gallop. Like a hawk's shadow falling on the ground in front of a chicken, it triggered a dollop of adrenaline even before I could realize what alarmed me.

Six feet above the water table, I saw two humongous bare feet and above them a pair of unbelievably muscular calves dangling in the air. My eyes followed up to reveal the megalith figure slumped on top of a fat concrete pylon anchoring the dock. The stature was slumped in the Rodin's "Thinker" position. I was facing the huge dark-brown back crowned with massive shoulders and flanked by arms whose triceps bulged like a cruise ship's shore ties. The creature's face, turned to the ocean, was despondently cradled in its open hands.

A monument! The colossus of Keehi! The alarming thought rang in my head. The State of Hawaii promised to do something about the pathetic condition of its small boat ports … and this is their solution!

But the legs were moving, the heels slowly banging against the concrete. As I inched toward the water edge to sneak a look from the front, the handsome face with a pair of big, black and very sad eyes turned toward me without a word.

"What's up, man?" I started hesitantly. "You comfy there? You might break a nail if you slip of this bar stool."

"Dead anyway," Hercules confessed. Then he added in a strangled painful whisper, "AIDS." His face hid again in his palms.

Oh, man! It … like struck me across the face. No human body is strong enough to resist the wretched silent killer. But my professional optimism kicked in.

"You know, AIDS is a nasty disease … but it can be treated now. I am a doctor; we can talk about it. But you have to come down."

His black eyes swept me with slight interest and he nodded. I prudently stepped back, so that a few hundred pounds of his body wouldn't fall on me as he scrambled down the pylon. But the colossus confidently jumped off and landed on the wooden dock where it was attached to the concrete embankment. A sunbaked board cracked in the middle but stayed in place, held by rusty nails.

"Kamekona," he said and timidly extended his hand, not sure if I would touch the condemned man. "Sometimes, they call me Shark." He smiled shyly.

"Chris," I said, grabbing his spade-size but amazingly delicate hand. Admittedly, I experienced some trepidation because his grip could put my extremity into a plaster cast for a month. But his touch was gentle. I was like a pat down executed by an airport security agent, the possibility of a severe discomfort understood but unrealized.

We sat down side by side on a pile of concrete slabs in the shade of a restroom building nearby.

There is no doctor—medical, naturopathic or of the witch variety— who is not bummed for a free consultation at least once a week. Medical boards hate it. Doctors despise it—as such advice carries a significant possibility of making an ass of yourself—but … it just comes with a territory.

A black tie dinner or a chicken wings bar—the locale changes but the routine remains the same.

The clue to a successful bar stool consultation is to get to heart of the problem immediately. Get the inquirer to stammer out her question, nod the head wisely once or twice, perhaps take a sip from a glass or blow a few rings of smoke. Then give a piece of your mind. One piece and one piece only. The first idea that seems reasonable at the moment—under circumstances that might include mild alcohol intoxication—must do. In fact, that's all that the inquirer expects.

A differential diagnosis or listening to the patient's grousing concerning the emotional problems caused by her spouse—all this brain-straining work belongs rightfully to a regular doctor, during his or her office hours. A possible exception to the rule could be made only if the whole enquiry is a scam, a ploy invented by a frivolous partyer who simply wants to screw with you, an event more frequent than the American Medical Association cares to admit.

The essence of Kamekona's problem fell right into this framework. His love-appendage started burning like hell when he pissed, and to make things worse, it dripped some fluid that looked to my patient like "this shit that comes on top of cottage cheese, when you leave it too long in a fridge." He astutely connected his symptoms with the quick but passionate love making that had taken place in the *wahine* portion of the very facility our backs were resting against.

"AIDS," he had concluded and decided to wait for the inevitable at his favorite place. High up on the pylon, he could take in most of his beloved Keehi Lagoon, caressed by a gentle breeze. Undisturbed, he watched life flowing below his feet, no passerby aware of the tragedy happening above. He looked over motorboats getting ready for a tuna hunt, coughing out smoke from their cold and damp motors. Sailors washed their yachts and dried fluttering canvass never feeling his loving eyes. Sunburned bums paraded through the gravel parking lot, fishing rod in one hand, a brown-bagged bottle in the other, not knowing they were the last witnesses of his days. The world kept grinding on in its usual way, even as his penis was rotting away.

To the jaded ear of an emergency room doc, his problem indeed fell into the general field of sexually transmitted diseases, but I strongly favored gonorrhea over HIV as the source of his misery.

"Clap?" The giant looked at me with disbelief, but his eyes were already losing this lead-dull glint of despair. "Do they still have *clap*? I thought AIDS was all there's now!"

His hope reborn, Kamekona easily agreed to go to the free clinic in Waikiki. Hell, he would gladly put his sorry member into some knowledgeable hand, if that could take care of the pesky burning. And having his premature death sentence commuted would surely beat sitting on his perch. Now, with the promise of his life renewed, Kamekona declared he had to go to Waikiki anyway. He was supposed to teach tourists the art of surfing in front of the Waikiki Sheraton.

As it always happens when a nose is being stuck in someone else's business, there were consequences to face. For my modest involvement into his affairs, Kamekona gave me full credit for saving his life and so adopted me as his friend.

For the benefit of mainland readers unfamiliar with Hawaiian customs, I have to state clearly that being a *kanaka*'s friend is not something to be taken lightly. It is not a simple social commitment in a *haole*'s understanding of the word, the kind of obligation that can be easily discharged by knocking off a few beers together once a week. This ritual is important, of course, but it does not even touch on the meaning of friendship in Hawaiian sense.

For Kamekona and his ilk, a friend is someone perhaps more important than a brother. After all, you cannot chose your brother and a miscreant lousy sibling may happen in every family. Nothing one can do about it but acknowledge graciously the blood ties without losing face and temper.

Friends, on the other hand; friends you choose. You must select them carefully because your friend's problem becomes your own predicament. You are up to your eyeballs in it, hundred percent, without ifs or buts, until the problem clears one way or another. A friend can take you to some nifty places or drag you under the ice, if such a metaphor is allowable in Hawaii. Your fate and his destiny are spliced together like fibers in a coconut husk rope, intimately and inseparably.

This understanding of friendship prompted Mele to tie the message to Caudillo's leg when, in her opinion, Shark's head had disappeared under waves of the legal system for a tad too long.

Chapter 2

Last night's shift, the unending stream of bigger and smaller disasters converging at the Queen's emergency room, screeched to a grudging stop only when my replacement, another ER doc, arrived. As soon as he crossed his heart, taking over my collection of Honolulu nightlife victims, now slumbering in their stalls, I dashed to the exit door.

Across the cavernous waiting hall smelling of pain and anxiety as much as of a disinfectant I stumbled out into the blinding sunshine. The trees in front of the hospital, like the rest of creation in Hawaii, seemed to be obsessed with one thing only—procreation. A soon as I took a big breath of the fresh pollen-laden air, I was gripped by a fit of uncontrollable sneezing. Half-blinded, rubbing my itchy eyes furiously, I eventually spotted the dented bumper of my Honda at the parking lot and found refuge in its air-conditioned cabin. Twenty minutes later, I keeled over into my bed and remained there perfectly unconscious until Caudillo started his racket, holding sacred his duty of mail delivery.

He did not calm down for a second until I squeezed my body behind the aquarium, cunningly placed between the apartment's front door and the cage to frustrate prying eyes. He suspended his clamor for a moment, like a toddler taking a deep breath before he carries on with his tantrum, when I reached for a small wire-mesh door. It opened with a squeak and, groping inside the cage, I relieved Caudillo of his red message pouch. I almost could hear him exhale with relief. But even then, he watched me carefully to ensure I open the message. Vigilant not to let me fall asleep, he was all ready to resume his fuss without delay until the blanket darkened the cage and shut down his senses.

According to one Keehi myth—and it could have originated with Shark looking for a commercial angle before he decided to gift the pigeon to me—the bird was a direct-line descendant of Argentina's reigning mail pigeon champ. Therefore, I assumed Spanish was his native language and he never let me believe otherwise.

How the precious Caudillo's mama had found her way to Keehi I did not know. She was a resident of the decrepit sailing boat my friend had won in the game of poker. One day she vanished, possibly murdered by a cat, leaving a tiny chick in Kamekona's tender hands.

Despite lack of any hard data, I was inclined to believe the pigeon's lineage. The little bastard had arrogance bred into his nature as much as his homing instinct. Even if it didn't register in his tiny brain, Caudillo's aristocratic pedigree had to be encoded in his DNA in big golden letters. He clearly knew his place in history and God help anyone who forgot it. Even I, his food provider, his landlord and the doting nanny during his fledgling weeks, could be allowed only so much slack.

I could not guess the exact chronology of Shark's arrest because Caudillo habitually flew out of his cage at the crack of dawn, when I was either hard asleep or hard at work. Then he would return home shortly before the sun disappeared behind the Barber's point on Oahu's western tip. He stuck to his timetable as rigidly as a shifts scheduler at the Queen's Medical Center Emergency Room where I worked.

But, despite our different lifestyles, we worked out a satisfactory solution to the potentially troublesome co-habitation. In fact, Kamekona devised it, feeling responsible for cramming the pigeon into my bachelor pad under the guise of a friendship gift. The three-day old chick could hardly stay alone on the vessel as his master trawled the back alleys of Waikiki, frequently an absentee owner for a few days and nights in a row. I had to agree with this argument and accepted the small gray furry ball as a tenant.

The next day, Shark brought a glass-cutting implement to my apartment and, before I could make a squeak of protest, he deftly outlined a six-inch circle in my window. Then he gently hit the pane with his elbow and a disk of glass exploded outside, leaving behind a hole and a fifteen-inch crack running through the glass, irregular like a frozen thunderbolt.

"Good," he assured me. "The super can't see it from the street. Just don't let him in."

We moved the cage so that its entrance touched the newly produced opening, transforming it into a comfortable—if small—pigeon loft. I positioned a big glass bowl—where my samurai fighting fish lived—on the table in front of the cage and, as long as I kept the super at the door, we were safe from accusations of unauthorized pet keeping, as well as charges of property damage.

A few days later, the chick—much bigger now than his initial ping-pong ball size—felt his oats, which I served soaked in water and enriched with crumbs of boiled eggs remaining from my breakfast. He stepped up to his window on the world and stood there for a few minutes, swaying slowly, hysterically clutching the cage's wire frame with his feet. After making a few fake, halfhearted head-lounges through the hole in the window, his fledgling wings tentatively stretching, Caudillo finally closed his eyes and made a suicidal jump forward.

I cannot be sure about his eyes closing, but I hoped he did, because he fell like a rock and for a moment it had to be a terrifying experience. He immediately dropped out of my sight, but by the time I could open another window and look down, he was gone. I was happy to see no gray-white-and-red splash on the pavement below. He nonchalantly clambered back through his hole in the late afternoon and gave me a mocking look, knowing fully well of my frantic dash to the window. Hysterical parents, he thought.

Caudillo never had much to say, so all I could deduce was that Mele had to trap him in Keehi as he was hanging around with the gang of common low-life pigeons, wasting his aristocratic wild oats on unqualified females. Mele's action could have taken place anytime today, between the pigeon's morning arrival at the lagoon and his late afternoon departure. His routine was inviolable. Not only did I respect his peculiar attachment to this timeframe, rigid like a crowbar, but Shark and I forged a private message system based on it.

Good communication is a foundation on which friendship can blossom, and here we had a problem. Kamekona did not own a computer to send me e-mail. In fact, his electric power supply consisted of an old car battery charged by the boat's archaic wind generator for the benefit of nighttime TV watching on his small black-and-white set. Sadly, windless days—apparently not that rare on Oahu's south shore— drove him into the multitude of boredom-driven bad behaviors, which Mele had to eradicate later with the power and endurance of a woodcutter clearing a primeval forest. It occurred to me once that Shark's decision to bring Mele into his life, and on board of his boat as a full-timer, had to have been taken in a bout of desperation during one of those windless evenings.

Unfortunately, Shark was not a citizen of the digital global village. This created a problem because my preferred channel of telecommunication is e-mail. Actually, this statement needs to be strengthened. I refuse to answer any gadget that might require an instantaneous response. I wear no chain someone could jerk. I do not carry a cell phone and stay away from fixed-line telephones. A telemarketer, the hospital's administrator and everyone in between them, all may send me e-mails, which I will answer whenever my time and mood allow. Of course, I have to wear a hospital-issue box at work, but once out of my emergency room … the only workable distance messaging would be yelling, "Hey, you!" after me.

My dislike of phones might have something to do with the abuse I suffered as a medical resident. During those few years of savage slavery, anyone who had a finger felt fully authorized to interrupt those measly few hours of sleep allowed to me once in a while. A phone buzzing had become the most detested sound of my life.

Not anymore. An emergency room doc *is* an island in the midst of humanity. I lower my communication drawbridge judiciously, as needed. No incidental traffic, please.

"Be a surgeon, good money," my mother implored. "Maybe a plastic surgeon," she added, looking into the mirror, pulling back her facial skin with fingers draped around her ears.

But I already knew better. Slaves, I thought with contempt. Once you touch a patient with a scalpel, you become his or her indentured peon—day or night, practically forever. They can call you five years later, claiming that this scar seems to be a tad too long. Well, it's almost three millimeters longer than the one on her sister-in-law, and she had the same operation! And if you, the surgeon, are not properly impressed with the complaint and profoundly contrite, her lawyer will track you down anywhere, even as you float in a canoe down the Amazon River.

Maybe it is OK for the right person but I didn't want to be anyone's slave, no matter how rich it could make me. I became an emergency room physician, working my clearly defined shifts and completely free once I stepped out through the door. This attitude might have something to do with my ancestors' obsession with personal liberty, which for generations extended right to the border of anarchy, and occasionally crossed it. But … since I have a few surgeons in my family, maybe it's my own mental quirk.

Thus Kamekona and I were stranded in communication channels that were unlikely to connect. The solution we discovered was low-tech but worked with amazing reliability. Caudillo's rigid commuting schedule between my apartment and Keehi Lagoon offered the unfailing method of passing messages attached to his leg. Just like e-mail, I wondered in awe, taking a tiny pouch of the pigeon's scaly leg. Every time I found a short, concise message spelling on a scrap of paper when and where the next round of our brotherly beer drinking would take place.

"Ala Wai. Seven," my friend would write.

"No can do. Sund." I would answer, feeling confident I would find him sitting on the edge of a floating dock, brown bag in his hand, on Sunday.

Shark figured it out very well.

But this time, the message was urgent, the fact underscored by a bright red plastic ribbon wrapped around Caudillo's leg. The precise timeframe of the event was not the only mystery. No matter how I strained my imagination, I could not figure out the acronym FBI. *Female Body Inspector* or *From Big Island* could come from Kamekona's repertoire of jests, but Mele was strict and stern like a fishery inspector. This was not her kind of a joke.

The *real* FBI? Why would they have any interest in Shark? There was not one plausible reason I could come up with. The Honolulu Police Department or a private hotel security—yeah, I could create a bunch of possible scenarios without breaking sweat, but the FBI? I drew a blank. There was only one thing I could do. I had to go to Keehi and see the situation for myself. Fortunately, the next day was my day off, a potentially important and convenient coincidence, if my intervention required more than a short visit.

Chapter 3

Nimitz Highway was constipated as usually at this time of day. Every office door in Honolulu slammed at the same time as, in effort to beat the traffic, workers rushed out to a hundred of multistory garages. They cranked their motors, spun the wheels and shot out on the streets, leaving behind the odor of burnt rubber, in a perfectly synchronized move. Once the small street tributaries channeled them into the big rivers of H1 Highway and Nimitz, the traffic calmed down. The ripples of a brisk traffic flow smoothed into a quiet mudslide inching to the west through a five-lane ditch. Now, everybody could finally relax and listen to some romantic, slack guitar tunes.

Only past the Sand Island Road intersection, could I gun the motor in a dramatic display of my rush to the rescue, but by then I was almost at Keehi. A few guys were sitting at the public boat ramp, taking refreshments from paper-wrapped bottles while fish ignored their plastic bates. I rolled up in front of the shuttered Harbormaster's office and its empty parking lot. Crawling along the shoreline toward my own slip, I passed entrances to a few piers—no sign of Mele, Shark or anybody else.

Live-aboard people were still cooking or eating on their boats, while the night brigade, the ladies dedicated to the business of carnal pleasures, had not arrived yet. The concrete strip along the shore looked abandoned. I parked my Honda at the road's end, on the gravel parking near my catamaran's slip.

Magic Carpet, which I had cleaned just two days ago, was covered with a thick layer of fine powder originating from both the concrete plant upwind and the nearby boatyard, where someone was still grinding his wreck with a power tool, filling the air with angry shrieks of abused plastic. Seeing the dust deposit undisturbed like fresh snow, I knew that no human foot had stepped on my deck recently. Apparently, Mele had not stopped by and, indeed, I found no messages on board.

On to *Water Whisper*, Shark's hideout, then, I decided. This would not be as simple as a walk or a drive, though. Since Kamekona's famous four queens had beaten Rattlesnake Bruce's four valets, Shark elected to lead the life of a boating gentleman, leaving behind the many attractions of Waikiki's back alleys. Perhaps he got tired of female tourists taking a double breath when their alcohol-dimmed eyes fell on his heroic chest. Or maybe it was the constant commotion and never dimming lights of big hotels. Whatever it was, his appreciation of Waikiki's glamour took a downturn. Given the opportunity of a simpler life at the Keehi Small Boat Harbor, Shark became a boatman. There was gossip at the marina that Kamekona had had a falling out with the cops incessantly trawling the tourist strip, but I did not know him then and he did not like to reminisce about his big city times.

Whatever it was, his decision to move to Keehi had been made the moment he threw his queens on top of Rattlesnake's valets. As the loser's right hand went searching for something in his pocket, Shark slapped his vice-like grip onto Bruce's left wrist. Turning white and sweaty, the poor man stopped making any menacing noises or gestures. He promptly took his shame somewhere else, a logical step considering he just had gambled away his crash pad.

Due to his mean, pockmarked face, as well as his ability to put on a scary bluff, Bruce had a significant following in Keehi, but after this poker game, the lagoon's political landscape changed irrevocably. There were some musings—mumbled discreetly under one's breath—that a figure as big as Kamekona's would present a great, hard-to-miss target for a bullet. A blade might need to be a bit longer than usual, some other jokers ruminated, but those big muscles offered no special protection for internal organs. In the end, though, no one was ready to put these hypotheses to the test. Rattlesnake moved to Guam, reportedly, to establish his new fiefdom there.

I unlocked the chain holding my kayak at the dock, took a paddle from my trunk and pushed off toward the dark patch of mangroves which—growing on a small island outside the harbor's jurisdiction—was free of official harassment and remained unencumbered by fees or any other financial burdens. Hidden behind dense vegetation, *Water Whisper* was basking in the last rays of the setting sun, her mast playfully wagging at me above the mangroves.

As I turned around the sandbar, a bright yellow sphere of light came into my view, hanging at the aft end of the boat's dark mass. It was benevolently illuminating the heartwarming scene of two people engrossed in intimate conversation, while hiding the ugliness of rotting plywood and rusty sheet metal patches in the deepening darkness. For many years, since before Shark was but a little minnow, the boat's original components have been slowly replaced with any materials the owner of the day could put his hands on.

A huge reclining black figure lowered its head onto a lap of another dark shade, D-size boobs overhanging his face.

"Oh, what da fuck? What you need me for? Something kinky on your mind?" I whined from my kayak below.

"Oh, Doc, good thing you come!" Mele pushed Kamekona's head away and moved to the gunwale to take my painter.

"I thought you were in the FBI dungeon ..." I started my investigation sourly, looking into Shark's serenely relaxed face. I had had a very promising shot at having my head on a female lap myself that evening, and I had selflessly canceled it. Mele and Shark had better have a good reason to drag me here and interfere with my mental health.

"FBI for real," Mele assured me, handing me over a bottle of warm beer. The luxury of cold beverages did not extend to this temple of domestic pleasures unless Mele had the wherewithal to bring a bag of ice from her Foodland. "So I watch Shark work with this *wahine* in the water and see this little pipsqueak on the beach. ..."

Since Mele had acquired claim on Shark, she kept

him under surveillance most of the time, even as he was teaching tourists to surf a hundred feet offshore. Can't be too careful with such hot property.

"So he keep his eyes on Shark like a *poi dog* on *da grind*," Mele continued, visibly agitated. "I see this sick-looking *haole* woman to paw Shark and da pipsqueak make face like he bit one lemon." She casted an accusatory look at Kamekona, who shrugged with the power of innocence. Work!

"So I watch him, thinking: *mahu* in love, or what? But I just keep watching. Shark come back to beach with this mainland lady and she drag him by hand to book another lesson. She be sweeping da beach she had da bloody tail!" Mele again gave Kamekona a sharp look.

"And then da little guy get up and go away. Three minutes later, a uniform come up …"

"And he tell me," Shark cut in excitedly, "I'm wanted for being a … public *newsence*. 'Are you *loco*?" I say. I had no problems with no cop since this *lolo bugah* they brought from da mainland wanted stick me fo' pissing on da sand. What, was night! Anyways, he now back to he come from, mainland."

Shark demonstrated his outrage then went on with the story. " 'Sorry Shark', da cop say. 'I know you good guy. But someone wants to talk with you. Don't give us no trouble, eh?' "

"So we go to this car in front of da Royal Hawaiian. Parked like shit, a mile long line backed up behind'im." Shark demonstrated the distance from *Water Whisper* to the lonely light shining now at the public ramp.

"The door opens and a small skinny guy shows for me to step in. I put my ass on the seat and he tells the driver, 'Go!' "

Kamekona turned at me his big black eyes wide in disbelief. "Where?" I yelled, and I grabbed the driver by his neck. And this fucking shrimp tasered me! And when I was trashing in the car he put cuffs on me!"

A rather dramatic story emerged from Shark's report, which suggested that some important guy at the FBI office wanted to have a conversation with him, but due to the skinny agent's nervousness, the invitation—probably intended to be polite—turned into an adrenalin-soaked kidnapping.

Even in handcuffs, Shark was a pretty destructive force, and I could clearly see why the person responsible for safety had serious qualms about unleashing him in their facility. A young guy, probably the lowest ranking in the detachment, nervously un-cuffed my friend in The Government Building, as his three colleagues stood at the ready with their Tasers drawn.

The bottom line was that after hours of holding him in an empty room, swearing, puffing and promising sudden death to all the participants in this escapade, they released him late at night. The big fish apparently decided that Shark's current state of mind was not conducive to any cooperation. On his way out, as he was passing the anxious group crowded at the door, he was told that someone would be in touch.

"And I break his neck," Shark promised. He slept the balance of the night in the bushes and showed his face in Keehi in the morning, after Mele had already stalked down Caudillo and put a message on his leg.

My own sexual frustration aside, I was glad Mele contacted me. Breaking an FBI agent's neck could not be the right answer to Shark's problem, no matter how liberating it might feel to his ruffled soul. The basic question remained unanswered; what—in God's name—the FBI might want from Shark?

Obviously, he was not a suspect in some heinous federal crime. They let him go without even a sham interrogation, as though someone had bungled the job so badly that it needed to be started from scratch. I saw such cases in my own field, after a bunch of medical interns screwed something royally. Does the FBI even have interns? I didn't know.

"Maybe it's something about my TV here." Kamekona pointed at a small portable set, made before Japanese had figured out which way a transistor goes into a box. "If the rabbit ears are set just right, we can catch ABC.

"Mele loves "Dancing with Stars" but generally signal's pretty shitty here in Keehi. Not like in Waikiki. All those antennas and dishes at the airport ... or maybe Pearl Harbor ... who knows?

"But sometimes ... it's like heavy rain ... can't see a thing ... and then a rocket come out among palm trees! Quite clearly! Barking Sounds on Kauai? China? North Korea? Who da hell know? But maybe they think I steal their signal? My cousin in Waimanalo had problems when they found out he hooked up to his neighbor's cable. But that only because he hooked up to the power line as well, and how could I do such a thing here?" He looked melancholically around the black water.

He was right. There was no electric line within a few hundred yards radius.

"You have something, Shark ..." I ventured. "Something they want ... but they can't take it without your cooperation."

Mele grabbed the boat's railing in panic, ready to protect her homestead with her life if necessary.

"I don't think so, Mele." I turned my head with doubt. "They have enough of their own tubs over there," I waved over toward Pearl Harbor. "We have no bloody idea what they want, but they will let you know soon, as they said. The important thing is not to break anyone's neck before we find out what it's all about."

"Just a figure of speech," Kamekona shrugged, his eyes shining with the law-abiding fervor, quiet pride and humble acceptance of this violent world. "Course I let them do da talking. If I have something they want …" he looked around his boat with puzzlement, "they can have it … for a price." I thought that a sudden flicker of greed flashed in his coal-black gaze, but he lowered his eyelids with an innocent smile.

"Kilika," Mele insisted on calling me my Hawaiian name, "but you must be here when they come to see Shark. Maybe, at least, they won't zap him with this cattle prod again. If he no talk to them without you, they will have to get you. Al Pacino never talk to anyone without his *consiglieri* …" she said with authority. "And he's a redhead … and your beard is kinda red, too," she added.

That did it. Considering the color of my facial hair, I had to agree to be Shark's *consiglieri* in his dealings with the FBI. But anyway, I would never turn down my brother-friend's request.

Chapter 4

"You don't have the dimmest idea who Kamekona is," Lala declared, carefully observing the bright-red nail polish drying on her left toes. Comfortably reclined on my bed, her right knee bent at ninety degree to support her left foot, she kept the tiny brush pointed at the ready for the last touch of perfection. Fully naked, Lala displayed the majestic innocence of a beautiful animal grooming herself in a moment of contend relaxation.

"He hoodwinked you into taking seriously this cartoon character he puts up as his front. In fact, he is a smart guy who has figured out exactly how to get what he wants." Lala switched her legs and started working on her right toes, now pointing them into my eyes.

"I met him three years ago, before his conversion into this clown, Waikiki Shark. He was a great surfer and a really good outrigger paddler, a waterman—as we say here. You saw him on the water, no matter if he was surfing or paddling an outrigger or just wading in the shallow, you knew he was part of the ocean, an awe-aspiring creature, a real shark, not this Waikiki joker."

Lala's toes shining like fireflies in the subdued light

of my apartment, she carefully screwed the brush into its jar. "But, I must admit, his guise works like a dream," she added. "The Honolulu Chamber of Commerce should give him a prize of some sort for promoting the Polynesian Dream. He does an exceptional job. Unfortunately, I suspect he might have recently started believing his own hoax. Even his English deteriorated to make him more of a Mythical Native Hawaiian."

"Why would he lie to me?" What Lala said was quite a revelation to me. In fact, I did see Kamekona as kind of a noble Last Mohican, reaching out to me, a white explorer, with an offering of peace and friendship. I felt a wave of irritation rising. Having been exposed to my patients' selective memories at the emergency room a lot, I considered myself a fairly astute judge of prevarications. And now Shark comes with his little joke to upset my self-esteem.

"Oh—" Lala noticed my hurt look. She stretched her brown arm covered with soft transparent hair to stroke my cheek. "I'm sure he is your friend! But maybe he wants you to discover his real personality on your own; perhaps you must prove to him that you can look through this silly disguise of Waikiki Shark."

She turned on her belly and rolled into the patch of daylight filtered through the samurai's aquarium. Like an expensive sport car, her body was two-toned, mostly deep brown except for the pink-white middle section. We are not talking here of a small bikini triangle with two narrow strips for bra strings. Lala's brown body ended abruptly at the waistline and did not reappear until the middle of her thighs. Her beach time —and she had a lot of it— was not spent working on her tan; she was a professional, hardworking, kick-ass defender of marine creatures. Her shorts, even if they were a bit skimpy, were her uniform.

I didn't need to worry about her wonderfully full bottom—even though its image kept returning to my mind frequently—being ravaged by melanoma, carcinoma or any other skin cancer. It was pink and safe, protected by khaki fabric, and I found that reassuring.

"What is the hardest question one must answer in order to have a successful life?" the bare-bottomed philosopher asked rhetorically. Without waiting for my answer, which would probably not fit into her argument anyway, she declared: "The question is this: what do you really want of your life?'

"Not now!" She caught a grin on my face and swiped away my hand creeping toward her pink section. "Kamekona has it all figured out. He wants to surf all day and play his ukulele at night. And believe it or not, he writes his own lyrics for his songs. So if he tries to make you believe he is illiterate, he is pulling a woolen cap over your eyes.

"But surfing all day and playing ukulele at night is not the lifestyle of a diesel mechanic, which he was when I first met him. Once they flew him in to Midway to fix a power generator that was giving my father hard time. He worked all day until the problem was fixed, didn't even have time for a dip in the lagoon. Next morning he was gone, without as much as a swim, never mind a few surfing runs. And I don't think he got rich on that contract.

"But now, converted into this caricature of a beach boy, he lives his dream. Women in Waikiki can't get enough of his muscles and he can make as much money off them as he wants. As long as he is not too greedy, he has all the time in the world to surf and play his ukulele. A genius, don't you think?"

"Sounds reasonable," I agreed. "But why play this game with me? I think he really wants us to be friends."

"Ah, human mind games … who understands those?" Lala reached for her t-shirt. "I'll stick to my monk seals; they really make more sense. Maybe he wants to see how long it will take you to see through this dumb mainland stereotype?"

Lala wiggled into her shorts and zipped them up. She bent over and kissed me softly. "Call me from the hospital after your shift," she said. "Maybe we will have breakfast together … if you are not too tired."

"Just as well you sleep here and I would wake you up …" I tried, but she just smiled and turned her head.

"Socializing and mating, that's what seals come ashore for," she said, like many times before. "But we live our lives in the wild."

This alien creature from Midway Atoll kept her *human* needs and routines private, or at least well separated from her animal desires that I was invited to play a role in.

I first met Lala in mid-December, a year ago. She was flown in from Midway with a nasty, rugged wound on her lower leg. Apparently, she had been thrown onto a reef by a big wave while trying to rescue a seal pup entangled into an old fishing net. I cleaned her wound, put some loose sutures to approximate the jagged edges and set her up for a follow up with the Queen's surgical clinic.

Two months later, an exotic looking woman in khaki shirt and shorts, her skin tanned into a coffee color and her hair sun-bleached into the shade of white, was waiting for me on the bench in front of my condo. I did not recognize her but she took my hand and said, "I'm Lala. You stitched my leg a few months ago. I am back in Honolulu for a while. By the way, Doctor Gorny, I do not consider you my doctor anymore. But I liked the touch of your hands."

As my marine biologist friend would say, we mated that day like two seals in estrous season, without a single rational thought, hungrily as though we might have no other opportunity in our lives. It was the longest, most passionate and sweetest love making of my life. I had taken the bait, hook, line and the rest of gear. Since that day, I have been always on a lookout for more.

Lala is certainly a very unorthodox woman and I found her thinking refreshingly different from any of my previous bedmates. I felt more wanted than ever, however she was anything but clingy. As I was trying to get closer to this extravagant person, out of curiosity among other things, I was being gently pushed away.

"Who's supposed to be a non-committal cockroach here?" I kept asking frustrated by her elusive attitude. "Don't you have dreams of a white gown and a house with a picket fence?"

But Lala steadfastly kept me locked up in the "mammal male" compartment. "I like your smell too," she confessed, when we woke up from a slumber on the first day of our relationship. Sometimes I wondered if Caudillo felt about me the same way.

Lala visited me almost daily—enthusiastically, I would say—while she was in Honolulu, but she kept disappearing for weeks, even a month. Whenever she got a contract from the NOAA or the University of Hawaii, she travelled to Midway Atoll. As a matter of fact, if a rich person woke up one day, thinking how good it feels to spend a few bucks on monk seals or green turtles or spinner dolphins in the Northwestern Islands, she would be available to help disperse his donation at a moment's notice.

Those trips were disturbing me more and more. The first few days were not too bad. I would have a beer with Kamekona, clean my boat and reorganize my wardrobe of four Aloha shirts and three pairs of long pants. But toward the end of the second week, I would start fantasizing about taking my boat, *Magic Carpet*, to cruise the archipelago with Lala. During the days she could watch over her marine friends while I was watching her. After the sunset we would curl together on *Magic Carpet* to check if my boat's deck could compete with beaches for socializing.

Chapter 5

A migraine episode with loss of vision, a nasty asthma attack, a bean in the kid's nose—usual emergencies kept me on my toes 'til 1 am, when I could finally withdraw to the staff room to sit down for a moment and eat my sandwich. I was still somewhat annoyed with the ease with which Kamekona had taken me in, but the humorous aspect of his performance was not lost on me. I would play along to see who breaks first. A diesel mechanic and a poet, eh?

I could recognize a gleam of my own instincts in his peculiar philosophy; maybe that's why we liked to hang out together.

"Work will make you free," my father quoted Goethe, whenever I complained about the tyranny of high school in my sophomore year.

Since he was occasionally right, I had found myself a job. Before going to school, I cooked donuts in boiling oil. Angry searing grease shot quick, unpredictable fountains whenever a cockroach galloped through the bakery's floor, and often without any possible cause. I was getting up at four o'clock, twice a week, for less than a minimum wage. I lived this American dream for a few weeks, tending to dozens of small burns on my hands and arms, but finally I confronted my father.

"This is freedom?" I whined. "It's worse than being in prison. There, at least you can sleep 'til six."

"Ah," he said with a clever grin. "This quote is not a full idea; it's just the beginning and quite misleading at that. Why do you think the Nazis put it on the gate of a concentration camp? You must work, of course. But as long as you have a boss, you are not free. There is no way around it."

He went back to his newspaper, but looking over his glasses, he added, "You wouldn't believe me if you didn't try, would you?"

That really made me mad because he had railroaded me into this stupid donut business knowing it would be a flop, but we made a deal, eventually. I quit the bakery job, so that my eyes could stay open during math classes, and he bumped up my freedom money, as my allowance was called.

The deal was conditional on my school never having a reason to distract him from his paper. Cleverly, he dumped all responsibility for my grades and overall performance into my lap, so that even when my friends took a day or two off to relax from school drudgery, I had to consider the unpleasant relationship between a likely call from the school's office and my ensuing state of being penniless.

Also, he intimated that he might stay a few more years on his soul-withering, blood-congealing job, if I solemnly promised to never, ever, move back into his basement after having finished my education.

He was a pharmacist in a big drugstore chain, the multilayered administration towering above his head. He hated its every layer. I think he had infected me with this idea of having a boss-less life. I wondered what Kamekona's father was like and what was his guilt.

Toward the end of my shift, when the new bright day was already heating up the world outside the artificial eternal spring of the Queen's Medical Center, a short, tense looking guy caught my eye in the waiting room. I was already running out of steam and I was looking upon the empty row of chairs next to the registration window with fondness. Usually, non-urgent patients are seated there, waiting for their turn. I had seen the last of them and sent him away with a prescription in his hand, but this guy with a jet-black hair and bristly moustache was still sitting on a chair, stiff and motionless like a coconut stranded on a beach. The reason why a wet coconut came to my mind was a small puddle of moisture gathering around the man's feet.

Now, it would not be the first time for me to see someone wet himself in an emergency room.

But this case looked different because due to male anatomy—and this individual seemed to be a man, albeit of a rather short stature— the puddle should form by one foot only, usually the left one. Moreover, he was dry from his knees up.

But there was no chart left for me; apparently he was not a patient. As my last act in the hospital, I was about to change into my street clothes and call Lala. I stuck my head past the door to call, "Aloha, Aiko," to the cute Japanese receptionist curling behind the glass plate, but the moment I touched the handle, the man sprung up from the chair like stuck with a red-hot needle. He leaped across the room, leaving wet marks on the shiny koa floor and put his dump shoe into the door.

"Doctor Horny, I presume!" He mispronounced my name, on purpose I was sure, just to piss me off. His small dark eyes shone belligerently a few inches above his black toothbrush-like moustache.

"Doctor Gorny. You could also say Goorny. I was called Horny on a few occasions in San Diego, but you don't look Mexican, or are you?"

I was not really rattled by being called Horny; one gets used to a joke repeated a thousand times. But this guy was projecting the aura of malevolent, jab inviting, provocation and my fuse was getting somewhat short after the night of work.

"Never mind who I look like," he spat then hissed like a king cobra "FBI! Special Agent Nakamoto."

He whipped up a badge with the three aforementioned letters and closed in, ready to inject his venom at the sign of my slightest resistance.

"You have bladder control problems, Agent?" I could not believe I said it, but this guy was provoking my worst instincts. I pointed to his feet.

The agent's hands went through a split second succession of movements that let me believe I would be momentarily destroyed by a martial arts master, but he asserted his self-control and instead of a war cry he cleared his throat. "*Uhm,* could we talk in private? Maybe in my car?"

The truth emerging from Agent Nakamoto's convoluted story gave certain justification to his foul mood. Apparently, he was the decision maker who had ordered bringing Shark to his office but had to abort the mission once it spun out of control. He decided to take the action into his own hands and had accosted Shark in early hours of the day, when Kamekona arrived ashore in his small dinghy.

An uninformed landlubber, Nakamoto did not realize that Shark was about to take a dump in the marina's public restroom. Proper small boat harbor's etiquette dictates that live-aboard boaters should be left alone when they stepped ashore in the morning. They usually have a good reason to row ashore, and one could never know how urgent the said reason might be.

But the FBI badge holder had no insight into this custom or—in majesty of his special powers— had chosen to ignore it. Too bad. Nobody was allowed to interfere with Shark's bowel movements. Undeterred by the shout, "Hold it, FBI!" Kamekona set his course on a rhumb line toward a toilet, brushing aside the federal agent.

The second encounter, a few minutes later, was more substantial. Nakamoto swooped in when Kamekona was already in his dinghy, unable to make any avoidance maneuvers. The agent's mustachioed face towering over Shark's eyes, he grabbed the untied painter from the deck. He was in full control now, preventing his subject's escape.

For a moment, Kamekona looked passively at him from below, listening to Nakamoto's persuasive invitation to talk. Then he shrugged. "No Doctor Gorny, no talk," and yanked his end of the painter, sending the agent flying over the water's edge into the lagoon, fortunately only knee deep by the shore. At this point— and in view of his minions' report concerning earlier events—the FBI man decided that the addition of any new element to stabilize his volatile person of interest might be beneficial. He came to fetch me from the Queen's Medical Center.

The prospect of missing another mating opportunity— a grave concern for any mammal male, according to the Atoll Creature—made me rather irritable. Also, the temptation to annoy the aggressive gnome was hard to resist, but Kamekona needed to find out about the nature of the problem before he hurt anyone and landed behind bars.

Chapter 6

Water Whisper's appearance proved that visitors were expected. Despite Mele being long gone to her station at the cash register of the Beretania Street Foodland, the meal remnants were conspicuous in their absence from the folding picnic table in the middle of the cockpit. Someone also had picked up loose clothing articles from the U-shaped sitting bench, and thrown them all down the companionway, creating a cozy nest on the cabin floor.

Kamekona's handsome and smiling face appeared above the railing when I yelled from my kayak and his hand warmly reached out to Agent Nakamoto to assist in boarding. As I turned to tie my kayak to the boat's stanchion, I heard a sudden yelp and a dark mass, ending in two wet black shoes whizzed by me, flying precisely through the open railing gate and landing onboard with a thud. When I looked over the gunwale, the federal agent was slowly detaching himself from the picnic table, his legs scrambling for support.

"Thank you very much," I declined Shark's offer of assistance. Express-lifting his guests onboard was one of my friend's favorite jokes.

"Vot I do fer yu?" Kamekona intoned in his best

Hawaiian pidgin, as Nakamoto settled at the far end of a cockpit, which offered him the greatest separation from the boat's master.

"There are two persons of great interest to us … can't tell you why." The agent raised his open hand toward us, as though he wished to stop questions pouring from our facial openings. "National security, you understand."

He looked gravely at Kamekona and then at me. "These two individuals are going to meet in Honolulu very soon. It is imperative … IMPERATIVE," he added for greater effect, "that we know exactly … EXACTLY," he stressed again, "where, when and what they are doing. And we MUST know if they come in contact with some other players." He raised his index finger but quickly folded it, noticing dark deposit behind his nail.

He suspended his voice, inviting our inevitable burst of inquiries, but Shark turned his confused face to me and I reciprocated with my dumb look, rubbing my unshaved face.

"Okaay… But what … what do you need *me* for?" Astounded, Shark forgot his pidgin.

"Well, Mr. Kalekona—"

"Kamekona," Shark corrected. "Kamekona Aku."

"Sorry, Mr. Kametona—" The agent resumed his explanation, but Shark interrupted.

"Eh, vot island you from, bro?"

"I am stationed on Oahu, now," Nakamoto explained obligingly, "but before that I resided in Alaska… and before that in Southern California, and …"

"You stay going pleny …" Kamekona showed all his indecently white teeth. "You real *makaikai,* traveler.

Your bossman like you pleny!"

"I try to discharge my duties well wherever I go," Nakamoto declared with dignity.

"So what's the rub?" I interjected in my *consigliore* voice. "Why do you bother this law abiding citizen?"

"The rub is," the agent sighed, "that one suspect, the woman who arrives from Texas tomorrow morning, told her contact, the Russian man arriving the same day, that she wants to learn surfing. Devilish. Think of it. What environment could be more hostile to the electronic means of surveillance? How do I plant a microphone in the surf? How do I keep track of a person tumbling on a board? Once above the water, a second later under the water, all the time surrounded by a hundred tourists. Any one of which might be the third contact. A moment and something passes from one hand to another, UNNOTICED. You just can't catch it on camera!"

"Devilish indeed," I had to admit. "Someone would have to watch her very close by, right there, in the surf."

"Right you are, Doc!" Nakamoto looked at me with pride. "I could do it myself," his chest bulged noticeably, "but as the agent in charge, I can't lose view of the big picture. I have to be at the command post, calling the shots."

"And those monkeys that tasered me?" Kamekona asked without a speck of sympathy.

"Ah, they can swim, but I don't know about surfing …" Nakamoto admitted with a sigh. The decisive moment in his recruitment drive was approaching and he leaned to us. "You see, Mr. Ka— could I call you Shark?" As Kamekona allowed with a nod, he continued in a conspiratorial whisper, "My plan is … since she wants to *learn* how to surf, she will need to hire an instructor to teach her. And who could do it better than you?" He finished triumphantly.

"There are a lot of guys on the beach who could try," Kamekona noted and added philosophically, "but no one can do it. It's like teaching a sack of rice to hula; those tourists are unteachable. Problem with the water on the mainland … don't know. The best I can do is to prop my student's butt up for a moment, then they squeal for joy and brag how they surfed all the way from the break to the beach.

"Texas, California … same thing; those mainland *wahine* have no sense of balance or feel for the water. You can keep her on board for three seconds and make sure she doesn't get hurt … well, that's the success of the day. We burn out on this job so quick …" he added mournfully. "Doc will tell you," he pointed at me. "A few months on the job and you're ready for the worker comp… or go crazy!"

Shark seemed to have started a bargaining session. "No, I don't feel I can do it. I am still not ready after the last experience." He shuddered and wiped his eyes with this big slab of his forearm.

At this point, the agent showed himself for what he was, a *schmuck* not to be entrusted with any form of negotiations. "But Mr. Shark," he whined, "you are uniquely qualified for this job. I seriously doubt anybody else would take it!" He reached into his chest pocket and reluctantly pulled a photograph. "This is she!" he moaned.

"Jesus Christ!" Shark moaned in harmony. "How big is she?"

"Baby—this is her codename—is six-foot-six

and weighs about three hundred pounds," the agent croaked in distress. "But you are pretty big person yourself, Mr. Shark," he added hopefully.

"Jesus!" Kamekona yelled, outraged. "So I'm about three-fifty but—you think—I would climb a palm tree to fall on someone? You know what three hundred pounds falling from above can do to a man? Jesus!"

I snatched the photo from his hand. The picture, apparently taken from afar, showed a nice kidney-shaped swimming pool filled with outrageously blue water and an expansive pool deck emitting the subtle shine of travertine marble. At the pool's steps stood a big woman, up to her fat ankles in water.

Her height could not be properly judged without any reference points in the picture, but she certainly was quite obese. She was walking away from the camera, but her face could be seen as she looked back over her right shoulder. This was not an ugly face; I would even say she had quite a bit of charm in those sunny, smiling features.

Her large hips, enhanced by generous rolls of fat, melded smoothly into a humongous but well-proportioned butt. No cellulite, I noted her good-looking smooth skin. She had a relatively narrow waist, which expanded into a broad chest. Only a part of her right boob could be seen in this position, but it was enormous and projected proudly upward, resisting gravity either by its natural texture or by the magic employed by the brassiere industry. Altogether, she might be considered a fairly attractive woman, if one were into this kind of abundant beauty.

I was not sure if Shark's outrage was the part of his bargaining effort or the real cry of a frightened man.

Damage inflicted by her fall could be substantial, no doubt.

"National security ..." Nakamoto groaned in distress. "Hundreds ... maybe thousands might die. Do it for your country ... patriot!"

Kamekona let his arms fall from the reach-to-the-skies gesture. "The orders come from Queen Liliuokalani?" he asked coolly.

"No, from the regional office, Los Angeles! But those negligent bastards don't even know what they are doing!" Nakamoto wept.

Shark looked at him with a slight but visible disgust for a longish moment then shuffled next to him. "Okay, boss. What you give me to save the nation?" He extended his right arm and started bending his fingers one by one. "One. You give me a badge like yours, and a gun and a Taser. I really want a Taser."

The agent shuddered, overcome by a sudden chill.

"Two. I cannot decide if I go on salary or take a contract. What do you think, Doc?"

Nakamoto's head sunk to the table.

"Three. This one is very important; if this woman falls on me, I get the worker's comp. Four—"

"Shark, I can't get you any of those," the agent whimpered. "An honorable citation, perhaps. But you can't show it to anyone. For the love of your country, Shark!" he exclaimed with the last shred of hope dying in his heart as Kamekona got up with an angry huff.

"King Kamehameha ask, I do. Queen Liliuokalani ask, I do. Regional office FBI... no can do!" He exploded. "You tink me *lolo*? I get bad back or worse ... and you turn big *kahuna*?" Shark's pidgin soared again, impervious to any argumentation in Nakamoto's bor-

41

ing standard mid-West English. He huffed again and sulked toward the companionway, disappearing in the cabin.

"There must be something I could do for you, Mr. Shark," the agent wailed into the darkness down below. "You are the one; only you can take on this woman!"

"Actually," the big voice boomed from below the deck, "let us see how sincere you are. Let us see how grateful my country can be."

A big head adorned with the wavy black hair re-appeared in the companionway followed by the rest of Shark's body. He had a yellow pad in his hand, its first page tightly filled with many lines of neat handwriting.

"Here," he handed the pad to Nakamoto. "You fix this and I'll be your spy for a few days."

I looked over the agent's shoulder. The first position in the long column was, "Failure to appear in court, traffic violation," followed by "Trespassing charges, Royal Hawaiian Hotel." A long list of Shark's altercations with the judicial authorities of Hawaii was neatly hand-printed, with dates, places and persons involved conveniently provided. The first yellow page was followed by the second, filled almost to the bottom.

"Oh," Nakamoto groaned. "This is … a long list. And this! Assault on a police officer!" He looked at Shark with terror. "I should arrest you right now!"

"Go ahead," Kamekona easily agreed and presented his wrists to the federal agent. "But I don't think I can surf with handcuffs on. Anyway, this was a stupid cop from the mainland. Didn't know shit 'bout Hawaii. Asked for it. Gone now."

"For God's sake! It's a major felony. How can I fix

that?" Nakamoto saw light disappearing at the far end of his professional tunnel.

"Oh, well …" Shark grabbed the yellow pad to yank it from Nakamoto's hands but the agent wouldn't let go. This was one of those times when bold decisions had to be made, the moment when great leaders rise like a banyan tree from the Wahiawa flat pineapple land of mediocrity.

"I'll take care of it!" he shouted, exhilarated by his own audacity. "I'll do it, even if I have to kidnap this officer. But you do my work here, tomorrow!" He extended his hand and Shark grabbed it in his paw. I almost had tears in my eyes at this display of courage and patriotism. The country would be saved.

Chapter 7

From the height of the fifteenth floor balcony, the strip of yellow sand below seemed quite narrow. Next to the vast blueness of the ocean—which further merged with the sky, just a shade lighter and splashed with a few measly clouds at the horizon—it looked … inconsequential. But the sense of proportion was restored when Colonel Boris Ossipovitch Kulagin turned his attention to the people on the beach, wiggling restlessly like worms where the water and sand touched. A lot of people, he thought. Through his binoculars, he could identify dozens upon dozens of pretty, almost naked women.

Amazing, he reflected. This is the same ocean I've been watching and cursing in Vladivostok for five years. He stepped back into the cool, shaded room, away from the aggressive brightness of the Hawaiian noon. As soon as he turned away from the balcony, he came face to face with a broad-shouldered, solid man in a striped undershirt whose broad face smiled at him warmly from the mirror. He sent his perfectly flat hand up to his head and the man in the mirror answered with a sharp salute. Nu, Boris Ossipovitch, you did well, ended up in general's quarters!

Looking around, he marveled at size of the bed. Why, his whole Vladivostok apartment would fit on this bed ... maybe without a toilet and shower, but those were shared anyway. He tried the mattress—firm but with a nice bounce. He smiled playfully. We will give it a better test later.

For a man rooted in the real world as firmly as the colonel was, it was next to impossible to accept this situation without a strong suspicion that he was still asleep. Maybe he was dreaming extra-long because Sasha in the next apartment hadn't turned his bloody TV on yet. Still drunk or dead; who knows?

He was about to test his disbelief theory an hour earlier when the arrogant bastard downstairs made fun of him, calling him *sir* like in some old American movie. A good punch on the nose would correct his manners right away; and in case it *was* a dream, he would wake up laughing about his brain's outrageous night tales. But at the last moment, Kulagin thought—wait! Dream or no dream—why spoil something that good? Let it run its full length. He swallowed the insult, pretending he did not hear, then took a plastic card and landed in this room.

So far, the whole operation was moving ahead smoothly like a Swiss watch. The ticket had arrived in an important-looking envelope, so impressive that the mailman—a despicable man known to open letters just to see if a few rubles were hiding between folded sheets of paper—did not dare open it over a steaming kettle, and slid it under the door with the flap still firmly glued.

The American visa arrived two weeks after he had sent his application, even without him having to trav-

45

el to Moscow. Such an event was unheard of, and—frankly—unbelievable, except that here he was, sitting on the room-size bed amid the unbelievable luxury of the Royal Hawaiian Hotel in Honolulu.

Royal, Boris Ossipovitch smiled. Maybe it is Tsaritsa Catherina the Great who wants to meet me! And this inner joke shook his belly with such force that he forgot for a moment about his hunger.

So, after all, his mother was wrong and his father was right.

"You learn, Boris," she groused all his childhood. "Study as much as you can, and sooner or later, you will come ahead. What you learn is better than having money under a mattress."

Silly old woman, he nodded. Top-notch high school grades, always on top of the class at the officer's school, each damn tank warfare field manual burnt in his memory like on a laser disc ... And where did it take me? To Chechnya, where any old hag on the street could whip out a Kalashnikov from under her rags and blow me into smatterings, on any given day, for four fucking years. Money under the mattress!

He placed himself comfortably in front of the TV and noted a small door under the set. It was not locked and when he opened it, row upon row of small bottles with exotic labels met his eyes. He grabbed a bunch and returned to the bed with a big smile clearly displaying his two golden molars on the right side of his jaw.

This is something Daddy would like, he thought. *Na zdorovie, Papa*, he said, raising a tiny bottle of Johnny Walker in salute.

The wily old fox knew better. "*Podpolkovnik*, he

mumbled disrespectfully, making faces like someone pissed on his boots. "*Comandir*," he mocked Boris when the second star, the insignia of lieutenant colonel, appeared on his son's uniform.

"Just see where it takes you. You know a lot … a lot of crap. And it will take you where crap usually goes … to a shithouse. And that's where you belong as long as you take orders like a good boy. I didn't raise you to be a dutiful idiot!"

The father apparently was not enough of an obedient boy, and he paid for it with all his teeth. Lucky to come back at all. Fate had it that his camp was not far from Vladivostok as well.

Unlike his papa, younger Kulagin remained on the Pacific coast voluntarily after President Putin decided that Mother Russia had too many tank officers. Vladivostok was his last army posting and, thanks to the generous provisions of his retirement, he was allowed to keep a colonel's last perk, the tiny apartment in a gray concrete beehive near the base.

He had tightened screws on Japanese cars coming through the port for a few years but that job ended as well. Then he had just sat in his one-room dwelling, sometimes staring into the gray sky and the never-ending rain against his window; and sometimes into the monitor of his old PC, trying to learn English for nothing better to do. That would make *matushka* happy!

Kulagin drained the last drops from the little bottle and pulled a chair right up to the big screen TV and turned it on. "Weder … wedzer …" he repeated, carefully watching the weatherman's lips, trying to mimic his intonation and gestures. His sincere look, reaching deep into the viewer's eyes, was as fake as *Pravda*'s article on the economy, but since this is how they talk … Kulagin looked back into the screen earnestly and intoned in a heartfelt baritone, "De wetser in Honolulu will be fer tonite … wit trade winds cooling de city to seventy-five degrees."

Not bad, he congratulated himself and turned to the anchorwoman at the table with a slight bow and a friendly grin, just like the guy on TV. It's not hard to smile at dolls like that, he reflected. A lot of pretty faces here, he thought, though women seemed mostly scrawny like harbor rats and had as many curves as a piece of wet plywood.

Irina, the full-bodied goddess of the Primorskij Kraj, who had graced his life for a few years, would get a fit of jealousy here. Kulagin would love to see her sneering and hissing at all those pretty girls stealing from her the men's adoring looks. Would serve her right … The bitch dumped Kulagin on the same day he had lost his job at the port, thinking his apartment would be lost as well. But *suka* was wrong. Boris stayed on to enjoy his colonel's quarters while she had to move back to her mother. Poetic justice, and she would have to endure the curse until her hooks sunk into some other apartment owner.

Only now, from the perspective of the fifteenth floor of the Royal Hawaiian Hotel, Kulagin could see that all those disasters falling upon him were a blessing in disguise. The end of army career, the loss of the port job, Irina's treasonous departure—all this shit raining on him for the past few years proved necessary to prepare him for this bold step. Without them, he would not have found the courage to jump out of the gray and grimy life in Vladivostok like a shiny trout leaping out of the brown waters of Amur River. For once, Papa would be proud of him; a docile idiot no more!

He turned off the TV and went down on the carpeted floor to do his customary fifty push-ups. This was not the time to get soft. He would need all the strength the army life had once crammed into his body.

Chapter 8

A huge crystal mirror, the apartment-size bed, a flowery carpet clean and soft to the feet like fresh grass in the spring—it was all lovely and well, but Kulagin had not eaten since breakfast was offered on the plane from Vladivostok. He was seriously hungry now. Cleaning up the funny pantry filled with small bottles of booze under the TV set helped somewhat, as did a few candy packages and chips devoured in a few gulps, but his manly body cried for a solid piece of meat with potatoes.

The instructions received—while still in Vladivostok—took him from the airport to the Royal Hawaiian Hotel, through the reception and up to this room like a general on an inspection tour, heels of black shiny shoes clicking all the way. But now, as the long arm of his watch came to rest over the little tank emblem adorning its face, and the short one pointed unequivocally to the number one, at thirteen hundred hours, he had every right to expect hearty lunch to materialize. No food appeared in the room however and—although it gravely disappointed his robust digestive tract—he accepted this failure almost with a glee.

So … they are not *that* good! They do have their screw-ups like the rest of the world, and he found it somehow reassuring, because he knew that in the field, things do not always—in his experience, actually, hardly ever—go as planned. The realization that he was dealing with fallible humans rather than with some champions of logistics gave him the much-needed dose of self-confidence.

It was his turn to grasp the initiative. A senior officer like himself would be expected to regroup in the face of the unexpected and outflank any stumbling block, be it human, atmospheric or logistic. His supply line appeared to be snagged but it should not be equaled with him going hungry. "Living off the land," was one of the topics he lectured on once to his junior officers, and this exotic hotel in a foreign country was nothing more than an interesting variation of terrain. The standard military approach—reconnaissance, risk analysis, planning and execution—would be as applicable here as in the mountains of Chechnya.

On his way to the room, Colonel Kulagin recalled, he had encountered a tray resting on the floor, which contained a generous amount of food remnants. It wouldn't exactly be his meal of choice, but undeniably it was a potential source of nourishment.

He inspected the empty corridor through a spyhole and slipped out. A bit unsteady on his feet after consuming contents of the bar, he nevertheless moved quickly through the darkened corridor. Silently, like a ghost, his steps muffled on the thick gray carpet adorned with brick-colored flowers and green leaves, he followed the passage to the right, where the abandoned tray had been detected next to the elevators.

It was still there, golden-yellow fries glowing softly in the subtle light of the corridor. He swallowed hard and accelerated, ready to pounce, when—like a tank concealed in an ambush—a gray metal trolley rolled out from the side-corridor, as silent as he had been. Poor Kulagin avoided a collision at the last moment, throwing himself on the wall. Two big shiny domes towering over food trays trembled as the trolley, propelled by a small Asian woman, squeezed by.

Like a second lieutenant straight from school, the colonel scolded himself. He had taken the bait and exposed the flank. *Svolotch.*

His hand was forced now; in order to keep his cover of a pressed-for-time guest, Boris Ossipovitch dove into the open elevator. He alighted one floor above and walked—did not run but marched purposefully—to the stairway, descended one floor and re-entered the corridor where the supply depot was last seen.

Alas, three short minutes later, not only was the tray gone but the food trolley which he preferred to think of as a supply truck— was empty and rolling away at the other end of the corridor, its distinctive domed trays unloaded. Only the faint smell of hot hamburgers and crispy fries drifted through the air, assaulting the officer's supersensitive nose.

But this was hardly a problem. Once the presence of supply vehicles was established and the pattern of their movements determined, it was only the question of patiently patrolling the area before a determined attack and swift fallback to a safe position. (Chapter 5, section 7b of the "Field Manual of Tank Warfare.") This one-man unit would be provisioned, eventually.

An hour later, an opportunity presented itself exactly as expected. A careless maid entered a room, leaving a loaded trolley unattended at the corridor. Kulagin swooped at it from around the corner like a diving eagle. Ready to snatch a burger and a handful of fries, he confidently pounced on the silvery dome. The shining cover came off without making a tiniest noise but his hand came to a standstill in the middle of a lightning swipe. Instead of a juicy brown pate on a bun and a pile of shining fries, his stunned eyes fell upon narrow strips of fried meat, sharing the plate with mashed potatoes soaked in brown sauce and green peas.

In despair, he dropped the dome on the floor, which mercifully dampened the noise with its thick carpet, and grabbed the whole plate. Then he ran with it, the thick, brown, greasy liquid splashing between his fingers on the plush carpet, corridor walls and his pants. He galloped away in a panic, but even before he turned the corner, the high-pitched voice of the maid caught up with him, as she was yelling her invectives—what else she could be shouting—in the way that reminded him of the Chinese longshoremen in Vladivostok.

He reached his room, his unassailable fortress, blood still pounding in his head but the song of triumph sounding its first bars. The green light flashed on the door when his magic card swiped through the slot and he barged in, shutting the door behind him in the face of any possible pursuit.

Almost immediately, he recognized some disturbing newness in his quarters. The smell ... this faint flowery smell mixing now with the rich heavy aroma of beef ... Not even aware that his hands had been burnt by the hot sauce, Kulagin softly put the plate on the floor and peeked from the vestibule into the main room. There was no one inside but three, big, hard shell suitcases were set in front of the mirrored closet, still unpacked.

She had arrived! While he was hunting for food, she had come and left again, God only knows for how long.

Go out and search ... stay put and wait ... go out ... Kulagin thought long and hard without reaching a definitive decision, while he ate a piece after piece of succulent, wonderful beef, scooping buttery mash potatoes with his fingers and, finally, giving the plate a good lick.

The more he thought, the heavier his head became and finally he decided to wait. Weakened by Johnny Walker and the other mini-bar characters, flooded now with the goodness of decent meal, Kulagin's alertness wavered. His head fell on a pillow and his legs kicked the shoes off. He spread his body on the bed, shamelessly displaying stains on his pants, so unworthy of a lieutenant colonel. But he was innocently unaware, submerged in a deep relaxing sleep.

Chapter 9

The message was very obscure, as Agent Nakamoto did not wish to talk in clear terms over the hospital's "unsecure line." What was clear though was that my presence was expected—indeed, demanded—at the war counsel he convened at ten forty-five, *Water Whisper,* Keehi Lagoon. Some most disturbing developments, he obviously could not reveal their nature over the said unsecure line, had occurred within the past twelve hours. Those harbingers of a possibly catastrophic event needed to be confronted with speed and resolve.

Not having been retained by the FBI for service in any capacity, I received this message with a very inappropriate expression pertaining to Mother Yamamoto's sexual conduct. However, as Shark had now been deputized into the federal service, I had to follow the rules of Hawaiian friendship. I took off from the Queen's Medical Center's parking at eight zero-five, my surgical greens still warm in the dirty basket of the ER change room.

The Nimitz Highway was crammed with cars slowly inching toward downtown Honolulu but I flew on the westbound lanes like a shearwater. I declined Shark's helping hand to get onboard *Water Whisper* twenty minutes later. He was serene, studying his rap sheet, apparently photocopied before the original was given to Nakamoto.

"Nice handwriting," I commented.

"Mele did it for me, " Kamekona answered, avoiding my eyes.

"What I noted, Shark, is that the most recent event on the list is dated January fifteenth, shortly before your "AIDS" affliction. Did the shot of penicillin cure you of your anti-social personality as well?"

"Mele." Shark shook his head. "She moved onto my boat. You wouldn't believe her temper. There must be some medication for that?"

He looked at me with hope, but since I couldn't promise any pharmacological solution to improve his woman's character, he continued. "After that clap scare, I decided to be a one-woman-man and I let Mele move into the boat. Now she lets me go to work on the beach, but she takes her Foodland shifts in such a way that she is always sitting under a palm tree, watching me. And if a lady tourist wants to book me for another lesson later on the same day, she puts up such a stink that it's not worth it."

He looked dejected and I felt for him; you just can't fence in a guy like that. It's simply not right.

"And if I want to see me brother in Waimanalo, I have to lie that I'm going to have a beer with you. For some reason, she thinks you are a good influence on me."

Cries from the shore broke our brotherly intimacy. Across the island, we could not see the source of noise but the yelling sounded like Agent Nakamoto had forgotten he needed a dinghy to get onto *Water Whisper*.

"Stupid jerk," Kamekona said, "but maybe he will get some of this nonsense off my back." He slapped the photocopy on the table. "Worth a try."

Ben, as Mr. Nakamoto had asked us to call him on his second visit, was as anxious as a medical intern before his first arterial puncture. Baby, the woman spy from Texas, had not flown into Honolulu as expected. How Ben got hold of her itinerary was, of course, privileged information we had no business to know, but she had clearly stated it herself in an e-mail to her male contact, who was already under the FBI surveillance in Honolulu.

Nakamoto and his crew of incompetents stood by the arrival gates since the first morning arrival at 5a.m., ready to pin a tail on her as soon as she stepped out through the arrival gate. But apparently she did not arrive. Even they could not miss a woman of such conspicuous appearance.

"What if—despite her e-mail statement—she came last night?" The question was eating into Ben's stomach like a gulp of hydrochloric acid. His boys were still on lookout at the airport but chances were she had given them the slip by arriving early. Unforgivable.

"Maybe she came on a submarine?" I ventured, now really worried we might have Ben's bleeding ulcer on our hands.

"Yes!" The agent beamed at me with a hint of respect. "Submarine! She could swim right into the surfing area in front of the Royal Hawaiian! Undetected. That was her plan!"

He put his hand on my shoulder. "Man, I should get your services too. This case can take every good man I can find. Do you have something I could fix for you?"

He winked.

Lost for the lack of ideas, I remained still for a moment with my mouth open. "Maybe you could kidnap the fucking clerk at the Queen's who puts me on a night shift all the time?"

But he was already spinning his wheels. "It's an emergency, men! She must be close, maybe even already on the beach. We must inject ourselves into the situation immediately. My boys will rush in from the airport ASAP, but with this traffic, it may take an hour."

Waikiki looked deceptively normal, the stream of cars easing off after the last stragglers had made it to their cubicles. Only a crowd of blurry-eyed tourists sloshed around from the coffee shops to the ABC store, from breakfast in a hotel restaurant to a street tree for a smoke.

Of course, there was not a single parking spot on Kalakaua Avenue, but Ben turned right and stepped on the brakes right where the street bifurcated into the driveway leading to the Waikiki Sheraton garage and the Royal Hawaiian Hotel's driveway. We spilled out like a bunch of drunks five minutes before closing time.

A policeman charged in our direction like a navy blue bull, the expression on his face screaming, "Are you fucking out of your fucking minds?"

Ben met him head on, fearless. He whipped out his badge and barked, "National Security!"

We ran around the astounded cop, haplessly left in charge of Agent Nakamoto's car and we rushed along the driveway, across the sumptuous bright green lawn, and into the pink building. The cacophony of insulted horns on the street followed us like harpies.

People leapt aside like scared rabbits as we charged across the hotel's main hall, hoofing it past the front of the old classic, wooden reception desks. Ben, in his gray military style t-shirt, led the steel point of our attack, followed by the threatening dark hulk of Kamekona clad into a yellow, cut-off t-shirt and surfing duds, and finally me, closing the assault team in my green, pineapple-patterned, Aloha shirt.

After running around the great flower arrangement in the center, the red and yellow bird-of-paradise flowers blurring in my eyes, we burst out on the beach side of the hotel. Only a green square of lawn separated us now from the low fence, which marked the sandy shore densely covered with umbrellas and recliners.

Ben stopped at the door, collected and in control. From this position, he focused and took in the big picture like a general before a battle. The crowd of tourists milling around the pool and on the pathways could not hide our big "Baby." No way. Our prey had to be further out, at the beach or in the water, hopefully unaware of the commotion we had incited in the reception area.

Stealthily, we dashed behind the cover of the grill chalet and moved along the wall until we reached the sand. And there, on the water edge, the platinum-blond female head lit up in the mid-day Hawaiian light like a beacon, sticking more than a foot above the black hair of two Japanese tourists in front of her.

"It's her, the Baby!" Nakamoto's strained whisper could not hide his emotion. He was elated.

Chapter 10

"Men!" Ben whispered in a way that a court reporter at Alakea Street could comfortably take notes. "She's already there; we have to think fast and clear." He gave me the long hard stare, like Ms. Stewart, my math teacher and the terror of my teenage years.

I broke in a cold sweat, searching for the right answer, and finally stammered, "Somehow, we have to be introduced to her." I did not even notice I was interjecting myself into this affair, with no good reason beyond Shark's friendship and love for my country.

"And how?" Nakamoto kept me fixed in his reptile eyes, Ms. Stewart style.

"If she takes a surfing instructor," I swallowed hard and speaking became easier, "… and she seems to be walking toward the Big Joe's board stand right now, we can slip a five into Joe's hand and he will give her Shark. That's easy."

"Very well," Ben decided without a second of hesitation. "Let's do it!" He abruptly turned to the surfboard stand.

"But she looks like a lot for an agent to handle … you may need two people to control her. I should get introduced to her as well," I added hesitantly. He sharply looked back, his eyebrows arching in the un-spoken demand for explanation.

"Sometimes, Shark's finger slips…" I explained. "No wonder, those butts are greasy with sun lotion," I acknowledged Kamekona's hurt look. "It gets him a nice tip from time to time."

"To the point, Doc, to the point!" The agent hissed. "She is almost at the stand."

"I'll be nearby and when that happens," I quickly explained, "she will squeal and I'll punch Shark in the face to save her …"

The brown wall in front of me, already on his way to see Big Joe, suddenly spun around. "You'll do what?"

"Not hard, just so she thinks I am her knight …"

Shark looked at me as if I suddenly sprouted green leafs from my ears. "Punch me up? I no care how hard you hit … Not half as hard as my sister would, any-way. But what if one of the guys see it? What if Big Joe catches the wind? Da haole punch me in da face and no ambulance to take him to a hospital? Even moving to Maui no help me … Maybe I go to Guam and chase Rattlesnake out to Palau? No go!" He firmly blocked the pathway with his body, causing a reflected wave of human bodies to bounce back through the chain of tourists behind us.

At this point, Agent Nakamoto stepped into our dispute and took a firm hold of Shark. "The felony case," he growled. "You do as Doc says or I'll cuff you right here!"

Kamekona rolled his eyes. "Okay," he said, "but we do this thing right past the break. I wait for a nice wave and let it pass. Everyone catches a ride, and when they are all gone *then* we do our stunt. You hit me when someone's around, and I'll hit you back! Then you see an emergency room from another side."

The big blond was already at the desk, speaking to Joe. The professor guys—so far waiting lazily for a client, relaxing and chatting—gathered around the desk, puzzled by this imposing woman. Then they all suddenly stepped back, apparently disinterested and looking away.

"Got scared," Shark murmured, looking suggestively to Ben. "Now, you write me da paper about this cop assault … you say I was innocent. I want it ready as soon as I am out of the water." And he swooped onto the rental desk, smooth and confident like a black panther, while I stayed two steps behind, blending into the crowd of beachgoers.

No more than three minutes later, Big Joe's business scored another success. Shark triumphantly escorted the beaming blond to the water's edge through the corridor of honor made by the other beach boys.

They cut a wonderful picture together; she advanced proudly wrapped in a dark blue swimming suit, her skin pink and shiny, a touch taller than Shark, while my friend floated beside her like a dark and menacing Titan from the Scheherazade stories of a thousand nights, except for his knee-long, green-and-yellow flowery shorts.

They stopped on the sand and Shark carefully put down the longboard. Big Joe was a mean bastard and could easily swipe ten bucks out of a teaching fee for mistreating his equipment. Kamekona put his belly on the board, demonstrating how to paddle the board, and then swiftly and gracefully jumped up into the classic surfing position. "Got it?"

She did. The spy-girl sprawled on the board, her majestic hips hardly leaving any free margins of wood on either side. She demonstrated her swimming moves, paddling like a green turtle lethargically travelling over a patch of seagrass.

"Now up!" Shark yelled, and she groaned loudly, breaking contact between her ample bosom and the board. Then she raised her heft onto one knee, both knees and, eventually, lifted all of her three hundred pounds to assume a surfing stance. It all took about ten seconds and the crowd watching the exhibition moaned in fear, looking at Shark with the sympathy usually reserved for a dying man.

Despite the slowness of her moves, "Baby" looked amazingly graceful on the board, which I thought could be related to classic ballet training, something to be expected from a Russian spy.

"Good!" Shark yelled. "Now into the water!"

It was easy to follow the platinum head in the water as they moved toward the shore break, the enemy agent on the board and Shark swimming beside her, cautiously maintaining distance in case she rolled off.

From the corner of my eye, I caught Agent Nakamoto's last discreet farewell and I followed the lead unit, swimming ten feet behind. Kamekona must have been doing some fine undercover work as I heard a female giggle and the massive pink butt in front of my eyes was quavering in spasms of laughter. Now I understood why Mele had a habit of keeping her eye on Shark at work; he had his way with women.

They reached a long row of surfers behind the break, everyone waiting for the right wave. Allowing a respectful distance around "Baby" and Shark, they quite obviously kept a keen eye on this conspicuous couple. Shark had to be uncomfortable under this surveillance but did not let it show. His left hand on the board, the right one crossing over the student's thighs to the other side, he was hanging in the water, waiting … waiting like a real predator of the deep.

One surfer after another took off, unable to resist the set of well-formed waves, but Shark still floated in the same position, only his right arm inching higher and higher.

Son-of-a-gun, I observed with admiration, he's going to do his finger thing even before launching her on a wave. I moved into position, two feet on Shark's left.

The last surfer casted a jaundiced eye on Shark and his charge, then pushed his student into action. It was the last half-decent wave of the set. Only then did Kamekona kick his big legs and push the board in the way of a weak ripple, unworthy of the name of wave. This coincided with his right hand moving up and I heard the squeal I was anticipating.

I swung into action, reached them in two crawl strokes and launched a wide hook into Shark's face. With me floating in the water, my unsupported punch had all the weight of a wet sponge thrown at a beach but Kamekona dramatically flipped on his back, his arms desperately flaying around. At the last moment, I saw his theatrical performance of pain changing into the expression of real hurt and fear, his mouth gaping in the cry of distress, his eyes open wide.

Blackness, wet blackness overtook me, no idea for how long. The next thing I perceived was the feeling of someone holding my head up, as I was coughing and taking air in big gasps. I opened my eyes and saw the expanse of the blue ocean.

A second later, a fist appeared in front of my face, but the big diamond sparkling on the hand stopped short of my eyes and the knuckles did not connect with my skin. When I turned my head around, I saw Shark holding my head above the water, trying to keep me out of reach of the blond monster sitting on the board, trying to punch the life out of me.

"You fucking moron!" she yelled without any foreign accent. In fact I thought I heard some Texan twang. "Look what you did to this good man!"

"Box jellyfish." Shark groaned into my ear. "Oh man, it's killing me! Can I let you go now? You can swim?"

I swam away, happy to put some distance between my face and the bitch obviously trained in close-range combat by the best instructors that the KGB had to offer.

Chapter 11

The voices in front of my door rose angrily. I could identify Lala's loud staccato whisper, "No... You don't! *No!*" as though she was trying to control a stubborn dog.

Then a male voice mingled in, pleading and threatening in turns. It sounded familiar but I got positive identification only when he shouted, "National security!"

Agent Nakamoto was there. Did he want to check on his contractor's wellbeing or was he planning some further action? As I was removing two bags of frozen peas from my face—a trick I had learned from my emergency patients—in order to open the door, Lala's angry huffs and Nakamoto's beseeching were moving away from my door. Apparently, she was displacing him toward the elevators.

A key made a soft noise in the lock and she stepped in, unobtrusive, tiptoeing softly, a true biologist entering the habitat of the beast under study. I covered my swollen left eye to avoid double vision, and watched her sailing noiselessly through my darkened room toward my bed. She was a fine female specimen of the breed originating in the north-European plains.

Her striking, almost white, mane of hair was the

heritage of her Finnish father and her freckled high-cheeked face undoubtedly came from the Vistula River valley in Poland, her mother's homeland. Below her neck, Lala's body could not be easily assigned to any particular geographical location, but one could safely assume that the evolutionary forces shaping it included six-foot snow drifts and hungry bears rummaging for frozen beetroot in her ancestors' gardens.

Four inches short of six feet, this young woman had breasts, hips and buttocks of the size very appropriate for her gender, as well as strong limbs with clearly defined muscles. None of the sickening thinness or weakness—reigning on the front pages of the fashion magazines—contaminated this alpha female.

Undoubtedly, she could pitch in for a communal reindeer hunt and would chase wolves away from her hut if the situation required it. In her present life circumstances, the ability to face down ocean creatures and an occasional law enforcement agent was sufficient. Whatever spare energy this wonderful body had, I was happy to help dissipate. Lala was an enthusiastic performer in whatever the activity she decided to partake in.

"You are not asleep," she stated, once her eyes adapted to darkness. "You've hardly slept for the past two days; always something going on after you leave the hospital."

She pulled away the heavy window curtain that let me sleep after my nights at the Emergency Room. "Remarkably little damage," she commented, having a look at my face. "I saw Shark's hand, swollen like a whale fluke. I thought it strange for you to rest in your place and not in the Intensive Care Unit. Mele was scared like hell that Shark had killed you when she called me."

"It wasn't Kamekona's hand." I pointed to my face. "In fact, if you look closely, this black point corresponds to a good size diamond." I indicated a tender spot below my left eye.

From below the green peas, I related to Lala the story of our beach adventure. I hoped to go back to work in a few hours, if the swelling around my eyes wasn't too great. I was sure my patients would forgive my black eye. This was not something that crowd would hold against me.

"What a screw up!" Lala looked at me unkindly. "But I'll have to call your current employer at one point. Your FBI boss made me promise to call him as soon as you are awake. He was about to call for backup to break down your door, otherwise."

"I heard your fight, Lala. Thank you for protecting my rest-time."

"You are welcome," she answered, reaching inside her bag. "I am used to facing bluffing bulls. It's all posturing … hardly ever do I need to poke one with a stick."

She pulled out a small glass jar and put it on the table. "Here, to cheer you up. I was about to buy some flowers to put beside your mutilated body, but for some reason this thing ended in my bag instead.

"Herring in oil," I read the label. "Gee, Lala, thanks. I always wanted to try herring in oil. What in God's grand design made you buy me this delicacy today?"

"You know, Horny," Lala was sitting at the table, holding the jar in both hands in astonishment, "I am asking myself the same question. It must be my subconscious talking. Have I told you of the significance that herring in oil has in my life?"

I rolled to the wall to make room for her and Lala assumed her favorite position, her right knee across my thighs, her upper body supported on the left elbow and her right hand holding my chin. A bit possessive, I thought, but I didn't mind.

"My mother was a postgrad student from Poland who came for a year to the Marine Biology Department at the University of Hawaii. You must know that the Baltic Sea, her likely future place of professional interest, is not a body of water known for its flourishing coral reefs or happy dolphins jumping across the bow of one's boat. No, the Baltic is a freezing hole in the ground between the Scandinavian Peninsula and Poland, where soles and herrings eke their miserable lives, their teeth chattering from cold.

"Since neither soles nor herrings are part of the Hawaiian fauna, it is not quite clear why she chose Hawaii to further her education. Maybe she wanted to learn hula or surf ... I don't blame her. Anyway, there she is ... blasted with the sun from the very moment she opens her eyes till the sunset when ukuleles start breaking out on the campus and the breeze brings smell of jasmine. One can go crazy, right?"

Lala looked at me questioningly and I agreed. That's exactly how I felt after having moved here from Rochester, NY. For a while, I considered sending water samples for pharmacological testing, just to make sure it was not contaminated with psychoactive drugs. It was that or a low-grade mania; I just did not feel normal. Eventually, I got used to it and accepted my happy affliction.

"So, she is getting homesick and thinks that maybe some familiar comfort food might help. And one day, she finds in the Foodland a jar of herrings in oil—just what the doctor ordered, like a sunny day on a Baltic beach!

"She reaches to grab the jar and ... her hand strikes another hand. She looks up and sees this dashing, seven foot, blond, young man in a blue officer's uniform, reaching for *her* jar of herring. And to make things really dramatic, there is only one jar left.

"He says something. ... It appears to her that he might be speaking English, but she can't understand a word, this poor foreign girl. She responds with her best Oxford accent and sees the vacuum of understanding in his eyes. But, obviously, she saw something else in those blue eyeballs, because she came through the curtain of misunderstanding like a steel harpoon. They treated their nostalgia together.

"They consumed the contentious herring in oil together and whatever else they shared, they found it very therapeutic. I was born less than a year later, slightly prematurely, on board a French research ship that was taking my pregnant mother from Midway Atoll to Honolulu for delivery.

"Not only did they manage to communicate in respect of reproduction—something simpler mammals can also do quite well—but she induced him to abandon his First Officer's position on a Finnish freighter. You see, she was the part of the University of Hawaii expedition to the Northwestern Islands and their research ship's first mate had appendicitis with complications, putting everything on hold. And here she reports to her professor with my father in tow. They checked up on him. Apparently, he was overqualified for the position and two days later they sailed away—course: Midway Atoll."

"A most interesting story." I sat up and put my peas away. "Why don't *we* share the herring and sail away? At least you could stay in my condo on a more permanent basis. I meant to ask you a few times."

"Glad you didn't," Lala sighed. "I would hate to turn you down, Horny. I enjoy the fact that your nickname suits your temperament so well, but …

"Do you know that my parents developed a language of their own? They think it is English but it's really made of Finnish and Polish words in equal parts, with generous admixtures and general grammatical structure of English. I speak this language, but you would need an interpreter. A strange language it is; there must be fifty expressions for making love, another few dozen for describing water and weather conditions, but considerably less vocabulary dedicated to financial terms."

She took my hand. "You are a bull, a strong and sweet bull, and you have a nice beach to share with your harem. Maybe one day you'll start looking to me more like a person. Maybe one day we will develop a language of our own. … For now, enjoy what you have."

She got on her feet and handed me her phone. "Here, call Nakamoto before he sends a SWAT team this way."

Chapter 12

A short conversation with Doctor Gorny lifted Nakamoto's spirits considerably. First, his growing anxiety about the operation slipping out his control was counteracted by the realization that even if its overall dynamic had changed, it was not necessarily for the worse. The attempt to observe "Baby" discreetly in the surf had flown widely off handle, no question. One of his agents slinked away with a black eye and the other beached himself like a demented humpback, swearing and huffing, holding his swollen limb for everybody on the beach to see.

And what "Baby", the subject of his investigation, figured out of this mess? Nakamoto could not be sure, but he had to admit to himself that, generally, bad guys don't become high-level operatives without a healthy dose of intelligence and a suspicious mindset. She was, oh, so concerned about Shark; one would think she had fallen in love with the muscled beast. On the other hand, a spy or not, she was a young female; maybe her hormones got the better of her. Shark did have his way with women, Nakamoto observed.

At least, Gorny admitted that his injuries were not serious. Having a civilian—not even a formally contracted help—injured under his orders was a certain way to face yet another disciplinary inquiry. But … he didn't need to worry about the doc for now.

Kamekona Aku, on the other hand … this situation suddenly acquired a few nasty twists. As soon as the giant dragged the longboard on sand with his good left hand, "Baby" dancing around him like some monstrous puppy, his blood-shot eyes started scanning the beach like searchlights. Nakamoto had the premonition that his identity would be trumpeted to the world momentarily and he dove beyond the lifeguards' tower. But he was a second too late. Shark took off after him, kicking big fountains of sand on sun-tanning tourists and leaving "Baby" completely unsupervised. The low hedge beside the lifeguard's tower proved to be an unsatisfactory hiding place and Shark grabbed the agent by his shirt, lifting him up.

"See what it did to me?" he thundered, tightening the grip on the agent's shirt and causing him shortness of breath. "You've got my paper?"

How could Nakamoto have the document prepared in such a short time? Impossible, even if he wanted to, which he did not. In response to the negative head nod, Shark gave a twist on the shirt until it burst on the back, squeezing the last of air from Nakamoto's lungs.

"We go to bench," he said. "You first. You run, I kill you."

The agent had no doubts it was exactly what the Hawaiian would do. His eyes were dripping murder. Happy to draw another breath into his collapsed lungs, Ben Nakamoto walked to the nearby bench on his wobbly legs and crumpled on it. A few seconds later, Shark sat next to him, a piece of paper and a ball pen—swiped from the Big Joe's counter—in his hand.

"You write," he commanded and Nakamoto could not find a single reason to object.

"Mr. Kamekona Aku … did what he did … with this cop in Ala Moana Park … for good reason. National Security …"

"What you waiting for?" he berated the federal agent. "You underline *National Security.*" Then after a while of reflection, Kamekona added, "He should not go to no court for it."

Nakamoto signed dutifully, but this was not the end of the affair because Shark pulled out a felt pen and demanded the agent's thumb. He thoroughly smeared the fingertip with black ink and carefully pressed it against the document. "Now is good," he declared. "I go piss on my hand, it's killing me."

That his recommendation would not be taken seriously in a court of law, the agent had no doubt. He also could claim he had produced it under duress, without even committing perjury. But what it would do to his career … better not to think. It is the eternal truth, though—he reflected philosophically— that winners are not judged harshly. The "Baby Operation" ending with a nice double arrest and the dismantling of a criminal or espionage network was the best solution to all his problems.

The positive twist to the situation was that "Baby" maybe, just maybe, had developed some sentimental attachment to Shark. Such a development would be a gift from heaven that Agent Nakamoto could not even hope for in his dreams. Meanwhile, Shark—no matter what his emotional attachments—would *have to* cooperate with the further investigations. Even a beach boy would understand that a document signed by an ex-special agent, dismissed on disciplinary grounds, would do him no good.

Nakamoto pressed the *play* button and the closing scenes of *Throne of Blood*, the never drying source of his inspiration and consolation in hard times, started flowing again. Immortal Akira Kurosawa was right— sacrifice, loyalty and obedience to his elders were his sacred duties, and he would do what's right, even if he had to commit a professional *seppuku*.

The second source of Special Agent's anxiety was the unclear nature of the subjects' criminal ploy. The message from the LA office was ridiculously informal and utterly incomplete, yet another example of the old boys keeping new blood out of the loop.

"Max," the message started, unprofessionally addressing the Honolulu office chief by his first name.

"As per our previous conversation…" Of course a phone communication—no records to keep, nothing to explain, Nakamoto chuckled bitterly.

"Baby" should be in Honolulu Tuesday afternoon, a few hours after Colonel Kulagin has arrived." Now this part, at least, could not be hidden from Agent Nakamoto. He used his own network to find out that the Russian was an ex-military officer who had spent four years in Chechnya.

What comes from Chechnya was not a difficult guess: either drugs or terrorism, or most likely both. Russki moved to the Pacific Coast, the port city of Vladivostok, building his organization for a final jump across the ocean, to Honolulu. Once on American soil, he just needed to link up with some homegrown crime organization, hence a reunion with "Baby," the

Texan.

A clever, logical plan with a good chance to succeed, especially because the higher echelons of the Firm were … let's say … lacking in diligence and imagination. For Max Bonner, the Honolulu Chief, to leave for vacation without leaving clear instructions and an active file on the subject was … ah … something that would need to be discussed later, after conclusion of the operation. No one is irreplaceable.

Negligence like that … even after the clear prompt from Los Angeles: "Keep your eye on this, Max. You know who would love to see "Baby" succeed. This hookup might produce a lot of good will."

Negligence or … Nakamoto consciously refused to go into the game of guessing *who* might be the person who wished for a successful hookup between the Russian mafia and a Texan mob. There is a right time for everything, and for now, finding out all the possible info about Kulagin and "Baby" was enough on his plate. Once he had fully explored the nature of this association, there might right time to reach up to the next level.

Fortunately, some new personnel had come to the station, a few young and enthusiastic kids. Admittedly, they were green and not very skilled, but on the other hand, they were refreshingly not corrupted by the old-timers, not yet anyway. Nakamoto could grab them for his service without worrying about some misguided loyalties to Bonner and his clique.

The last credits rolled off the screen, forcing him to get up and eject the tape. There was no question in his mind; this affair was of epic proportions, an act worthy of Kurosawa's talent. The genius was unfortunately dead, but life has to produce drama before it can be turned into art, and he would not run away from the challenge.

He saw it many times on screen; even a simple samurai could become a great general if—in addition to courage, dedication and self-sacrifice—he had the balls to seize the opportunity when it occurred. Special Agent Nakamoto had heard a battle cry from afar and felt his hands tightening their grip on his *katana*. The moment of greatness was approaching.

Chapter 13

On my way from the Emergency Room, I stopped at the Foodland on Beretania Street. "How many jars of herring in oil do you stock?" I asked the manager.

"A box of forty-eight every month," he told me. "Sixteen already gone," he added, glancing at the shelf.

"I'll take the remaining thirty-two," I said. I decided to be well stocked with this stuff; it did wonders for Lala. Also, I would feel better knowing that nobody else could get them. She would always be welcome to share the delicacy with me. I might even give them as gifts for her parents from time to time. I thought of accumulating small crumbs of good karma here and there, until my personal account was so full that I would become irresistible.

"A crate of vodka with it? What's your brand?" The manager asked, but seeing my confused eyes, he added apologetically, "That's what usually goes with herring in oil."

But I had different plans for the oily fish. The day was ending with the usual golden-orange blast of sunshine above Keehi and I was ready to hit my bunk but first I decided to catch up with Shark.

As Caudillo should check in any moment, I wrote a short message to put it in the mailing purse for him to take it to Keehi the next morning.

"Hi Shark, how's it going? We've surely got a rough deal from Nakamoto. You think there is a way to make him pay for damages?" I knew this thought would cheer up my friend; he had to be pretty pissed as box jellyfish burns are wicked. Caudillo was quite groggy by the time I finished, and went to sleep with no more than perfunctory bitching.

Kamekona loved my idea. He dropped by early, Caudillo having delivered the message soon after sunrise. He was nursing his swollen and itchy paw in a small beach cooler, with a few cans of beer crowded aside. As we sat on the bench opposite the Ala Wai marina, he pulled out two Heinekens from the stash and we contemplated the morning, sipping slowly from the cans hidden in brown bags.

We were thinking how to get to Ben Nakamoto but we were making no headway. "Good thing I got my paper, at least," Kamekona tried to find some satisfaction in our misadventure.

Then, as I was catching up with the *New England Journal of Medicine*, he went to see Big Joe to find out if his ravaged hand would qualify for some form of compensation, or paid sick leave, or whatever. Back less than an hour later, he sat down even gloomier.

"Joe told me to go and fuck myself," he confessed in response to my unspoken question.

And that's how the Special Agent, patrolling Waikiki from inside a free tourist trolley, found us. He jumped spritely out of a slowly moving vehicle. "Men, I've been looking for you all over the place," he snarled. "We have to act without delay."

Shark pulled his hand from the cooler and presented it for the agent's inspection. It was seriously swollen
and covered with hundreds of small bubbles that itch
like hell. "See? This I got for working for you. Not even
a tip. No work for you no more." He turned away with
studied determination.

"Amnesty! Don't forget the amnesty I had granted
you!" Nakamoto was sorely disillusioned by Kamekona's ingratitude and let us feel it.

"I was in no jail even before your amnesty," Shark
replied. "And now can't even work. What will my family do? Who will give me a job with this?" He stretched
his beefy arm as though it was a paralyzed and dried
up limb; his eyes almost turned wet.

There was no slush fund that Nakamoto could uti-
lize for the noble cause of motivating his ace in the
hole, but without Shark's dedicated cooperation, he
had no hope of taking on the disease that was already
infecting his beloved organization.

"A hundred dollars a day," he shot, looking hard
into the Hawaiian's pain-filled eyes.

"And expenses!" Kamekona returned fire.

"Breakfast and lunch only. Dinner's on Baby!"

My head was spinning as they haggled hard, like
two hard-nosed Yankee traders, though neither had
roots in the Eastern Seaboard. The result of negotiations was that, in addition to his one hundred dollar retainer, Kamekona would be on a food-plan but
with exclusion of dinners, which—they both hoped—
would be financed by the enemy forces.

In fact, this was the centerpiece of the Grand Plan.
Now that Shark befriended "Baby" and she had shown

certain weakness for him, evidenced by punching me out, it was only natural to follow up with a sentimental entanglement.

"You will have an incidental encounter with her," Agent Nakamoto was thinking loudly. "As soon as she sees your hand, her heart will overflow with sympathy for you. Spy or not, mobster or something else ... she's a woman and that's what women do."

I wondered where our friend Ben had discovered this truth, and he was very secure in his belief, but I kept my silence. My less optimistic opinion about women was based on female nurses I knew at work. I would have to admit that a sample of less than hundred individuals could not be a fair representation for a XX genotype population of a few billion.

"Then," he continued, "she's bound to invite you for dinner."

"So far, so good." Kamekona easily agreed.

"You eat ... for free," Nakamoto raised his finger in a jocular admonition. "You drink ... and make sure she drinks a lot. You are not exactly a machine-gun mouth ... that's good; let *her* talk, talk, talk. Whatever she feels talking about ... She will start leaking information sooner or later."

"But if Shark drinks much, he will not remember what she said," I objected. "Moreover, *he* may start talking too much. You, Ben, haven't seen Kamekona after a few drinks. He might even sing ... and grab a ukulele from a band."

"I thought you were my friend, Chris." Shark didn't like my interjection. "And if you are so concerned, I can carry a wire. This way you'll hear all she says. It should work, at least until we go to ..."

81

Alex Modzelewski

"Shsss," the sound coming from Nakamoto's mouth reflected the sudden deflation of his hopes. "Go to her room ... and who's there? Colonel Kulagin is there!"

Now, clearly, counting on some kind of a three-some with the Russian infiltrator would really be too much to hope for. Even the best undercover organization in the world could not pull that off reliably. We sat silently on the bench like a building crew slapped with a stop-work order by a building inspector.

"Unless ..." Nakamoto mumbled, "Unless we lure him away." His scrunched face lit up in a triumphant smile as—to my concern—he winked at me. "Doc and I will take care of it. And you, Shark, get to work. I am not paying for your lunch to get in a bit of idle chat. You've already had your breakfast, right?"

As soon as Kamekona directed himself to the beach, where Baby had recently been seen, the special agent leaned into me with his cobra smile, which made me feel very uncomfortable.

Chapter 14

Kulagin woke up to the sound of some moist matter being sucked into a wide-bore pipeline and, as he opened his eyes, he saw Faith at the table, devouring a big plate of waffles, hardly visible under the landslide of bright red raspberries and snow-white cream. A plate containing a bare steak bone and a lonely burnt fry was already pushed aside, toward the table's edge.

One silvery dome was still uncovered on a tray, containing a remaining mystery dish. With the smooth confident moves of a champion, Faith released chocolate-colored jelly from its shiny prison and propelled it down her gullet with a large glass of orange juice.

This amazing woman had an appetite for food as great as her desire for love. Boris Ossipovitch has had his fair share of love stories to reminisce about, even though he never married, but he had never encountered such a tsunami of enthusiastic, overpowering femininity. It was only logical to presume that this mountain of passion had to be powered by a suitable intake of energy, but the glorious truth he observed was bigger than his assumptions.

He watched Faith's broad back glistening in the early sunshine with admiration and followed it down, where it expanded into her imperial butt. A spongy, soft behind could be justly expected in someone of her body build, but here Faith again defied low expectations; her buttocks were hard like a truck's overinflated tire.

These parts had been created for tough, all-terrain service and—God be my witness, the atheist colonel thought—she knew how to use them. After many years of searching, after the countless semi-satisfactory trials, Boris Ossipovitch Kulagin had finally met the goddess of love and fertility. What would his *mamasha* think of Faith? He really didn't care. She surely could help me with English; Boris showed his teeth in a flippant smile.

Was this kind of beauty somehow unique for Texas? Or, perhaps, the American nutritional supplements had something to do with it? Or was she simply a recipient of divine touch, a phenomenon as rare as inexplicable? Whatever might be the explanation, she was a *krasavica*, he made a mental note, a beauty.

To top it off, as soon as she caught his eyes in the mirror, Faith declared she would take another lesson of surfing in the morning. Irina—here he had to admit not being quite fair, as she was at least thirty kilo below Faith's weight category—certainly would not think of surfing after such a heroic night of love-making. She would stumble to a half-open window on her wobbly legs to feverishly suck on her long stinky cigarette, only to return under the duvet a moment later to continue in her coma.

He remained in bed, enjoying the view of Faith's enormous semi-naked body, but not feeling any excess of energy remaining in his loins. Nothing to be embarrassed about, he certainly deserved some extra rest after last night's maneuvers. He felt confident he had not brought shame on his tank brigade's glorious crest. A special gift had been bestowed upon him, as though in compensation to the young man for his really lousy, mostly fatherless, childhood. Those women who knew his secret endowment, and there were more than a few, made him feel proud long before the colonel's insignia shone on his shoulders.

Now Kulagin allowed himself something that would have gotten him kicked out of the Communist Party ranks twenty years ago, a very dangerous event in life of a second lieutenant. He ordered breakfast to be brought to his bed. He committed this act of decadence not so much due to his laziness as out of the desire to probe this exotic world. Boris Ossipovitch wanted to observe someone in the act of obeying his extravagant orders, even though this person was not motivated by threat of a kick, slap or court-martial.

Faith, on her way out to the beach, didn't stay long enough to observe the experiment. Maybe her mind wouldn't even have the capacity to understand her lover's curiosity, but she smiled and put a twenty-dollar bill on the table. "Give it to the maid, Boris, and see how it works."

It worked like fairy's gold dust. The colonel had never had anyone in his life, even his mother, look at him with such adulation. If one twenty-dollar bill could produce such a profound effect, Kulagin philosophized while chewing on his hamburger, what would a fistful of green notes do? To push the theoretical limits of his thought experiment, what extremes the human behavior might reach if a briefcase filled with

Alex Modzelewski

banknotes were offered?

His personal experience showed that people were exceedingly responsive to the business end of an assault rifle or the possibility of having a tank track driven over their body part. Clearly, with this kind of motivation, the subjects' love and compliance extended all the way into infinity. But even a tank commander would have to admit; this was a dirty and troublesome business.

Had he stumbled on a more elegant method of persuasion? Now, what would be a graph to describe the relationship between love and money? Kulagin had always been gifted in mathematics, able to predict the ballistic curve of his tank's cannon with one look at the graph, while his fellow students diligently sweated over their dog-eared tables.

The coordinates might start at zero dollars, zero love, he scribbled on a napkin, sharply turning up at X = \$20. But where would the love value go as the money axis grew? Would it ever reach infinity, just like with a barrel of Kalashnikov? His right hand trembled and the curve went sharply up on a moon-shot.

The urge to work on this problem grabbed his heart because, since his early days at school, he was passionate about science. It had landed him temporarily, in a tank brigade but now ... now he could dedicate his life to study the pure—not polluted by the foul smell of diesel and the coldness of wet mud—abstract forces, the phenomena of money and love.

Right there, Colonel Kulagin resolved to make a personal sacrifice and stay on this subject, so much in need of further exploration. He congratulated himself again on the bold decision taken weeks earlier and gathered strength to start his research project without any further delay. A logical place to start would be the open bar by the pool, where he could practice his English and observe local customs, draining glasses of colorful liquor charged to the room.

His chase of a food trolley made him shake with laughter. Now he knew he could have as many burgers and steaks as he could eat. The only lasting memories of this first day's adventure were the stains on his long pants. But he was wearing shorts now.

Filled with newly found energy, Boris Ossipovitch stood up and turned to the door. At that moment, a thought occurred to him that froze his smile and chilled his heart. Colonels of the Russian Army, even the retired ones, were not supposed to drag their sorry ass wherever they wished, and graze in any green field that caught their fancy. He got his passport as an unemployed grease monkey—quite likely someone would get his wrist smacked for this blunder—but that did not change the fact that he was still an ex-senior officer of a tank brigade.

There were things he knew … and there were people who knew what he knew. … Kulagin's frozen smile slipped of his face in one swoop like a patch of wet snow sliding off a heated windshield. For those people to reach across the Pacific, grab him by his balls and twist them off like a mushroom under a birch tree … it was as easy as gulping down a shot of Stolichnaya with black caviar. He sighed painfully but straightened up defiantly and marched out of the room. If he would have to run, he would run forward. Ura!

Chapter 15

Sometimes Lala accuses me of having a death wish, a misconception because neither sky diving nor motorcycle racing is that lethal. My still walking around without so much as crutches proves it. At that particular moment, however, I preferred not to know her opinion on my current arrangements with Agent Nakamoto and his faithful contractor Shark. Our friendship with Kamekona could carry my explanation so far; the rest of my involvement in the national security business would be credited to my addiction to high adrenaline sports.

Despite my initial misgivings, I nodded approvingly when Ben Nakamoto explained his plan to use me as a diversion for Colonel Kulagin, so that he would stay away from his room and his cohort "Baby." Once I had assented, Shark already dispatched to his duties, Special Agent succinctly presented my obligations.

"Doc," he said. "I don't give a fuck how you do it, but when Shark and "Baby" step out of the restaurant to go upstairs—and I believe they will, for I've noticed Shark's magnetic influence on women—you have to get Kulagin out of the way, even if you have to wrestle him."

Wrestling a foreign agent, especially after my first experience with KGB-trained "Baby", seemed to me somehow ungentlemanly, something that perhaps Sean Connery might do as 007, but I saw myself more along the lines of an intellectually superior and classier operative, like Simon Templar.

We agreed that I would need a solid cover story to procure for me a credible excuse to approach the colonel. Then I would lead him astray for a goose chase; I hoped to not become the goose.

"It's his second day in Honolulu," Nakamoto offered. "He has not accomplished much so far. Our audio surveillance tapes prove that the suspects mostly were screwing their brains out all night. The technician almost blushed when she handed me the tape - and she has heard a lot of the hanky-panky before. It is suggestive, I'd say, of a mob enterprise rather than any government-sponsored organization. The government employees, even foreign ones, would not allow themselves this kind of unrestrained behavior.

"Anyway, no significant information was exchanged. It was mostly moaning, clacking and squealing ... until the lady left for the beach in the morning."

"An athletic bastard," I noted. "And you want me to wrestle him?"

"Got your point, Doc," Ben admitted. "But remember—for national security, personal sacrifices must be made."

Then he got to the nitty-gritty. "Kulagin must be antsy—no progress with his business, whatever it is, while his costs are mounting. The Royal Hawaiian is not a cheap hotel. If you offer him an interesting lead to make a buck, he'll follow it."

"You mean ... I could try to sell him some state secrets?" I offered.

Nakamoto looked at me, disappointed, "Doc, when he buys your secrets, *he* must pay *you*! That's how it works. Don't they teach that in a med school? For him to get some fast cash out of it, you must buy from him!"

That really escaped me. In my line of business, whatever I do, money always tend to move into *my* hands.

"The question is: What he might have for sale? Drugs? Contract killing? Human trafficking?" Ben was just floating the balloons of possibilities.

I felt coolness spreading below my knees, even though noon was approaching and our bench emerged from the shade of a palm tree. We were sitting in the full sun.

"All these lines of business are hard to break into. What would you do if you said you wanted drugs and he opened a suitcase filled with neatly stacked bags of heroine? Would you have enough cash to buy even one bag?"

"Not in a hundred years," I admitted embarrassed.

"Exactly. Your cover is blown and so is your head. Poof!" He did not seem to be concerned with this possibility and I felt a twinge of dislike for his cavalier attitude. "Same with a sex slave or a contract assassination. Big money is required up front.

"But there is one element that unites all these cases. Whatever he does, he has it, or he can easily obtain it. And that would be ..." He looked at me expectantly, judging my readiness for this operation.

"Weapons," I whispered. "He has guns ... and I don't have to show my cash until he comes up with a crate of Kalashnikovs or bazookas or whatever …"

"Brilliant!" Nakamoto shook my hand. "You're ready!"

I swung past the beach and saw the platinum head bobbing next to a surfboard and Shark's big teeth glistening on the other side. "Baby" was into Kamekona, big time.

Big Joe presided over the scene, his bold head fixed on top of a pyramid of flesh, its wide base starting right at the level of the booking counter, extending up to his jaw like a cone. Even close to its top, just beneath Joe's mouth, his neck was still wider than his head. Where exactly was his neck was a very difficult question, surely somewhere below his jaw and above his chest, but its exact anatomy would be a very imprecise science. I just hoped I would never have to attempt a tracheostomy, a breathing hole, on him at my Emergency Room. Let his airways be blessed with eternal health.

I started patrolling the hotel grounds, looking for a tall man in his early forties. According to the description, he had big shoulders, a small beer belly and a tiny Hitler-like blond moustache. Nakamoto's picture was not bad and I was confident I would pick Kulagin up sooner or later. Shark's end of the business was not advanced yet, they hadn't even gone to a restaurant; I had time.

Searching for Kulagin was more exercise than I thought it would be. At noon, I sat at the grill to have a cold beer and a slice of pizza. I didn't even bother to take a tab. My tightwad employer, Nakamoto, was sure to decline my expense account.

"Y enoder one," I suddenly heard behind my back. Studiously, I placed my knife in a position to see the man behind me. I was grateful I was carrying out my operation in the Royal Hawaiian; a lesser hotel would have plastic cutlery at a grill.

Yes, my subject was sitting directly behind my back, nursing a Mai Tai in his hand.

My midday tiredness shot into a thousand pieces by a jolt of adrenaline, I turned around slowly, faking boredom. "A nice drink you have," I opened up. "What is this?"

His eyes focused on me with some sluggishness. "Shit know this," he answered nonchalantly. "Vont try?" And he gestured to the bartender, "Give one my friend. On room."

I was in the game! We were sitting and chatting. Slowly, our communication lines were opening. He did not hide the fact of being from Vladivostok and gave me his real name, Boris, without any tricks on my side.

Boris had good things to say about Hawaii; he was awed by the local women and loved hamburgers. We developed some empathy on this basis; the conversation was speeding up when I reminded myself of my job. Not interrupting our amiable exchange, I started doodling a crude image of a submachine gun on a napkin and decorated the edges with a garland of hand grenades. I hoped he would take it for a typical, subconscious drawing of a man preoccupied with his inner, undisclosed thoughts.

Boris fell silent, observing my hand with this sort of undivided attention that a poker player displays when the stakes are getting really high. When I finished my last grenade and thought about adding a simple bazooka, he grabbed my knee under the table with his spastic hand and said something in Russian in a strange, strained voice.

"C'mon Boris," I smiled at him, "your English is pretty good, and it's getting better every minute. In a few days, you will be a regular local guy. You are moving really fast!"

He spat a few more words in Russian, looking like he was on a brink of having a heart attack. That got me really alarmed; Nakamoto wouldn't be a happy camper if his subject died having a Mai Tai with me. I had to get him out of this anxiety attack, perhaps redirect his thinking. "So, can you get me a few of those?" I pointed to the napkin. "And, speak English …" I teased him a bit. "I'm sure we will be good friends." I winked warmly at him.

The hand on my knee relaxed and let go, then without saying a thing, the colonel turned around toward the hotel. I followed him into the lobby only to be confronted by the spectacle of Shark, standing in front of the elevator, intimately holding "Baby" around her waist, as she was swaying around like an oak tree in hurricane. They had to have had a pretty high-octane lunch.

The worst nightmare Nakamoto could imagine was just coming to pass in front of my eyes. *National security!* I told myself and leaped forward, between the sloshed couple and Kulagin, who seemed detached from reality, his unseeing eyes glued to the marble floor.

"Boris," I grabbed his arm and shoved my napkin before his eyes, "How about my guns?"

The colonel raised his head, his pupils big like holes in a death mask, jerked his arm free of my grip and galloped out through the hotel's front door, knocking tourists down and jumping over suitcases until he disappeared in the midday crowd.

Beats wrestling, I thought. But I was not quite comfortable with the service I had provided on behalf of the FBI Fortunately, Shark and "Baby" didn't notice a thing; I saw their backs in the open elevator. Her head slumping on Kamekona's shoulder, she looked pretty tired.

Chapter 16

Nothing more soothing, relaxing and romantic has been invented so far that could beat an evening on a boat in Keehi. Yachts anchored in the lagoon or tied along jetties are mostly dark, as their owners live somewhere in Honolulu. There are a few bright halogen lights over the gravel parking and a dome of harsh brightness produced by the battery of spotlights over the loading dock, but they are away from *Magic Carpet*. The point of luminosity closest to us was the warm glow over La Mariana, a small marina with a pleasant unassuming restaurant by the same name.

With your back turned to the land, you saw nothing but the night sky, splashed with the faint blush of smoldering orange on the right, over Barber's Point, and a faraway flush of lights on the left, over Honolulu.

If the night happened to be clear, as most of them are, a shimmering phosphorescent blackness started right overboard and extended to the solid pitch-black line of the mangrove islands. Over and beyond those, the huge sky begun, a humongous canopy crammed with brilliant points blinking on and off. You could not decide if the particular disappearing star, picked just for the fun of it, was hiding behind a wisp of a passing invisible cumulus, or it was blotted out by a swinging mast of a boat dancing in the lagoon, or maybe the tired eyes stayed closed a moment longer than thought.

But that night was of a different kind. Lala and I were submerged in the dense thick darkness, the blackness bearing more resemblance to roofing tar than to watery ink or airy coal dust.

I like all nights in Keehi, but the very dark ones hold a special attraction for me. With my eyes completely shut out of the business of observation, other senses—unaccustomed to having the field for themselves—recover their confidence. They start bringing wonderful and unexpected news and images to my brain. A night like that paints in unusual detail the steady low rumble of waves breaking at the far-away surf. The warm moist wind feels on the face like the gentle sigh of a puppy. But more than anything else, I look forward to the concert of delicate smells that can be hardly ever enjoyed while eyes overpower the brain's sensory circuits.

As soon as the sun disappeared over Barber's Point, I set up a nest for us in the *Magic Carpet's* cockpit, wedged my back where the walls meet in a rounded corner and scooped Lala in front of me. My nose in her hair, my arms and legs around her, I could not experience her any closer, unless I morphed into an octopus.

I am endowed with a very sensitive nose, which—marginally speaking—is a very useful faculty in my emergency room work. Often, I can identify people with diabetes or certain infections before any tests come from a lab, drawing accusations of witchcraft from the nursing personnel.

My face buried in her hair, I tried to itemize the smells I could detect on her.

- Chloe perfume—check. The fragrance is well known to me. I'd prefer a bit less, as it interferes with her natural aroma, but I won't complain.

- The soft, warm whiff of a young mammal … I could swear I sensed estrogens, even if my professors would have ridiculed me. … A female mammal, a *hot* young female mammal—a big check.

- Irish Spring soap—an easy check.

Then I sniffed suspiciously at the unexpected odor—herring? "Lala, you had some herring in oil? I wonder who else shares your obsession," I asked nervously, feeling a painful tag on my heart.

"My parents flew in from the atoll last night," she responded, turning her head up, toward my face. "By the way, my Foodland ran out of herring. They told me some jerk bought all they had yesterday. Talk of obsession. Didn't even buy any vodka with it, an ignorant fool."

"If need be …" I swallowed hard, "I happen to have a few jars. I could share with your parents, since it seems to be a ritual food in your family."

"I didn't think the list of suspects would be very long," Lala nodded. "And it is not a bad thing to have family rituals. Look at the outcome," she spread her arms in darkness for me to behold. "But they swore that they held that particular communion without vodka, so if I seem to you strange on occasion, it has nothing to do with the alcohol-fetal syndrome."

A dense white beam of light shot into the moisture-saturated darkness and a searchlight cut across the lagoon. The light was coming from the direction of mangroves and groped the shore around us. "Shark's coming," I said and got up to light a reading lamp; it should be enough to guide him here.

Mele climbed onboard first, refusing Kamekona's assistance, a *wahine* on a warpath, apparently.

"He and you," she pointed at me, her index finger like a pistol, "what you did all day? I wait and wait on beach for Shark to come to work. Big Joe say, no see Shark after ten. And make faces like stupid."

One didn't want to make Mele angry. It would be just bad politics. She was not an aggressive person on a daily basis, but I strongly suspected that unduly agitated she could be dangerous. Shark had confirmed my premonitions no more than a day earlier.

At close to six foot, Mele was a big woman. One could not really call her obese, her body was solid like a trunk of royal poinsettia, hard and full of knotty muscles. I have observed her easily grab a boatful of heavy bags from her ancient station wagon to fill the dinghy to the brim in one turn, no groaning, no straining. And when she dropped her head low and bit her full lower lip … even Shark stepped back.

"Working," I volunteered cheerfully. "A special assignment, government job."

Kamekona nodded enthusiastically. "See? Told you!"

Mele threw him a jaundiced look of an old prosecutor worn out by countless lies. "If you worked, where is the money?" She considered the investigative part of the trial successfully completed; what was left was the penalty phase.

"Here!" Shark pulled his gray nylon wallet out of

his back pocket triumphantly. He searched in it for a moment then … ta-da! He produced a one hundred dollar bill that had left Agent Nakamoto's bill holder in the morning.

Mele took it with distrust, rubbed it with two hands for a moment, crinkled and examined it against the reading lamp, as though she suspected that Shark had produced it in his underground high-tech laboratory. Eventually satisfied, she folded the bill carefully and placed it in the back pocket of her own jeans. "I buy food," she explained.

I understood the disappointment that was overtaking Shark. The proceeds of a whole day's work, a dangerous day in service of the country; it was all gone down the drain. Not even a few bucks left for a six-pack. "What you gonna buy?" he asked with a grudge.

"Celery sticks and carrots," Mele answered spitefully, still knowing deep inside that some punishment was due.

"Filet mignon," Shark demanded petulantly. "I like filet mignon."

"You can have baloney," Mele sneered. "Anyways, where the hell you got taste for this kind of expensive shit?"

I knew but—in the national interest—I kept my mouth shut.

The evening lightened up somewhat over the next thirty minutes, in social terms at least, as the sky remained black. The girls went to the galley where Lala wanted to show Mele the virtues of a juicier as a tool likely to switch Shark's preference for steak into enthusiasm for pureed vegetables.

"Have you?" I mumbled in the tiniest of my voices

making a small but suggestive movement with my middle finger.

You crazy? Kamekona's face twitched in alarm, as his eyes shot into the companionway. Then he turned his head for *no*, shrugged and mumbled back, "Like a log ... in coma ..."

We dropped the subject as two heads emerged from the cabin. Mele had a juicer in her hand and announced she was going to her sister, who lived in Kaimuki, to try this new approach to nutrition. Besides, she was just starting some courses to finally get her GED and she might sleep at her sister's for a while. Then she might consider the continuation of her education in a community college. We were allowed to infer that her continued living on *Water Whisper* in Keehi Lagoon would be detrimental to her academic career. Obviously, even if his standing has improved somewhat, Shark was still in the bad books.

Lala wanted to spend that night with her folks and they both left.

The sound of a rotten silencer on Mele's Dodge was still reverberating through the harbor when we heard, "Hey, Doc, Shark! Over here!"

The special agent emerged from the blackness behind the announcement board. Son-of-a-gun was hiding within a few feet of my boat, heard every word yet remained completely concealed. Superior intelligence training, no question.

"We've lost Kulagin," he announced honestly, without any false pretenses, an earnest leader openly communicating with his team.

"What did you tell him that he jumped like a spooked deer and ran so fast that my men had no chance to get on his tail?" He addressed me gravely, allowing no misapprehension of the fact that I was accountable for the alarming turn of events. It would be only logical for me to assume now that I should be responsible for fixing the problem I had created.

"He was just about to walk into the elevator where Shark was hauling wasted Baby," I said. "I reminded him about those guns I wanted. You think I should have wrestled him in the lobby?"

Nakamoto shrugged with resignation.

"Besides, maybe he just hurried out to fill my order?" I added, but I had to agree with the agent's acid smirk that it was an unlikely explanation.

"What did you find on the tape Shark produced? Did she leak?" I knew I was nowhere close to the level of security clearance necessary to share in this kind of info, but Nakamoto's face indicated he needed all the help he could get.

"Tough bitch," he complained. "Not a word about her and Kulagin's business. But there were some interesting parts; your friend is apparently a Hawaiian prince." He looked to Shark with biting irony, his black moustache twitching suggestively.

Whether Kamekona blushed I couldn't say due to the ambient darkness and his natural complexion, but he sounded rather defensive. "She kept bullshitting me about her daddy who owns most of Texas. ... And how she has those spare ribs with the Bushes. And that W. prefers his burgers without cheese, because he's such a great biker and can't gain weight ... and that Jeff would not put any mustard on his steak. I just couldn't listen to it anymore, so I let it slip out that Queen Liliuokalani was my grandma."

Ben was nodding, smiling sardonically, his gold fillings shining in the reading lamp. "So, now her papa and you are going to clean this Hawaiian mess?" For the first time in months he had a bit of fun.

Kamekona looked at me for help. "I mentioned the problems that the queen had with those fucking sugar planters and Faith, this is her real name, just took off from there."

"*Real!*" Nakamoto snarled. "The only real and honest thing about her is her appetite!"

But we did not pay him any attention.

"'My daddy had a ton of problems with those stupid farmers, as well,' she said." Shark decided to present his investigative experience honestly and without withholding any juicy elements. "And on she went, about those stupid peasants objecting to her daddy putting oil jacks in their fields, and sabotaging his gas drills, and dragging him to courts because of pipelines … I could not take it anymore, I thought of escaping from this restaurant. Anyway, I had already two steaks …"

"Duty, national security, man!" Special Agent Nakamoto growled.

"I know," Shark agreed. "And this hundred dollars you gave me. … Anyways, so after this second bottle of wine … Do you know," he turned to me, "that they have wine for hundred-twenty dollars a bottle? So after this second bottle, she decided to ask her daddy to come over here and clean up this dirty business with sugar planters as he did in Texas."

"How did he do it in Texas?" The idea of cleaning Hawaiian politics caught my imagination. We could dig out those fucking planters; what's a bit of exhumation if that might give Hawaii a fresh start, remove all this simmering discontent about stealing the King-dom. It's just … what, a bit over hundred years, not that much in the life of a nation.

"Ah, as far as I could understand," Kamekona thought hard, "Immigration decided the farmers were illegals and deported them to Mexico."

"Oh, they were Mexicans." Disappointed, I reflected that this route might not be available for Hawaii.

"No, not that," Shark objected. "They were U.S. citi-zens, but the INS *made* them Mexicans. Just took their papers, pushed a Mexican driver's license in each guy's pocket and kicked them out. Oh, and put them on this bad list so they wouldn't ever come back."

"How's that possible?" I looked to Nakamoto, hop-ing he would deny the very possibility of such a scam, but he just smiled mysteriously, silently saying with his eyes, "You have no idea what we can do, buddy. National Security!" Eventually, though, he could not take the silence that followed and changed the subject. "Looks like her daddy has real clout in his home state! Hard to believe it could be pulled off anywhere in the good old U.S. of A."

"This is exactly what this journalist dog said in his paper! She couldn't remember whether it was the Houston, Dallas or San Antonio rag." Kamekona had the second installment of the cleanup story. I hoped this might contain some elements usable in the State of Hawaii.

"So when they kicked out this lying piece of shit to San Salvador, they had something tattooed on his forehead: 'FUCK MARA' or something like that. That, according to Faith, would ensure he wouldn't come back to do any more mischief."

Alex Modzelewski

Ben Nakamoto had a fit of laughter. Now that was *esprit de corps*! His colleagues in Texas surely had a sense of fun running as deep as their sense of duty. "He will surely not bother anybody anymore," he said eventually, wiping his eyes. "*Mara Salvatrucha* will make sure. An exceptionally nasty gang in San Salvador," he added for our education.

I imagined myself being released from the jail on Dillingham with a tattoo saying in big blue gothic-styled letters: "FUCK KALIHI." I would not see morning, I suspected, and neither would that guy. I would put my knife to *Magic Carpet*'s dock ties right away, if I could make it to the port. I would push off without so much delay as to take a piss in the public toilette. With this kind of urgency, I might have a chance. I would make a big circle around Honolulu, sailing around Mokapu'u Point to Kailua in order to pick up Lala. She wouldn't mind my tattoo as long as we sailed toward the Northwestern Islands right away.

Silence fell on *Magic Carpet,* heavy and dull, without any original thoughts or new information shared. That moist dark night, looking so tender and congenial an hour ago, had become clammy, gloomy and downright depressive. I was bothered by the image of the tattoo on my forehead, while Shark deliberated on the impossible dilemma that providence had thrown into his path—the choice between the two big and powerful women, each perfectly capable of turning his life not by a mere ninety degrees but spinning it by a few hundred, in either direction.

Agent Nakamoto fell silent after his outburst of good humor because a poorly defined anxiety started gnawing his gut again. The idea was crystallizing in his consciousness that his personal prospects were becoming less and less inspirational. The rope he was splicing so skillfully was now mysteriously coiling around his neck. This case was going nowhere and he needed a breakthrough before Max Bonner, the Honolulu office chief, returned and botched the "Operation Baby," dumping his failure on Nakamoto's lap, as was always the case. A few short days … no more time could be wasted for feeble measures.

Chapter 17

A double row of colorful silk kimonos swayed gently like a double line of sunflowers, the dancers making exquisite small steps one way and another. Their beautiful, white powdered faces—whenever coyly revealed from behind a long line of pink, red and yellow umbrellas—did not lose their charming smiles even for a second, while the graceful silhouettes floated across the stage on their half-bent legs.

Shit, Ben Nakamoto thought. It's hard on legs; their thighs must be burning... And yet, they were smiling as though someone was swinging an overtime check before their eyes.

A joyful discipline and radiant obedience. Ben wanted a woman—no, let's be straight about it—a wife like that, a good, refined Japanese girl. They would watch samurai movies together, the good ones, by Kurosawa, which he already owned, but some new titles could be purchased as well, so she wouldn't consider him an old bore.

His *okusan* might explain to him some intricacies of the dialog in her singsong voice, as English subtitles were probably just a crude translation from *Nihongo*, the language of a thousand delightful nuances. Unfortunately, Ben did not speak the tongue and felt cold sweat pearling on his forehead every time he thought of the task of learning it.

He was in command of a small vocabulary, useful to drop a word here and there, just to keep up the general belief that he could speak Japanese. But in fact, his conversation skills were even worse than those of his father. And that was something to say, as the older Nakamoto brought eternal shame on his family once when he bungled a polite conversation with a visiting Buddhist monk.

Considering the agent's name and reputation, nobody thought of giving him a language skill test. It was a very fortunate presumption indeed, as his presumed Japanese language mastery was the single thread by which he was hanging in his position of a special agent. After a few less-than-voluntary transfers—from South California, to North California, from there to Alaska and finally to Hawaii—Nakamoto's position was rather precarious, but that was about to change. Operation "Baby" would be his *coup*, an inflection point in his career's trajectory, as well as a sharp turn up in his love life. An umbrella dance girl, even if the exact person was not selected yet, had been already self-promised and she was almost within his loving arms.

The wheels bumped on a metal board and the car's front bumper brushed against the floor, as the agent swooped into the underground garage on Kuhio Avenue. That was his favorite operational spot, despite the driveway being too steep. It had one exit onto Kuhio Avenue and another onto Kalakaua Avenue, offering this fox the choice of discreet ways in and out. Moreover, there was a busy Internet café above from which dozens of people streamed in and out all the time. From here, the agent could move all over Waikiki like a ghost—sometimes a Japanese tourist in a loud Aloha shirt, sometimes a faceless local guy in a dirty baseball cap, and on a few occasions a clown totally concealed behind his mask with big red nose. He was the invisible man who could see everything, floating through the streets undetected like a ghost.

On that day, his area of interest was located upstairs, the busy Internet cafe where thousands of people hailing from around the globe accessed the net. Any one of them could stick his thumb drive into a computer's USB port and cause anonymous mischief.

Those people, Kulagin and "Baby", felt just too comfortable in Honolulu, Nakamoto had decided. Appearing from nowhere, like the Texan woman did, disappearing without a trace like her Russian cohort managed—they had way too much field in which to play their dubious game. Even he, an FBI special agent, could not keep up with the rascals. This problem required an urgent remediation and would be addressed promptly.

What troubled Nakamoto most was time, or rather its lack. While he felt the rising heat of Max Bonner's return on his neck, the suspects seemed to concentrate on fun rather than on their proper objectives. The special agent abhorred such an attitude of duty abrogation, even if their employers were evil.

Nakamoto decided to focus their minds on the business at hand, while he was wrapping his—temporarily empty—tentacles around them. Nothing stimulates a person's interest in his or her vocation like cutting off money flow. This is a well-understood principle, especially true when one is used to generous living expenses. Nakamoto was about to radically boost his suspects' professional ambition.

He pushed his baseball cap deeper over his eyes, inconspicuously but thoroughly scanned his neighbors for presence of any hostile agents, and slid his mini-drive into an USB port.

Five seconds later, not only all credit card issuers in America but also hotels, banks and even department stores in Hawaii received his message that charges and payments made on behalf of Ms. Faith Kruger of Dallas, Texas would be not honored. Now he felt confident that those double filet mignon lunches, with multiple bottles of the hundred-twenty-dollars-a-bottle wine, would make "Baby" call her employers pronto. Whether her controllers were hiding in some blasted submarine offshore or in a luxury suite next door, he would have the transcript of this call on his desk in no time. As far as the electronic means of communication were concerned, he had Honolulu covered pretty well.

The surveillance measures would apply to the other actors of this drama as well. He had Shark's cell phone tapped, and the doc's e-mail monitored, just to make sure nobody tried to play a double game. Only Kulagin was still running in the wild, free of any surveillance, but he was bound to come home too. By the time Bonner has fitted his lazy ass into the chief's chair, the case would be tied up, wrapped and delivered.

He felt like rubbing his hands with a devilish giggle but instead stood up, bearing all signs of profound boredom, and left the café through the Kalakaua exit, directing his steps to the Royal Hawaiian.

Right place, right time, this was his maxim, and it

was achievable only by spending many patient hours waiting, like a hunter in his duck blind or a ninja in ambush.

This time, his reward came with the most satisfactory speed. He was hanging around the hotel lobby, a tourist wearing a small round fabric hat and a khaki canvas vest over his polo shirt, pretending to read a Japanese newspaper, when he became aware of the commotion near the elevators.

A big angry woman stormed out of an elevator. Dressed in an expensive-looking white dress tightly draping her very generous curves, she held a red lizard-skin purse in her hand. She was aiming squarely for the middle of the reception desk, where amidst the row of black heads, one blond clerk was standing behind the counter.

The impetus of this large, and highly charged, mass produced the effect of an express locomotive suddenly rushing into a busy railway station, where, unaware of danger, a crowd pulsates with random activity from one edge of the platform to another. Fear and a sense of foreboding lashed across the throng of guests, who threw themselves out of the big woman's path, opening a clear track to the hapless clerk, who shrunk in her battle station but bravely did not flee.

"What d'you mean, my card is no good?" The platinum head stooped a foot above the top of the pale blond girl, emitting a hostile growl.

"It has been declined, ma'am," the girl whispered, after a moment of panicky tapping into her computer terminal. Now she was seriously considering an emergency evacuation. Damn the health benefits when one's work becomes *that* dangerous.

"I'll be ..." Baby huffed and slammed another titanium card on the counter. "Take this!"

The clerk swiped the new card through a reader ... then slid it again ... and again, while the crowd watched the scene with growing interest. She looked up and timidly shook her head for *no*.

This went on for a few minutes; the static electricity increasing in the lobby to the point of blue sparks ready to jump off any pointy metal object. Baby kept pulling out new credit cards from her red lizard purse, one after another. She slammed each piece of plastic onto the marble top, only to observe the sweaty girl shaking her limp long blond hair, *no*.

The reception hall crowd, intimidated by Baby's first appearance, relaxed and started enjoying the show. Keeping a respectful ten-foot distance, the throng of tourists coalesced into the dense mass of colorful shirts tightly packed against each other, enclosing the proscenium in a watertight fashion.

Every new card emerging from the scaly purse was greeted with a low, rising in pitch, oooooo...ended by the dry slap of the plastic on marble. Then a minute of silence ensued, interrupted only by Baby's furious breathing, while the clerk fed the card through a machine.

The first sign of *no* was greeted with the collective groan of short "ough!" The second try evoked a louder and longer "aaaaah," coming with the unmistakable tinge of joy that the mob experienced in retribution for the initial moment of undignified panic. The third *no* was met with the exited and loud "ooah!" which sounded very much like "ole!" in a bullfight.

The pack felt blood and was ready for the cruel

conclusion of the show, while maintaining its respect-ful civilized manners. But they misjudged this victim. Baby slammed her red purse against the counter, bare-ly missing the shell-shocked clerk and splitting her ac-cessory at the bottom. A lipstick, coins, a mirror and a dozen of other objects women habitually carry in their purses spilled out, but she was not about to pick up the wreckage from the floor.

A half-pirouette put her red, blazing like a furnace face in front of the giggling crowd. Even before Baby made the tiniest movement forward, her tormentors splattered against the walls, dove behind pillars and hid beyond the big arrangement of bird-of-paradise flowers in the middle of the hall. This time, the throng did not face a powerful and dangerous but self-con-trolled mass. Now, the locomotive was out of her tracks. Stumbling and careening, she was converting her tremendous kinetic energy into the force capable of dismembering anyone in her unpredictable path.

"Manager! To my room!" Baby shrieked like an, "All Aboard!" whistle blown by a mad conductor on steroids. She disappeared into the elevator and only then did the shaken spectators start emerging from their shelters.

Special Agent Nakamoto smiled serenely and qui-etly left the hotel. It was time to go his office, put the headphones on and listen to the important call that would take place anytime soon.

Chapter 18

By 1am, the flow of patients at the Queen's Emergency Room had slowed down. The patients under observation started nodding off in their cubicles and the anxious crowd in the waiting room thinned out. The pace of work eased, not enough to sit down and enjoy some coffee, but sufficiently enough to go to a restroom and have a few deep therapeutic breaths.

As I was ambling toward the cubicle sheltering the nice lady who had stepped barefoot on a broken glass in the Ala Moana Park about midnight, we received notice of an ambulance heading our way, carrying victims of a major car crash.

A crazy rush, the phenomenon always following arrival of a major accident victim, must be multiplied by three if there are two seriously injured persons. Personnel, equipment, consultants— all resources are suddenly in short supply, while the poor guys on stretchers can't wait.

While the whole world spins around the critical patients, all less urgent cases wait ... and wait ... And as they are waiting, new folks arrive, each one convinced of his case's absolute priority. By the time the accident victims are in an operating room or at the Intensive

Care Unit, the pent-up mass of frustrated sick people and their families has grown hostile.

It looked to me that the midnight stroller would have to do a bit of healing on her own before I would be through with the new critical arrivals. But before the car accident casualties arrived, another ambulance brought two men with burns on their faces and upper bodies. They were shirtless and their skin was shining red like boiled lobsters, but there was hardly a blister to be seen. Their hair and eyelashes were singed but, after my examination, I could see that their eyes were normal.

Though they were scared as hell and, I was sure, quite uncomfortable, they did not strike me to be in serious trouble. There was certain chemical smell about them that I could not identify and their shorts were soaked with water.

"What happened?" I asked.

"Eeee ... Ah ..." The victims made mewing noises but did not produce any coherent answer. The ambulance crew could not say what had happened either. Someone had called 911 and they scooped the pair up on Sand Island, close to Dillingham Boulevard. They seemed so confused that the attendants had to practically force them into the ambulance.

"Happens with an explosion," the paramedic assured me. And since I knew he had done two tours in Iraq, I was pretty sure he had seen more big blasts than I ever would.

Maybe a cooking gas blew up a kitchen, I thought. The skin looked burnt by a flash, a fireball of a very short duration. Then someone hosed them down to extinguish their burning clothing, thus the wet shorts.

It made sense. The poor devils had not regained their bearings yet but they should be all right. I ordered some painkillers and cold packs and put them to rest. I intended to keep them under my wing to make sure they didn't develop a respiratory distress or symptoms of unsuspected head injury. They would tell me their story a bit later, after having recovered their senses.

I just had enough time to look at the X-rays to make sure there was no glass hiding in the midnight stroll aficionado's foot, when the car crash victims rolled into the ER and sucked all the oxygen out of it.

Once I had them stabilized—more than an hour later—and sent to the ICU, I went to the soundly snoring Ala Moana Park Barefoot Countess. On my way, I peeked behind the curtain of the first of my burn patients. The bed was empty, a white blanket carelessly spilled onto the floor.

Was he entertaining his friend? I turned to the next cubicle and its bed was empty as well! My lobsters had disappeared! Only the mysterious chemical smell lingered in the linen. How could they have vanished? Excluding the possibility that they had de-materialized and disappeared like ghosts, they had to have sneaked past the nursing station, as well as the registration desk, in order to slink back into the streets of Honolulu from which they had been forcibly removed. Why?

I had no idea, but I knew the facts would come out later. Either a police detective would spill beans during his obligatory visit to the ER, or a nice fat rumor would tell the tale in all its glorious details, or an article in the Honolulu Star-Advertiser would report on some shameful situation and sternly demand improvements in the public safety. The story would come out as it always does, satisfying in its gory detail, truthful or not.

Now I was looking forward to having a few hours of more relaxed business. The Barefoot Countess was less than grateful when I woke her up to do some stitching on her foot. A tourist appeared with a superficial stab wound to his shoulder--a cut acquired on Liliha Street. What where you doing in that part of town by night, buddy? Not enough of the nightlife for you on Kuhio Avenue, where the watchful eyes of undercover cops and hotel security keep you and your wallet safe? Are the girls prettier over in Kalihi?

Speaking of which, I could see the peroxide head of Ailine through the window of the door leading out to the waiting room. Clearly uncomfortable, she was squirming in her seat. It had to be at least four weeks since we had last met at the ER. I thought she had taken to heart my exhortations about the use of condoms, but apparently I was wrong. Now, the remaining two or three hours separating us from the sunrise had to feel to her like an eternity spent in the gynecological hell.

My nose diagnosed the trichomonas infection even before she put her feet into stirrups. She was out in no time, clutching the prescription for Metronidazol in her hand, happy for this horrible itch and burning to stop soon. The labs would come in their own sweet time, while Ailine had her instant relief. She was no different in this aspect from anyone else.

It is my professional opinion that people—not all, of course, but a good portion of my patients—land at emergency departments for reasons of their own silliness. Considering how many stupid and reckless things I had committed in my life, I am quite sympathetic to them and understand an occasional attempt at self-immolation. Boredom, laziness or simple lack of common sense—whatever their reason, it usually fits comfortably into my liberal understanding of human psyche.

Pretty Jack, on the other hand, jerked the chains of my ethical restraint. The moniker "Pretty" was obviously given to him in the fit of irony, as he was devoid of any shred of physical beauty. Short and skinny, but with a potbelly, Jack was missing his front teeth and had had his nose rearranged a few times, every episode adding its unique twist to the big shnoz gracing his face.

The usual reason for our meeting was a facial trauma on his part, suffered at the hands of a small-time drug pusher or pimp he was trying to dislodge in his unrelenting drive for economic success.

Many repeat trauma patients are people with mental disorders, victims of our screwed up psychiatric care system; but Jack was not one of them. By my non-expert assessment, he was not crazy, just stupid. Jack could not recognize the fact that a career in petty crime demands a certain amount of talent and skill, like any other vocation. Apparently, he lacked both. In effect, his visits to the Emergency Department were frequent and utterly devoid of any professional satisfaction on my side. Predictably, my handiwork would be undone sometime over the next few weeks.

His appearance in a cubicle number three put me a bit on edge, and then the unit clerk waved to me from her desk, performing a pantomime of having a phone at her ear. "Call for you," she mouthed.

"Who the hell?" I squashed my desire to utter a vulgar phrase. People were not supposed to call me at work; even Lala didn't try. Every poor soul on a stretcher in front of me, no matter how serious her or his problem, has a damn right to one hundred percent of my attention. Social callers are intruders and I made sure people I knew understood that.

I put the last stitch in Jack's split upper lip, where the soft flesh compressed by someone's fist met his, standing proudly alone, canine tooth. I felt like a glazier repairing the same broken window for the fifth time. Maybe you should board it with plywood, I felt like saying to Jack, or consider moving to a better neighborhood.

"Yes!" I barked angrily into the telephone.

"Ah… Chris… Sorry…" It was Shark's mortified voice. He had never called me before. Normally, Caudillo was good enough for him.

"Come soon you can. Big job. Bring scuba. Bye!" He shot out his plea and cut off the conversation with obvious relief, not giving me the opportunity to give him a piece of my mind.

I discharged Mr. Pretty and saw his greasy ponytail bobbing across the door. What now? Did Shark find Baby's supposed submarine and I was expected to sneak onboard for reasons of national security?

I did not even bother to go home in the morning. I just stopped at the public storage place on Dillingham to pick up my scuba gear. Not knowing what was going on, I had no choice but to go, grumbling about Shark drawing rather heavily on the account of our friendship. How many times had I had seven uninterrupted hours of sleep that week? My tired brain could not recall.

Unlike its night incarnation, Keehi Lagoon has all the charm of an old industrial plant in the morning. It is exceedingly rusty and clunky but seemingly not bad enough to be flattened with a bulldozer.

The incessant cloud of dust floats from the concrete factory upwind, covering all surfaces within a mile or two with fine grime. A gnashing low-frequency noise vibrates from the same direction, fighting against the competing high-pitch whine of plastic-grinding tools at the boatyard on the opposite side of the marina. This duet is regularly interrupted by the staccato of a jackhammer where the pile of concrete, that used to be a pier during Eisenhower's administration, is being replaced. Jets roar, taking off from the Honolulu Air-port—no more than a mile away—every few minutes and it comes almost as a relief, one big noise instead of that wildly textured cacophony.

"DINGI SCUBA OP CAT" These were Shark's instructions drawn with his finger on the dusty table in *Magic Carpet*'s cockpit.

"Take your dinghy and load your SCUBA gear on it. Meet me opposite this big catamaran, you know which one..." I decoded his message. I was sure he also intended to add, "IF YOU PLEASE" but ran out of surface on my dirty table.

Grinding my teeth, I undid the straps on my din-ghy and wrestled it onto the water. I loaded the tanks and regulators, threw in two buoyancy compensators and lead belts. Then I carefully lowered my body inside; the small rubber boat crouched under the load like a little donkey burdened with an elephant's cargo.

Finally, I jerked the motor's starting cord and,

miraculously, it fired on the first try. Coughing and expelling blue smoke, the dinghy turned her bow to our rendezvous point opposite the blue catamaran, a permanent fixture and landmark on the lagoon. It was already there when I first cast my eyes over Keehi and will probably remain there after I have died.

As soon as I turned around *Magic Carpet*'s stern, I noticed a small boat in the middle of the lagoon with a big guy sitting in it motionless. That would have to be Shark ... doing what?

I realized, when I pulled closer, that Kamekona was sitting in the middle of the harbor like a big dog over a bone, staring down smaller mongrels flitting nervously along his eye periphery, not daring to challenge the top animal. The landscape has somehow changed. I became vaguely aware that something was missing.

Shark's arms flew up the moment he noticed me. "Ove hea! Ove hea!" He was signaling wildly, almost falling out of his dinghy.

He seemed to be anchored in the middle of the harbor but I knew he had no anchor. Ah! I experienced the flash of understanding; I knew what was missing. There used to be a boat there, a nice forty-footer with two guys living on it. This boat had disappeared ... but on closer examination ... it was still there, only twenty feet lower, sitting on the bottom. My friend's dinghy was tied to the tip of her mast.

Now everything made sense. The boat had sunk last night and Shark was officially in the maritime salvage business now. He had claimed the wreck and now it was his job to keep looters, thieves and other scoundrels away from *his* property.

"When and how?" I asked, seeing him worn out and

seemingly shrunk. It had to have been a long night.

"After eleven last night. A loud boom and a big orange flash. Even on my boat, we heard the whoosh of a big fire. But before I got out from behind my island, the fire was gone. She went down like she got a torpedo in her belly."

"And the guys?" That sounded like a gas explosion, a bad, bad thing to be around.

"Saw them in the water, swimming like crazy. Won't be back."

"How can you be so sure?" I asked, thinking there was a nice chunk of money sitting on the bottom of the lagoon. "They will be back with an insurance adjuster."

Shark let out a puff of air with contempt. "Not unless the cops get 'em. Why you think the boat blew up?"

"Gas explosion?" I ventured with my theory.

"Maybe gas too… but there was a lot of other shit down below. It blew a hole so big that she went down like in a minute." He looked me over carefully. "You really don't know?"

Now he had this expression of concealed disregard reserved for an elderly parent who just cannot figure out which button to push to Skype someone. "They were cooking ice … and they had a … work accident."

Lobsters! I'd treated those guys. Having narrowly escaped their on-the-job accident alive, they fully intended to evade police as well. Shark was right; the boat was as good as his, unless the cops got to her first.

"She sits straight on her bottom, but it's damn murky in this stinky mud," Kamekona explained his predicament. "I snorkel down, but no can see much.

121

And good stuff is in the cabin. That's why we need your scuba.

We geared up, strapped the tanks on and dove. The roof above the bow, where one would expect a front hatch, was practically missing; just a fringe of melted plastic was left along the hull's sidewalls. We looked through this big hole into the front cabin where a V-berth should be. We saw no remnants of sheets, blankets or sail bags—the stuff usually kept in this compartment. Instead, we saw a few bent metal bars coming out of the bulkhead and spanning the space. On this frame there were still shiny clamps, struts and beaker holders attached. Clearly, this was not a place meant to be anyone's living quarters or storage for sailing equipment. This was a lab.

Filled with the fairly clear water now, as the brown muck had settled on the floor, the front cabin was striking in its emptiness, crossed by horizontal beams of faint daylight let in through the blown out portholes. Its contents had to have been blown up, showering the lagoon with pieces of glass and metal, or they were pulverized, shot into the thick mud seeping inside through a foot-wide hole in the bottom.

My lobsters were very lucky they were not too close to their factory when the blast occurred. Had they been anywhere close to this inferno, there would not be much of their skin left to apply Flamazine on.

Interestingly, the lab door held, probably reinforced just in case of such an unfortunate event. The main cabin seemed intact, if flooding with the ocean water was disregarded. I looked inside it through a porthole, while Shark squeezed inside, hauling my tank behind him.

VHF radio, GPS plotter … all the electronics were naturally ruined by the salt water. I wondered what things of value Shark could salvage from the wreck. And I was amazed.

He put me to work in the cockpit, tasked with removing the steering wheel. This normally simple operation turned out not to be that easy when performed underwater. Feeling for the parts in dark water rather than seeing them, I worked clumsily, my wrench maliciously slipping off the nut.

Shark emerged from the cabin five minutes later with a big bronze barometer in his hand. He lingered behind me for a moment then stabbed his thumb up, twice. Get up to the surface, he meant.

"You keep eye on those thieves," he gestured toward the competition, who—encouraged by his disappearing underwater—had closed in on our dinghies in a very intimate fashion. "I bring stuff up. You take it to my boat. And bring Mele if she shows up from work."

What he did not say, but I understood, was: It's waste of the air on you, man. I can dismantle this baby like a piranha as long as I have some air to breathe.

I followed his instructions because I knew he was right; my efficiency in stripping the boat was nowhere close to his. But he was not Mr. Right anymore when Mele arrived. I found her on board of *Water Whisper* when I delivered the first load of treasures Shark had recovered from the wreck. I laid it out on the deck: a boathook, two sadly unused fire extinguishers, a steering wheel that I'd failed to remove but Shark swiped off like a wristwatch, and a number of other useful and salable items.

Mele watched with approval, but the moment I gently placed on board the hanging lamp, an elegant piece made of brass and porcelain, she gave out a groan like she was delivering Shark's first son and heir apparent. She threw her big body into my boat, almost tipping us over with her momentum. "To this boat," she commanded, urging my hand to open the throttle wider.

Her knowledge of the boat's anatomy and the location of equipment shocked Shark as much as me. She steadfastly remained on top of the operation, in a figurative and literary sense, perched on my dinghy's side, directing her partner to nooks and crannies I had never discovered during the few years of my boating experience. Whatever could be unscrewed, unhinged or ripped off—enough to fill my dinghy three times— had been removed and joined the pile on *Water Whisper*.

The salvaged stuff was divided into two categories—useful and beautiful. Mele's heart was on the side of the beauty. Each table cover, pillow, berth sheet, pot and lamp had been lovingly examined and folded for washing, cleaning, drying or whatever work might be needed to restore it to its original beauty.

Her yearning for bourgeois trappings transformed her into a merciless slave driver. She kept sending Shark to search for pretty things in the muck, even as the air gage on the second tank implacably planted itself over zero. He tried, the brave man, to continue his scavenging with a snorkel, but his lungs failed to cooperate. Finally, with great regret, he had to leave a fine brass handrail in place, for the time being.

I, on the other hand, was waiting for the inevitable end with impatience. By twelve o'clock, my eyes were coming to full closure as I was motoring between the wreck and *Water Whisper*, the two points separated by few hundred yards of water. I also developed this funny feeling that taking the next breath was optional and I might rest a few minutes before doing it.

A soon as Shark scrambled on his rubber boat, gasping for air, I motored straight to my *Magic Carpet*, leaving all the SCUBA gear with Kamekona, in case he would like to have the tanks re-filled and keep going with his plunder. I had only one thing on my mind: throwing myself on a berth and sleeping without any further interference. And as I was almost at the point of fulfilling my plan, I committed a crime against national security.

I was just stepping out of my dinghy into the water, disregarding my new sandals, yearning for the touch of a pillow under my head, when Special Agent Nakamoto sprung out from behind a poster board, shouting, "Doc, you must find Kulagin!"

I do not believe it, because it is not consistent with my nature, but some witnesses reported that I roared like a wounded bison and charged Nakamoto like the same, knocking him into the water. The agent actually believed that I tried to trample him to death. Then I jumped back into my dinghy, yelling, "You can kiss my ass!" and took off, the motor yanked into FULL POWER.

I vaguely remember streaking past Mele and Shark, who were paddling toward their mangrove home, then racing next to the airport end of the lagoon, my motor temporarily overpowering all other noises of Keehi.

There, I made a sharp right turn under the Nimitz Bridge. I knew the place where Pretty Jack hid from time to time. He told me of it once while semiconscious under intravenous sedation.

If he were there, I wouldn't mind, because out of all the inhabitants of Honolulu, he was the only one I could trust not to flap his lips at me. I could trust him because I had personally put a lot of sutures into his mouth just a few hours ago—3-0 chromic catgut into his lip muscles, 5-0 nylon monofilament on skin and 4-0 gut for mucosa. I was safe with him and only him.

Why the details of his lip repair resurfaced in my mind, I was not sure. Possibly, because I was already on autopilot. All the components of my brain capable of critical thinking had shut down, my eyes had closed. I rammed the boat into a bulrush at the end of the short dead-end channel right past the bridge. When the motor stalled, I slid onto the rubber bottom, fully unconscious.

Chapter 19

Ben Nakamoto understood that the voluntary support civilians might extend to an FBI agent had definite limitations. The glorious spirit of Bushido could hardly be found among the semi-anarchistic citizens of the Eastern Pacific and to believe otherwise, despite proof cropping up every day, would be foolish. But this samurai's back was against the wall and he could almost feel a spear grating against his bones.

As soon as he had established himself comfortably in his cubicle, a headset within his reach, Kathy from the electronic surveillance unit called; the suspect was dialing a number in Texas.

Things fall into place once you give them a little push, he smirked, putting his headphones on. To his surprise, almost disappointment, the conversation he tapped into was carried unscrambled over an open line. What an unprofessional, arrogant bitch, he thought unkindly of Baby.

A sniveling female voice flowed without a moment wasted on breathing, like a stream jumping on rocks and turning into eddies but never interrupting its run. The whiny music of Baby's monolog sounded like a piercing flute song countered by the low-pitched irritable grunts of a bass, originating in Texas.

It took Nakamoto a few seconds to understand the gist of this conversation. His suspect was calling a man, whom she addressed Daddy, in Texas. The intimate familiarity of their conversation sounded to the puzzled agent quite genuine. A business-like exchange between an agent and her controller was replaced by the mushy rapport of a terminally spoiled brat with her overindulgent father. A display on his desk showed the telephone number and the name of its owner, Mr. Rick Kruger.

"And Daddy, my cards do not work, and the hotel manager says I have to pay cash … and they are very, *very* rude…" Baby's complaints never slowed down even if their essence had been already stated and re-stated. This essence was directly attributable to Naka-moto's action.

He just could not reconcile in his mind the image of the fiery locomotive in the hotel reception with the small prepubescent voice lilting in his ears. His mouth started to dry because with every second of the sus-pects' conversation, it was more and more apparent that his read of the situation could have been quite faulty.

But the agent's anxiety was still very low on its tra-jectory, short of the point of its rocket-like takeoff. Daddy started consoling his little one by telling her home stories and those accounts produced a tingling of Nakomoto's scalp, which spread quickly toward his face and neck and continued on down to his heart.

The Bushes were apparently planning another ranch brush clearing with a big BBQ, while Charlie Dougal, the godfather …

The name Dougal buzzed in the agent's mind for a moment like an annoying fly before it stung him with the white-hot punch of an angry hornet. The Homeland Security Agency Deputy Secretary's name was Charles Dougal. Not that Nakamoto had ever met the bigwig, but he had seen the dignitary on internal videoconferences on a few occasions. Those mean pale-blue eyes set in the round face would not even blink while he was stomping a humble civil servant like Special Agent Nakamoto into dirt. He was quite sure of that. If this Mr. Dougal was Baby's godfather, Nakamoto's skin was already worth less than he had paid for the dragon tattoo on his left shoulder last year.

He listened to Papa Kruger babbling about happy family events, and Baby whimpering and laughing like a ten-year old with the quiet resignation of a man with terminal cancer. He was well past the prescribed stages of denial, rage and whatever else he was supposed to feel. The next world, that's what he was already looking towards.

Seppuku, this is what a decent samurai would undertake without much delay, he thought, nodding his head sadly, his headphones abandoned on the desk. But before he set out looking for a friend ready to cut his head off at the end of the ceremony, a thought blazed across his consciousness like lightening. *Here I am, thinking of my own glory, but have I asked what my master would want of me?*

He blushed at the realization of his shameless self-love and complete lack of responsibility. But at the same time, he could not suppress the odious sense of joy that this thought brought to his heart. Foul as his duty would be, this warrior would have to wait for his chief. He would suffer through all the humiliation and the cruel abuse heaped upon him, and only when fired from the Agency, a free *ronin,* would he let his guts spill in glory.

The decision to delay the settlement of his debt of honor had an unexpected effect on the agent; his frozen mind started working again. There were bizarre holes in this story, which could not be explained in terms of a rational world. He must have missed something, perhaps a lot, and it was his business and duty to fill those holes with facts.

To start with, how does Kulagin fit into this high-powered family? What the hell happened to him, anyway? Secondly, how did Baby arrive on Oahu? And the supplementary question, what is the source of Kruger's money and political connections? Kruger's record on the computer screen that Nakamoto had summoned—unfortunately, the last entry had been made ten years before—simply described him as a businessman, the owner of a few bland, oil-related enterprises.

And what if, the agent felt his hair rising, what if he had stumbled on a plot so big, so far reaching, that it implicated some *extremely* powerful people? A lot of money could be made if some well-positioned political figures kept honest agents like him under the thumb. Uncovering *this* kind of a plot could surely resurrect his life, even if the danger of it would be extreme.

"The way of the Samurai is in desperateness," Nakamoto whispered. "'Ten men or more cannot kill such a man.' Thank you, Yamamoto Hagakure, for spelling it out so clearly." He was certain now what his duty was;

he had to find the way to uncover the deadly affair before Bonner returned, as he was obviously in league with the traitors.

The first breakthrough arrived ten hours later, when he received a transcript of a cryptic message from Shark to Gorny: "Come soon you can. Big job. Bring scuba. Bye."

"Son-of-a-bitch," Nakamoto mumbled surprised. "On my pay, after all I have done for him … turns out to be a double agent! And this emergency doc! You can never, *ever* be careful enough!" Once more, he congratulated himself about the wiretap, technically illegal, practically priceless.

To know the exact meaning of the message, one would have to be in Gorny's head, but the agent promised himself to be there before long. What he should do right now was clear enough. He slipped into his black, night operations— shirt, put on a pair of extra padded, dark sneakers and donned a black baseball cap. Then he drove to Keehi Lagoon to assume position behind the notice board close to *Magic Carpet*.

This could be a long wait in the humid darkness but no ninja ever thought of complaining. The agent lay in ambush, watching the single figure of Shark, sitting morosely in the middle of the black lagoon, through his night goggles. Whatever was hiding under his dinghy, it could be the first link leading to that nasty man in Texas.

Nakamoto imagined the spiteful, pale blue, watery eyes and drew strength and determination from one singular thought; someone was going to be crushed like a bug, and there still was a chance that this annihilated person would not be him.

131

His job indeed required a lot of strength and determination because Doctor Gorny did not arrive until eight forty-five, when the sun was already blazing through the haze of dust spreading from the concrete factory. Nakamoto remained as still as a rock, and did not even shift weight on his sore swollen legs when the doc passed him on the way to his sailboat. Undetected, Nakamoto watched the suspect struggling to lower his rubber boat on the water and load a lot of diving equipment onto it. Gorny drove it to the spot where Shark was doing his guard duty. Could the submarine that had brought Baby be sitting beneath? Perhaps it's damaged and requested an emergency assistance?

The doc and Shark disappeared under the water. The tension was becoming unbearable but the agent persevered like a warrior standing guard on his watchtower, ignoring the peril of a treacherous arrow aimed at his heart at any time.

Finally, the water broke, startling him, and the suspects emerged, hauling up a variety of objects. Unfamiliar with boats and ships, Nakamoto couldn't tell what objects were recovered even with help of binoculars, until a steering wheel appeared. It was a great relief because, quite clearly, the sub could not leave the lagoon without this critical part. The importance of recognizing a good number of other items, most of them looking like nautical equipment, was not that essential anymore.

The agent would love to get this vessel and its crew under lock and chain, but now, knowing the submarine could not escape before getting its steering wheel back, Nakamoto decided to wait. He needed to find more details about this audacious operation before shutting it down.

When in unknown territory you need a guide; it's that simple. And when you need to move through a dark unfamiliar place fast, it is even more important. Nakamoto needed a guide to walk him through intricacies of this treasonous enterprise, and he had already decided who that would be—Gorny. Doc was not as physically threatening as Shark, and—as all intellectuals—he would be easier to manipulate into becoming his collaborator. Willing or not, the traitor would *have to* help Nakamoto unravel this plot. The agent had just a few ideas of how to motivate him.

The decision had been made but the agent still had to wait for three more long hours, standing in his post and suffering from heat exhaustion, until the middle of a Hawaiian day. Nakamoto endured his dry tongue sticking to the palate, his feet melting in his padded tennis shoes and the sun turning his black-clad back into a baker's oven. He ignored the smart-ass remarks of the local bums wandering around with their fishing poles. He suffered through it all, waiting with the determination of a *kamikaze*, until Gorny's rubber boat touched the shore.

Then he jumped out from his hunting blind to apprehend the prisoner, blinding his mind with the confusing demand to search for Kulagin. Search for Kulagin, ha! There would be no more aimless running around; his steel trap had shut! Now it was time for Gorny to sing his story in a windowless room, again and again, until the agent was sure that its last note has been extracted.

At this moment, a terrible and unanticipated event took place; the traitor unexpectedly turned on the agent of law and order. A full body slam—delivered by a taller man moving with a lot of momentum—knocked Nakamoto into the water. The assailant trampled over him viciously with a wild war cry, and left him in the water for dead.

The distraught agent rose to his feet, cleaning his flooded sinuses and checking his bones for fractures. Doc Gorny was speeding away in his dinghy, the motor's roar shaking drops of salty water off his cap. Actually, Nakamoto's body—suddenly cooled off in the lagoon water—felt better, but his soul was howling to the heaven with anger and pain. There were times when a samurai could cut off a commoner's head on grounds of disrespect, and Nakamoto wished he had lived in those times.

Chapter 20

No soldier ever regretted escaping from under enemy fire fast enough. Not a real warrior, that is; the uniformed clowns working on their poems and motivational stories in propaganda units do not count. Of that Colonel Kulagin was quite sure, and that's why his frantic run from the Royal Hawaiian Hotel did not bother him at all.

There are times to attack and times to take cover, and knowing which one is which is this rare quality that defines an officer as a leader of his men or their executioner. He washed his soiled underwear in Argun River just like his men, without any feeling of shame because he knew that all of them, a lieutenant colonel as much as a shaved-head private, felt the same euphoria at surviving the rockets and machine gun fire that the Chechen devils poured on them from above. And hey, they pulled their wet boxers back on and were ready to kick ass again. A front-line soldier's story, nothing exotic.

Boris Kulagin felt he *was* a leader, unlike his failed-poet old man who hatefully and persistently kept hissing into his ear, "You ran like a rabbit, Boris, like a fucking scared rabbit!"

Why is it that the father, who had so little to say to his only son when alive, now could not stay away from him, buzzing around his head like a fly circling a plate of hot soup. The mysteries of parenthood—both in biological and philosophical terms—held very little interest for this mechanically inclined tank officer. "Shut up, you stupid old son-of-a-bitch!" the colonel wanted to yell at his father, but you can't have a loud argument with a ghost in the Ala Moana Park. Theoretically, one could but not without people staring and possibly having a policeman come over for a closer look.

Kulagin didn't wish either. He would not welcome any interest on the part of the cops, but would hate even more any civilian curiosity. A bland looking fellow with too much interest could turn out to be a government worker, after all. Worse, you wouldn't even know what government he worked for. Therefore, under his current circumstances, all Boris could afford was to mumble and whisper spitefully, as many people did, pretending there was a phone-plug in his ear.

He wished to explain to this old and thoroughly dead dog of a father—oh, so important, because he spent a few years in a *gulag*—that to move fast is to survive. Maybe a general has enough time to take a cup of *chai* from a *samovar* and carefully consider this option and then another. On the frontline, you either run like a rabbit or get a posthumous decoration.

And he could also add, "You, dear Father, fucked up your life in a way so spectacularly stupid that you should keep your mouth shut." There was no need to retell this story because it was an urban legend anyway, but Boris would bring it up anyway, for no other reason than to drown out the obnoxious whisper.

Shark of Waikiki

Year 1950, dear Papa, Ossip Pavlovitch Kulagin is a student at the Moscow University. A poet, they say.

"A young man with a brilliant sense of humor, a poet with great imagination and a fiery heart, the real hope of our Communist Awareness." That's the university paper. Then, in April, this great poet looks through a window in the student lodge …

Here, younger Kulagin, the colonel, envisioned looking sardonically into his father's blue eyes.

And what does this poet's great imagination bring into his mind's eye? A likeness of Comrade Stalin rendered in the snow on the sports field outside, no less. His high cheeks made of mounds of shoveled slash and ice, two patches of dogwood for his bushy eyebrows, and his eyes marked by trashcan covers, a striking likeness.

"If you had a shred, a gram of a brain, you would hide under your bed like a rabbit, YES, like a fucking rabbit." Boris was choking with anger. "You would suck on a bottle of vodka until you've passed out … and I might have had a normal father." Now Colonel Kulagin started kicking into the grass, making green clumps fly, drawing worried looks from passers-by.

"But *no!* Your famous sense of humor demanded that you go down four flights of stairs and add a nice handlebar moustache, made of burlap potato sacks. How very funny!

"Five years of camp was in fact a pretty lenient sentence for this desecration! Someone really liked your poetry! Lucky you, Comrade Stalin took his last breath in fifty-three, so you had less than three years of rehabilitation. Without teeth, but still young, you were back, right in time to snatch my mother, before she was even out of a high school. A really famous poet, you were quite a catch! Unfortunately, you'd left a good portion of your brain behind, somewhere around Vladivostok, maybe so that your rotten teeth would have company."

Now Kulagin's eyes unexpectedly turned wet. He stopped arguing and discovered with relief that his father's hostile whisper stopped as well. The argument stopped just in time, because a stooped old man dressed in a long and exceptionally dirty coat stopped by.

"You better get out of view," he mentioned in a friendly tone. "You look like a fuckup, bro. Cops will hassle you here. See those two?" He waved toward two men on bikes, wearing navy-blue shorts and helmets. They were still fifty yards away but already looking in his direction.

"You may stay in my place," the guy declared magnanimously, and smoothly slid over a black four-foot-tall plastic pipe running along the street. "But only tonight. Tomorrow you must go and find your own place."

Kulagin followed over the pipe and the policemen glided past without giving him a second look.

"See?" the old man noted proudly. "Have to know where to hide and they won't bother you. I'm Charlie."

In fact, Charlie was not old, perhaps fifty or even less. His old age impression, intentional or not, was due to his thin hunched figure enveloped in an ancient black trench coat. His skin was also dark and wrinkled, evidence of years of exposure to harsh sun, but his long greasy hair tied into a ponytail was still mostly black.

"Are you a local citizen?" The colonel formed his question carefully.

The vagabond looked him over carefully. "You French? You speak funny."

"Russian," Kulagin admitted sadly. Hiding his identity would not be easy. "My name is Boris."

"*Na zdorowie!*" Charlie yelled joyfully. "So happens, I grabbed a bottle from a deadbeat. Was already smashed out anyway, sleeping. So here we have better than half a bottle of booze. We celebrate friendship between our nations!" He patted a place next to him invitingly, leaned comfortably against the thick pipe and took a swig of brown liquid.

Not much to celebrate with half a bottle for two, Kulagin thought, but sat down and took a big gulp from the bottle. "What is in this conduit?" he asked, considering his words carefully and articulating them with care. He knocked on the pipe behind him with the bottle.

"Shit," Charlie shrugged his shoulders. "Bothers you?" And when the colonel made an ambivalent face, the vagabond went on to elaborate. "See, Boris, you are sitting less than a foot away from a bag filled with a gallon of shit. I know what I am talking about, because I am the bag, and I have not crapped for three days, even though I still eat. So you are sharing a bottle with this shitbag, and it is even not tied up that well." He farted loudly. "This pipe really should not bother you. It should be underground, but like all emergency measures will likely stay here for a longer while."

Kulagin started feeling strangely tipsy after only a few gulps, an unnatural development in view of his well-hardened head. But it did not bother him; it rather made him mellow and relaxed, so he listened amiably to Charlie's theory about the role of excrement in public life.

"Take those two cops," the vagabond stabbed his thumb backwards, toward the street, which was filling now with tourists smartly dressed in their new Aloha shirts. "They know I'm here, but as long as I don't start dancing in the street, they pretend I am a ghost, an immaterial being.

"They would go after me if the Mayor told them, but he won't do such a thing. Why? Because he knows that if he orders such abuse, I'll go where his office is and take a dump on his stairs, the whole gallon of it. First, of course, I'd call a TV station.

"So, tell me Boris, what would be the chances of him getting elected to *any* office if he becomes known as the Shit-Mayor, or the Mayor that people crap on?"

"None," Kulagin mumbled, amused by Charlie's devilish plan. His back was sliding off the black pipe, his head seeking rest on the ground.

"Forgot to tell you, Boris," Charlie snickered. "I figured … not much booze for the two of us, so I put in some pills the doctor wants me to take. Guess you're not used to them, eh? Hope you have good night. Sometimes, if I take that shit, I have some wild dreams."

The colonel completely missed the remaining portion of Charlie's political theory as all his senses shut down under the potent mixture of booze and psychotropic medication.

His body was quietly resting, but his mind had to endure another visit from the other world. The old man was still putting in his fake teeth, covering his mouth bashfully with the left hand, as though the visitation caught him by surprise as well.

"Boris, I'll give you that … I screwed over my life, no question about it." He started in a conciliatory tone. "But it doesn't mean I haven't learned anything. I was picking on you not because you fled but because you ran like a stupid rabbit, doing exactly what they wanted you to do.

"In my *gulag* times, if I found a rabbit hole, I put a snare in front of it and made the critter run. Smoke or noise or anything I could come up with, the stupid animal did what I expected of it, it ran almost every time. That night, my friend, I ate like a king. Had I discovered this method earlier, maybe I would have kept some of my teeth. And I don't have to tell you that rabbit stew tastes much better than the soup made from the leather belt you have already boiled twenty times.

"My trap hardly ever failed because the little fuckers were so predictable; a small brain doesn't have that many ways to respond to fear, I guess. But your head is like a melon and for years you were cramming every damned book you could find into it. So it really pissed me that you acted like a rabbit."

Father was reasonable now, Boris thought, and it was quite nice of him to bother to share his experience from his grave. Therefore, he volunteered that his mad dash from the hotel was, indeed, rather pathetic.

"A well-timed dive into a foxhole before an incoming shell slams is one thing; but it is a completely different thing to jump under the table because someone knocked a beer mug off the bar. It seems rather unfair, because making a split second mistake might have unpleasant consequences in either case. Being too proud,

Alex Modzelewski

or even just too slow, could easily result in one's ass smoked in the first case. But having survival reflexes too keen would make one a butt of jokes in the officer's club for many years to come. It all comes down to the context, which could be apparent one second too late."

Boris saw his father nodding with understanding and he gave up a bit more ground in his self-criticism. A man with his experience *should* have realized that if his pursuers wanted him dead, he would already be cold, with his cock crammed into his mouth. Or maybe his balls, one never knew what was the proper routine. Kulagin suspected that a cock meant official business, while balls signified a more personal dislike. For example, if his unit commander had ever found out about his wife's admiration for Capitan Kulagin's special talents, he might have been choked on his balls.

"Irrelevant!" The old man lost all the appearance of reconciliation and shouted through his ill-fitting dentures, waving his arms wildly. He was clearly losing his patience. "My point is if you let them set a wire noose and then do what they expect, well … you are going to be made into stew. They are creepy and scary bastards, true, but then it's even more important that you outwit them! And you won't do it if you act like a frightened rabbit, shitting on your heels. A spine, man, you must have a spine! You must surprise them. Go right for the jugular; they can be intimidated too!"

Old Kulagin, the poet, was losing steam; his speech was getting slow and his voice gravely, as though it was coming from an ancient crank-driven gramophone that was grinding down to stop. His figure was breaking up as well, but he made an extra effort to stay a moment longer.

"After watching you these past ten years, I wouldn't even bother with you anymore." He waved his hand with contempt. *"Comandir,* fuck you very much! But you surprised me by taking on this Hawaii business. For a moment, you made me feel like you were my son. You took a jump over the camp's wire! So now don't lie there under this shit-pipe like a homeless dog! Finish the business!"

He snapped his fake teeth playfully. "There are worse things than losing one's teeth."

Already almost invisible, he added with an increasingly bad temper, "Don't make me feel like I could have just as well shot my load into the ground instead of chasing after your mother." And then he disappeared in a small cloud of malodorous gas.

At these words, Boris Ossipovitch shook in a familiar rage at dear papa, but—credit to Charlie's pills—he slept well under the shit-pipe for the rest of the night, having no more dreams.

He woke up in the morning pretty well rested and barefoot. His nice Argentinean leather sandals, purchased especially for the occasion of visiting Hawaii, were gone. Whether it was his last night's friend or some other early riser, someone liked his expensive footwear well enough to walk away in his sandals, kindly leaving behind a pair of old rubber slippers.

Ah, good enough, Kalugin thought, the leather sandals were a bit too ostentatious anyway. He was right. In his new footwear, he could blend into the Ala Moana landscape like a pineapple on the Dole plantation, at least until he opened his mouth.

His new strategy could not be too complicated, he figured, as his freedom of maneuvering was very limited. How long might it take someone to find him in the park? This strip of grass and sand, sparsely punctuated with bare trunks of coconut palms, was crammed between a busy street and the ocean, nowhere more than two hundred yards wide. Three men could comb it within an hour. He had to act immediately.

The starting and central point of his action had to be Faith. She was the only lead available to him, and only from her could Kulagin follow the strings leading to the puppet master, now completely submerged in the darkness.

He had to get back to Faith, even though she was a part of the plot to ensnare him. She was nothing but bait, he understood it clearly now, but at the same time, she emanated from her expansive persona strangely positive vibes. No question, she was a beautiful woman, the kind he liked best, an abundant generous dollop of femininity, but in addition, she had certain quality that Kalugin considered even more important. For some reason, he did not perceive her as a threat, even as he discovered her being an agent of the enemy organization.

The colonel trusted his intuition, because he was the guy who stuck his head out of a tank's turret for quite a few years, and it remained attached to his body. If someone had a good antenna for unknown dangers, that would be him. Faith did not raise hair on his neck. Significant!

Thinking of her, Boris could not help interrupting his war planning with some irrelevant thoughts, even if it meant losing valuable moments. A sly smile creeping on his face, Boris thought that perhaps he had met his equal. He was awed by this contender's sexual appetite, endurance and imagination. The KGB trained their female spies well but the Federal Service, the old spy workhorse's successor, apparently knew their business just as well. KGB, FSB … new name, old company, he shrugged.

Chapter 21

I felt the scheduling clerk pulling me out of my bed by my right foot. I was kicking and loudly protesting, "I'm not on call! I'm off until Thursday!" But she held my heel in a steel grip, shaking it viciously. I had no choice but to open my eyes if I wanted to walk again. Black smooth surface ... smells like rubber. Still quite disoriented, I lifted my face but all I could see around me was the same black wall. Alarmed, I sat up and looked around.

Above the black surface there was a green barrier closing around me. When I managed to focus my eyes, it resolved into a thousand individual stems, each one sporting its special shade of lime, emerald or bottle green. I realized I was in my dinghy, which I had wedged into a field of bulrush. The narrow open space behind my transom was filled with the sun setting into the water, but it was mostly blocked by a big dark blob, which just let go my foot.

"You OK?" The blob asked in Shark's voice. "Mosquitoes will suck you dry here when the sun comes down."

I stretched my neck and cracked my fingers. "How did you find me here, Kamekona? It's supposed to be a secret place." I felt remarkably better after my little snooze.

"First place I looked." My friend sounded surprised. "Everybody hide in this dead-end one time or another. So busy, people stopped coming. Like hiding behind the same trashcan every time you play hide-and-seek."

"So much for my secret place." I was disappointed. "In any case, Nakamoto didn't find me here and I slept like a log."

"Nakamoto ..." Shark mentioned with concern. "He might be crazy, I think. When you took off like a breakaway marlin, he started making an awful racket on a jetty. He was yelling and waving his arms at me, so after I took the last load of the stuff to my boat, I thought I would see what the hell that was all about. He was all wet and kept jumping in this black outfit like Count Dracula on Big Bird. What did you tell him, anyway, that he was so foamy at the mouth?"

"Nothing more than to kiss my ass ..." I was thinking hard how to understand this strange turn of events but no explanation came to mind.

Kamekona was also at a loss. "As soon as I came to the shore, Nakamoto yelled that I was under arrest ... and pulled out a pair of metal cuffs." He shrugged but he was obviously somewhat disturbed. It looked like his rap sheet was getting even longer.

"What did he arrest you for?" I could not believe Nakamoto's ingratitude as well as his lack of self-preservation instinct. "Wait - national security!"

"Not sure." Kamekona made a gesture of ignorant innocence. "He slipped and fell into the water again. Bumped his head on the way, but only a bit ... dropped his gun into water too. You know, a fool and a gun are a bad combination.

"And know what, Chris? He wanted you, too. Kept calling you names, like ... fern coat ... I think. Loco?"

"Maybe a turncoat," I sighed. And I realized that Nakamoto did sound like someone with paranoid ideations ... A tricky situation; those guys with paranoid schizophrenia sometimes behave like they are all right and then, boom! Something sets them off. We sat among the bulrushes, safely ensconced for now, trying to make some sense of the transformation that our friend, Ben, had undergone over the past few hours.

"He could get a new gun and handcuffs," Kamekona noted. "We better keep away from him for a while. Maybe he should have an accident before catching us."

"No, *no!* Shark," I protested, as he made a hesitant but telling gesture, his two big hands twisting in opposite directions. "We rely on our luck; he might fall head-first in a sewer by himself."

We agreed to change our environment for a while, at least until we knew what was going on. Keehi was out of the question. By now, Nakamoto felt at home here. He could even bring his own dinghy or kayak to pursue us on water.

Waikiki did not feel safe either with all those Russian and Texan characters running around and the FBI boys on their heels. Who could even say whose boys they were? Nakamoto himself could be a North Korean agent for all we knew. All we could be sure of was that his hundred bucks was legit; it passed first Mele's and then Foodland's scrutiny.

Kailua and Waimanalo were our next candidates; both were far enough from Honolulu but still could be reached by public transportation. Since Nakamoto could easily follow my or Mele's car from Keehi, we decided to outsmart him by jumping on Da Bus.

Although Kamekona's brother lived in Waimanalo, he was against that location. First, my *haole* face would stick out over there like a spruce in a coconut grove; second, he didn't think he could spend more than three hours with his brother without a fight. Then the police, ambulance … those were not good things for the two fugitives from the law, or whatever it was we were running from.

Kailua, in that case, we decided, especially since Lala lived there and she could be our keeper/courier. She had not exactly invited me to her house yet, but the circumstances were extraordinary and I wouldn't mind meeting her herring-loving parents.

This choice of location and my enthusiasm to visit Lala produced an embarrassing moment. "Lala—" Kamekona started haltingly. "I know you kinda like her. Maybe you even wannah go serious on her … so I better tell you … so you know. She's crazy, *loca.*"

My eyebrows arched and hands automatically raised in a shocked surprise, as I yelled, "What the hell, Shark? Just explain what you mean!"

"I was at the atoll … two, three years ago. Doing some work, they had a problem with a generator." He smiled sheepishly when my face contorted in the grimace of utter surprise in reaction to the revelation that he was an expert on power plants now.

"She was crewing on a research ship … something about seals. She's always around seals, turtles, dolphins … you know. This tiger shark wanted to get a seal pup, and the pup was trying to hide around the boat. First, she was trying to jab the shark with a boat hook and then … she jumped in after it. It got scared and got away. But she couldn't know that. The fucking fish could'a just turned around and had a meal." He shrugged. "I thought you should know."

I imagined the scene and to my concern, I clearly visualized the slick brown body with a white top plunging head first, trying to scratch out the shark's eyes. Could she be *that* crazy? Alarmed, I could not clearly answer—no.

Darkness completely cloaked our under-the-bridge hidey-hole and mosquitoes started seriously going about their business. The lagoon seemed as quiet as usual, no suspect boats, searchlights or dark figures in the bushes onshore. We paddled quietly to *Water Whisper* to drop off Shark's dinghy. If Mele, all spiffed up for her cash register at the Foodland, didn't find it there in the morning, she could be more dangerous than the whole network of spies—FBI, Russian or North Korean.

Then we motored out on my dinghy through the mouth of the lagoon into the open ocean, dark and mysterious now, glimmering under stars but hardly revealing our small black craft. The shore break was amazingly loud, which suited us well, as I could kick the motor into the high RPM.

Twenty minutes later, lights came up on the Panic Point, which marks the entry canal to the Port of Honolulu. *You a sheep, you hide in a shipyard*, was Kamekona's motto, and so I tied my dinghy to the ten-foot concrete embankment in front of Aloha Tower. Once we had scaled the wall, built with passenger ships in mind, balancing precariously on big rubber fenders, we melted into the crowd of tipsy tourists sloshing between the Hooters, Gordon Biersch and ten other drinking holes. Now a whole battalion of agents might have problems following us.

Bus 56 was almost empty, not many people had a reason to go to the Windward side that late. In the back seat, an acne-afflicted young man with a flat top haircut was trying to get into the pants of a girl with wise eyes who was hiding her boredom with professional courtesy. On the way to the marine base in Kaneohe, I presumed, but they might be done well before reaching his quarters.

If they were the agents following us, it was a case of major dereliction of duty.

Lala had given me her address once, just in case, and we found it easily. It was an older, unassuming bungalow screened from the street by a thin, terminally sick hedge of spindly plants unrecognizable in the darkness. A dim light beamed through the half-open door and we heard low-pitched female laughter inside. I stepped forward from the shadows, leaving Shark behind a tall, thick croton bush. His un-announced appearance from the darkness might give someone a heart attack.

A very tall, slim man appeared at the door, his hair so white that I couldn't say if it were silver-gray or just white-blond. He wore a beach towel wrapped around his hips and nothing else.

He addressed me in a strange sounding language and smiled encouragingly. It took me a moment to understand that he actually said, "Vot kan I do for you?"

"My name is Chris Gorny," I introduced myself. "I am Lala's friend. Is she home?"

His face lit in recognition; he stepped back and

waved for me to come in. "Lai-ne!" he yelled. "Your friend is here, Chris Gorny."

A single standing lamp illuminated the large room filled with mismatched furniture. Two guitars leaned against the bookcase and a number of large objects, which.I could not identify at the moment, hung on the walls. A woman dressed in a blue one-piece swimming suit was sitting at the round table in the middle. The lamp light illuminated her blond hair from behind so her face was hidden in the shade, but I knew she was grinning ear-to-ear when I heard her theatrical whisper, "Lala, come, your friend is here ... and he is horny."

I was not an unknown quantity in this home and my nickname apparently had provided some healthy entertainment before. She stood up and approached me with an outstretched hand. She could be a well-preserved fifty with a generous hourglass figure but strong legs and toned arms. She changed her mind whcn I was about to take her hand and grabbed me into a bear hug.

"Good thing you've come, Chris. We'd heard about you, but Lala always refused to show you off. We thought you might be missing some body parts ... but you appear to be all right!" She looked at me from the distance of her stretched arms, her eyes sparkling with laughter. She was warm and smooth like a bottle of Irish Cream on a winter Baltic night.

The welcoming atmosphere did not last. Lala's voice in the darkness was alarmed and not quite friendly. "Mooom! Let go of him. And what the hell are you do-ing here? You can't send your pigeon ahead?"

She emerged from the side-room, dressed in her

customary white t-shirt and delightfully skimpy shorts. She swept her eyes over her towel-dressed father and her mother beaming in her beachwear and moaned.

"Kamekona is here too," I said and coaxed Shark from the darkness of the garden. Huge, dark and imposing, he materialized at the door, drawing a gasp from Lala's family.

Captain Heikki Tuukkanen, this was Lala father's official name, was firmly on my side as far as Shark's and my situation was concerned. "You people," he looked at Kamekona then at me and finally at his daughter, "don't understand the power of time and seasons."

Twenty minutes into our conversation, we sat around the table. Lala had prevailed on her parents to dress formally and put on shorts and t-shirts. Now I could actually understand most of her father's utterances, pronounced with a hard guttural accent.

"You are handicapped in this sense." He looked at us sternly. "In Finland, we understand it so well because of our climate. Without this internalized knowledge, hardly anyone would survive the winter. After a few months of darkness, cold and misery, you finally reach the point when you are ready to make this rope you keep under your bed into a noose.

"You are ready to open the barn door, so that the animals taste freedom before wolves have their party, and then ... suddenly you remember, the spring is coming! It will be here in ... what ... only another three months! And you put your rope back under the bed, and you make another baby, because the seasons change!

"It's not that things *might* get better; they will! Guaranteed!" He started laughing happily, as though his Scandinavian genes determined that he had no choice but to be happy, as long as the warm sun is shining.

"So, I think you should hide and wait. This situation is too—" He was struggling for proper words, "—too … surreal to last long. But if it does, you can always come with us to Midway. Nobody can sneak upon you there."

Since the U.S. military had left the Midway Atoll, Heikki and Kasia Tuukkanen ran the place, playing hosts to scientists buzzing around the Northwestern Islands. They worked the radio, oversaw the airstrip, ran a small restaurant for the regular atoll occupants and occasional tourist groups. They did whatever needed to be done for a few dozen humans, in addition to mothering a few million goonie birds, a few hundred monk seals, a pod of dolphins and other sea creatures hiding from poachers under their wings. Adding Kamekona and me didn't seem a problem to them and Lala was already a part of the seal colony.

They fed us a nice dinner; no herring in oil for us, I noted. Hoarding for some other occasions perhaps. … However, confronted with our hearty appetites, they did not have enough dry food for us to take up the mountain, where we intended to set up a camp. No problem. Lala offered to go shopping in the morning and visit us for breakfast, hot buns and coffee in her hands.

After the streak of my back-to-back emergency room shifts interwoven with Nakamoto and Shark's machinations, living in the bush sounded like a nice vacation to me. Equipped with a small tent and water, we were ready to hit the trail leading into the hills of

Lanikai, when Kamekona decided that, since he was so close to Waimanalo, he could visit with his bother for an hour of two.

That would give me some time to spend with Lala and I warmly supported his family sentiment. We watched him sprinting away on the captain's bike and we turned to the dark beach.

"Now you see what I went through in my childhood," Lala said apologetically. "My folks consider dressing optional and do it basically to save others from embarrassment. You must know that most people on the atoll are biologists and a naked mammal body hardly shocks anyone. I didn't realize how emotionally damaged I was until I went to college in Honolulu." She winked at me. "There were no missionaries on Midway."

We found ourselves a nice ditch in the sand that some kids had dug out during the day. The sky was different here than in Keehi. A half big shiny moon with a tinge of pink was stuck between two islands, rising from the ocean less than a mile offshore. It backlit the unending, fast shifting sheet of fantastically shaped clouds, which were projecting a film of abstract figures onto the beach below like in a drive-in movie theater.

We wedged our bodies into the ditch, watching the show above. "So what's the story about this poor tiger shark that you had attacked at the atoll," I asked innocently.

Lala sighed. "That again … I'd found this seal on a beach with an old piece of nylon net wrapped around her upper body. She had put her head through the hole and got stuck in it. She didn't eat for a while and was quite thin and weak, didn't even look at me when I

Alex Modzelewski

came closer to inspect her. And then I noticed that she had a pup, thin like an old shoe and half-dead.

"I cut the net off her; she hardly paid attention. So far this was a standard management, that's what we are supposed to do." I saw Lala's white head nodding in self-approval.

"Then I thought I would give her a fish; she wouldn't even notice I did it. We were not supposed to feed animals. So I gave her a fish a few times, hiding it from everyone, and she got stronger. She dragged herself off the beach and went hunting; her pup made it too and went with her. OK, I said, good for you, just don't tell anyone.

"I saw them now and then; she was easy to spot, having this fresh raw mark on her neck from the net. I didn't feed them anymore, but I liked to see them around, somehow I had bonded with her—a no-no for a biologist.

"Then one day, I was on deck of my research ship and perceived a quick movement in the water. I looked overboard and saw a shark, eight or nine foot long, stripes on the sides – a tiger. And he was trying to double up in his turn because he was hunting a seal pup, which can move pretty fast and is very agile.

"In the open water, this would not be much of a contest, but the pup was maneuvering around the boat like a weasel, forcing the big bully to go into real contortions to keep up."

Lala squeezed her hand under my arm. "Now, I'm not particularly proud of it. The shark had a right to his meal as much as the pup was entitled to object to it. The business was between the two of them.

"But it was *my* pup! I grabbed a boathook and as

156

they were almost brushing against the hull, I tried to poke the tiger from the deck. They made one pass, then another … I was a bit too high above the water and stepped outside the railing. I was *this* close to reaching the bloody fish … and then … I slipped and fell into the water with a big splash. I was so scared I almost peed myself because this tiger was pretty excited by now. But he decided that being fallen upon by a big blob from high above was not a fair part of the hunting game and went somewhere else.

"I hoped nobody saw me but nothing goes unnoticed on the atoll. My mother gave me hell for disturbing the wildlife and I was deported to Honolulu a week later with a group of tourists. How demeaning," she whined, burying her head on my chest.

"So what's your status on the atoll now?" I asked. "Can you go there whenever you want?"

"Well, no one can really go there without a government clearance." She shrugged. "You can go if you have a job there, like my parents, or for a few days as a tourist, though it's damn expensive. But I know most everyone that has had anything to do with the Northwestern Islands over the past twenty years. They were either my babysitters when they were young researchers, or hit on me when I was sixteen of seventeen, or I helped them with their field research over the past few years. I've had my finger in a lot of doctoral theses, so the Marine Biology department in Honolulu is more like an extended family for me.

"Anytime there is a research project planned in the Islands, I am pretty much guaranteed to get a berth. So I spend a lot of time there but it is irregular and not very conducive to any regular work in Honolulu.

I didn't even get my bachelor's degree yet, still have some courses missing."

'I might report you to the authorities as being infected with rabies," I thought loudly. "That would surely help to keep you away from the Midway and more in Honolulu." I felt her body shake with laughter.

"I might choose not to be quarantined in your apartment, Horny. My mother got a kick from your nickname; it's very much in my family tradition. Remember how I told you about the herring introduction of my parents? They landed up on the same research ship, where he—the first mate— shared a cabin with the machine chief, while she had another female Ph.D. student for a roomie.

"Somehow, they all got confused about who sleeps where, but my parents liked it so much that they stayed behind on Midway when the research team returned to Honolulu.

"I was born—a week too early— onboard a French vessel steaming from Midway toward Honolulu; they offered to give us a lift so that I could be delivered at the Kapiolani Medical Center. Oops, *fait accompli*, they had probably said."

"Ehm … Speaking of which, how about if we make my pad into *our* castle?" I started casually, but Lala put her hand on my mouth.

"Not a word more, Chris. You are a strong, resourceful individual, a quality male that most females would like for a mate. Being a biologic entity with her animal needs, I do enjoy you this way. But long term … I won't settle for anything less than they have," she pointed her finger in her home direction.

"I watched them for twenty years brushing against

each other in a ten-foot passage and pawing each other under any silly pretense. We would be watching a video—there was no TV on the atoll as you might guess—and my mother would declare a headache. She had to go her bedroom. My father would get bored with this silly movie five minutes later and then leave me alone. I would turn up the volume.

"You know what it does to a growing girl? Stupid and perverted people could say it might make her twisted sexually. I say, it made her want the same kind of crazy fascination that goes on and on for decades. You know there is this Spanish song that goes: *Que cada noche sea noche de bodas, que no se ponga la luna de miel.*

"For every night to be a wedding night and for the honeymoon never set. Until I know we have that, I will be a female seal visiting your beach."

We heard Shark whistling in the darkness; he was back from Waimanalo. He had had a rather short visit.

Chapter 22

No point stumbling all the way up in darkness, we thought. We decided to hike up to the first place on the hill flat enough to set our tent. We would climb the rest of the way in the morning. Lala recommended a place around the pillbox—as the second-world-war bunker was known—where homeless guys sometimes resided for a few days, until the lack of water and electricity rectified their romantic notions about living the life of noble hermit in the world's most beautiful location.

For us, it should work just fine. Not only would we enjoy the gorgeous vista of Kailua Bay, therapeutic for our frazzled nerves, but we would also have an unobstructed view of the only pathway weaving to the summit along the hill's ridge. We would see Nakamoto long before he could climb within shouting distance. With Lala volunteering her courier services, we were assured of a steady supply of basic necessities like water, freshly cooked meals from Mama Kasia and charged batteries for the camping lamp.

As long as she could see the ocean, no physical effort seemed to scare Lala, and I fully intended to keep her motivation to visit us on high. Shark had no hope of receiving a conjugal visit from Mele; she was way too practical to waste a day on hiking up the mountain in Kailua, while her treasure store on *Water Whisper* was exposed to attacks by envious competitors in the wreck salvage event. The necessity of going to do her shift at the Foodland store was bad enough.

I took the tent and two sleeping mats while Shark strapped the backpack with water and, in the last moment, grabbed a loaf of old bread our hostess had put aside for the horses on her friend's farm.

"You have quite an appetite, Kamekona," I noted. "Still a growing boy, eh?"

"Starving," he answered curtly. "Almost weak from hunger." His mood improved for a while as he was chewing on the loaf, but then started turning darker and darker while we were trudging uphill. I followed him and we kept going up the steep trail in the darkness for forty-five minutes, stumbling, falling into thorny bushes and swearing.

We had not covered a long distance when Kamekona snarled, "Good enough," as soon as the six-by-eight area of fairly flat dirt appeared in the moonlight. His hands were empty; he had already finished his stale bread.

Shark was never a smooth talker; the concept of making noise just to be social was foreign to him. I appreciated this feature of his because I didn't have to pretend to listen to some empty chitchat. If he had something substantial to say, he said it. His message was loud and clear and I gave it my full attention. Meaningful silence was just fine with us.

This time, however, he had no messages for me at all. In fact, he was as silent as an ironwood on a quiet day—not a squeak, not a rustle. The visit in Waimanalo didn't go too well, I thought. Shark's mad and doesn't want to talk. Fine. I set up the tent while Shark swallowed a few pills and washed them down with water.

"What you taking?" I asked.

"Vitamins," he grumbled. Then he stepped two paces away to piss into the bushes and crawled into the tent. I followed him ten minutes later and, as he was not asleep, I asked, "Kamekona, since when are you so concerned about your health?" It was a simple question without any dubious implications. Since he didn't answer, I jabbed him in the ribs and to my surprise, he violently pushed back.

This was not the big, good-natured Shark I knew. "Bastard won't push me around anymore," he growled, somewhat slurring and not exactly on the subject. Then he got up and I heard him rummaging through his backpack.

What the hell is going on? I wondered. He was acting completely out of character. The pills that he was taking by the handful ... were not vitamins, I suspected. Shark returned to the tent without a word but strangely excited. I heard pills rattling in a hard container next to his body as he turned impatiently from one side to another, as though we were sleeping on bare ground. I could smell his sweat, even though a fresh breeze was blowing over the mountain and we were not hot.

Finally, as he settled down, I reached over the sleeping body for the container. The pills made a soft noise and my wrist got caught in a vise. "You touch them again and I break your neck," Kamekona roared without lifting his head. He seemed to be asleep, his eyes closed, but he maintained pressure on my arm.

His grip loosened over the next minute or two, and I slowly pulled my bruised arm back. I was still holding the flask and I made very certain that pills wouldn't rattle. Shark was snoring loudly now, irregularly, with frequent twitching fits.

Like a snake, slowly, without a sound, I crawled out of the tent and pulled a flashlight from the backpack.

"Anabol." Oh, shit. Anabolic steroid, this is what's making Shark such a giant of a man. And maybe this is why Mele didn't like him to see his brother. Whatever Kamekona's reasons were, I had seen him take a fistful of the stuff and he might have taken some earlier, before he returned from Waimanalo.

My recollection of this drug's pharmacology was not quite clear—amazing how I came to rely on internet searches whenever something less common fell into my lap—but of this I was sure: anabolic steroids could produce hypoglycemia, a low sugar condition.

That could explain a lot of strange things happening that night. He had a wolf's appetite; the loaf of stale bread had disappeared for good reason. And he was sweating in a cool comfortable temperature … and he was acting like a jerk … Undoubtedly, Shark was confused like a drunk waking up in a dark room.

He was hypoglycemic, I decided, and since his last—and huge —dose was just making its way from his stomach into his bloodstream, the blood sugar was certain to fall much lower. At one point, pretty soon, he would fall into coma.

Being comatose or confused, as Shark was now, and being in a coma are two *very* different things. A patient does not fall quietly into coma in order to rest like a log, awaiting peacefully his or her fate, quite possibly death. It may come to that eventually, if things go very wrong, but first, those guys and gals turn into the most quarrelsome, hell-rising individuals in an emergency room. They cannot be reasoned with, but they still may have a lot of physical strength that just slips out of their control. It may take a couple of hefty security guys to pin down an average size lady in order to start treatment. For a guy Shark's size … the whole Hawaiian Warriors football team would not be too much. An hour later, after getting some sugar on board, they are the sweetest folks, reasonable, model patients happy to cooperate and ready to rest peacefully.

I was sure that no security personnel happened to be hiking in the darkness of Lanikai ridge, and even if they did, a tranquilizer gun would be the more reasonable approach to this petulant buffalo of my friend. The whole drama was going to happen between him and me.

Had he actually fallen into a coma—a very likely outcome—there would be no way for me to carry the three-hundred-plus pounds of his un-cooperating bulk down the steep slope.

Go for help? It would be hours before an ambulance crew could get the stretcher up this mountain and safely lower him back to the bottom. They would have to rig a contraption like mountain climbers do and set it in the darkness. Helicopter? Not until the morning.

"Shark," I yelled and rattled the bottle outside the tent. "I've got your vitamins and I'm going to throw them out!

He threw his arms around incoherently, trying to get me with an angry roar, but his hands kept closing on the fabric of the tent's wall. Eventually, he figured out that he had to get out of the tent to get me and started scrambling out clumsily.

I was waiting for him on the pathway and shook the bottle. Kamekona, filled with the single-minded desire to break my neck, followed the rattle. We raced down, doubling up on our trek, falling over rocks protruding from the ground, wading through the fields of thorny acacia bushes and bumping into boulders in the darkness. Fortunately, the trade wind shredded clouds into a tattered thin sheet and we had quite a lot of moonlight by which to gallop down the precipitous pathway at break-neck speed.

Kamekona, released from his usual confines of self-preservation, plowed through our obstacle course driven by pure fury. The reason for this chase had possibly escaped his mind by then, but his desire to break my neck remained undiminished.

My salvation was in the big rocks around which the path was weaving. Shark treated those big lumps of basalt like all other impediments on his trajectory, to be bulldozed through. That, of course, didn't work too well for him. A few times a minute I heard the muffled thump of a heavy but soft object bumping into a wall, followed by Shark's groan and a few seconds of stunned silence. Those brief breaks allowed me to catch my breath and keep a safe distance between Kamekona's hands and my neck.

We went through an almost-an-hour hike in less than ten wild minutes and we were approaching the last steep segment of the trail where falling headfirst might end in a lifelong wheelchair ride. Kamekona was clearly slowing down and my breaks were getting longer and longer. Was he just physically exhausted from the running, bumping and falling, or was he slipping closer into a coma? I couldn't tell.

I waited for him at the last ridge, hoping his rage had run its course and he might be safely helped down. He stopped abruptly seeing me so close, hesitantly turned to me and took my hand. But a moment later, his other hand landed hard on my shoulder, groped for my neck and squeezed hard. Apparently, he still wanted to break it.

I threw myself at the middle of his bulk, the hundred-eighty pounds of my body propelled with all the scared energy I could master at that point. He staggered; his heels planted on the steep slope slipped, and we both tumbled down, sliding down the incline until we landed at the road level, separated by no more than a foot.

Somewhat stunned, but feeling no pain signaling any major damage to my body, I bounced off the ground. We were already at the edge of asphalt pavement and I was ready to run again, sprinting toward the town until Shark gave up. But he stayed down on his back, slowly moving his legs and arms like a beetle flipped belly up. His respiration was fast and shallow. Undoubtedly, he was getting worse. Now he was in a real coma and my dash to the closest telephone was needed more than ever.

Two hours later, peaceful as the first morning of January, Shark was taking a sponge bath at the Queen Medical Center. Glucose solution dripping into his vein, he was smiling beatifically, tired, but happy with himself and the world around him.

His face was banged up pretty well; bruises were not so obvious on his dark skin, but his upper lip was double its usual sensuous thickness. His arms and legs looked as though we had run through a carwash equipped with metal brushes, but miraculously he needed only a few superficial stitches and no casts for broken bones. He looked almost respectable, for an emergency room patient.

I, on the other hand, was the sensation of the night. Nurses from other departments were finding perfectly valid reasons to parade in front of my cubicle, trying to get a glance at this naughty doctor Gorny.

As soon as we had arrived at the Queen's, I exchanged my t-shirt and shorts—shredded on acacia bushes—for a pair of hospital greens, while a small crowd of nurses, technicians and doctors gathered around Shark's body like a flock of vultures. The change of my clothes did nothing to cover up the spectacular angry-red scratches densely covering my arms and legs, or camouflage a big bruise on my neck. My face escaped any major damage—proving the advantage of being conscious during a controlled roll down the rocky hill—but my whole body was generously powdered with the red dust of Lanikai hills. My hair had acquired a distinct reddish coloration and I felt fine dirt grinding in my teeth. And the worst part of it, I could smell the sharp stink of my own sweat—generated in large quantity by the mad rush as much as my fear—running down my body in a thousand small rivulets.

I abandoned Kamekona in favor of a shower as soon as Mele stepped in. The miraculous soothing quality of a stream of tepid water falling on one's sorry body was not known to me until that moment. Right there, I promised myself to incorporate it into my medical practice.

Shark was asleep when I came back. Mele was holding his hand. "Thank you, Chris," she said softly, then added, "He would do it for you too."

I knew he would, that's what friends in Hawaii are supposed to do. "Now, Mele," I started delicately, "how about this shit he is taking? How long he has been into it?"

"Three years maybe …" She was not that sure. "You know, until the last six months, we met from time to time but we were not that close. He was such a superstar! He could have any girl he wanted!" She looked at him in such a disagreeable way that I thought she would slap him as he was sleeping in a hospital bed.

"He wanted to be in this Molokai six-man canoe race; it was very important to him. He was a good paddler and was very strong, but other guys were just as strong, or maybe even stronger. But the worst of all, it came to this: either he would be on the crew or his brother, Palani. They are twins and they have been competing since before they could walk. It really had come to a boil over this canoe race.

"At the end, Palani got the spot on the boat. I think he came up with this steroids shit first. Kamekona must have started using his 'vitamins' not much later. Within a few months, he became like another man. Not just big, that he always was, but …" Mele was looking for words, "like great big … like this Schwartseneger in California. And his fuse got pretty short, too.

"*Then* the girls really liked him!" Mele rolled her eyes theatrically. "All those mainland *wahine* went crazy. Big Joe was charging half as much for surfing lessons with Shark, and there was always a lineup waiting for him. I still saw him from time to time, but I wouldn't touch him with a three-foot stick then. He was like a fucking public toilet!"

Mele's hands started shaking and Shark's face was again in great danger of a solid smack, but she controlled herself. "Then of course he caught gonorrhea from this stupid bitch Jenny. I let it slip my lips that it could be AIDS … let him worry a bit. It *could* be the next time.

"I thought a month would be a right punishment but you came along and "saved" him a week later. I don't hold it against you, though, Doc. He kinda grew up since he started hanging out with you. He asked me to move in on his boat a week later after they gave him the shot. Afraid to touch another woman now…" Mele made a sweet face and stroked Shark's hand tenderly. "But I made him bring a paper from the clinic that he's clean before … you know."

Nothing could be hidden from Mele, I suspected, and she had not seen any drugs on *Water Whisper.* Quite possibly Shark did not use anabolic steroids regularly anymore, and the night's episode was an isolated reaction to the massive dose.

It was my duty as his friend to make sure it would be his last one. We could start by discussing the size of his balls; the steroids would shrink them to dimensions of a green pea, certainly no more than a lima bean.

Doctor Chiu, my department head, took one look at my arms and commented that I looked like someone who spit chewing gum on the pavement in Singapore, and they ran out of my healthy skin for flogging, hence the markings on my arms. Therefore, he decreed, I would not be allowed to bring shame on this fine hospital and I would be banned from the Emergency Room until all my scratches either healed or could be disguised by application of a suitable base powder.

I could hear the scheduling clerk's molars going into the slow, painful, protracted grind until they slipped into silence on her own chewing gum. I was out of her clutches for at least seven to ten days, depending on the quality of my diet and night rest.

I was going to use this time to tie up all the loose ends in the ongoing FBI drama. They were numerous and tangled, twisting mysteriously like wires in my *Magic Carpet's* electrical board. And I was sure there were more hot leads hiding, waiting patiently to snap back and burn my fingers in their own sweet time. Not that I had any special knowledge of the future, but this is the way the electrical things usually go.

Chapter 23

On the long stretch of human life, as much as in the vast watery expanse of the Pacific Ocean, big waves collide occasionally, causing an extraordinary loss of life and property in the midst of fair weather. Those rogue waves being rare, many people—sailors and ordinary bread-eaters alike—are not aware of their existence. But even if they have heard of the phenomenon and acknowledge its theoretical possibility, few would consider such a momentous event as a real danger.

Expected or not, these calamities do occur, however. Mountains of water arise seemingly from nowhere and rush at each other like the bulls from hell to clash with vicious violence. A murderous wall stands up then, tall like a building, and barrels ahead with great speed. It grows in the unfortunate victims' eyes for a second or two until it spills outside their visual field and swallows them whole. Life or death, the outcome of such a tragedy depends on pure luck.

Faith Kruger was one of those blissfully unaware people. Even though she was well aware of two big waves rolling through her life, she experienced no anxiety because each of the powerful forces was propelled by sentiments favoring her wellbeing. She did not consider the way they might interact, a common mistake with grave consequences.

A brief meditative moment spent atop some isolated Hawaiian rock, even a cursory thought dedicated to the mechanics of surrounding waves, might allow her imagination to jump from the world of oceanic currents to the course of her own life.

Seeing the seas split in front of her would not cause her any intellectual reflection. That was just a law of nature; everybody and everything in her life accommodated her presence. But if she looked behind her rock, she would shudder in fear.

As soon as they have streamed around the islet, the currents collide like two hostile armies. Driven by the same Alaskan storm, the angry white foam-spitting forces have no awareness of their shared nature and clash like mortal enemies. Other, more insightful person may see this turmoil as an allegory for her own future, but this prairie-born Texas girl had interest neither in the ocean mechanics nor in poetry. The metaphor connecting two waves generated by a storm in Alaska with the two men filled with love for Faith Kruger was lost on her. She had sufficient time and means to avert the danger, but instead she went to pursue her favorite morning activity, breakfast. This was what her cheerfully placid nature dictated.

She missed Colonel Kulagin by five minutes. He was stalking through the corridors of the Hawaiian Royal Hotel to meet his destiny in her room. His plan was very simple because he knew from past experience that malevolent fate would use the smallest opportunity, the shortest untied ends, to screw up any complicated design.

He hoped to find Faith alone. KGB or FSB or whos-ever agent she might be, there was an undeniable spark of empathy between them. Heck, he would even have said passion, if he didn't know how well these people were trained. She had had more than one opportunity to squash him, suffocate him like a newborn kitten in the course of the night they had spent together, but she hadn't taken it.

Having a bit of intimate time with his very recent lover, free of the threat of physical assault in her room, Kulagin hoped to cajole her into spilling the beans. All he wanted to know was this: *What do you people want of me*? Was that too much to ask?

Unfortunately, the more realistic assumption had to be that the operation's handler was there as well. He would not cooperate, oh no! A slippery bastard, a false friend one minute and a hostile bully the next moment—Boris knew the type. Most of them were ex-political officers of the glorious but defunct Red Army. They were waiting for their retirement in some intel-ligence units, poisonous snakes until the last day.

This kind of opponent had to be approached by an intimidating full frontal attack, guns blazing and die-sels roaring, until out of sheer fear he would vomit the details of his devious scheme, like a seagull attacked by a frigate. And he, Lieutenant-Colonel Boris Ossi-povitch Kulagin, was going to lead this panzer charge because he would not be a rabbit anymore; the wire loop would not snap on *his* neck.

Kulagin walked casually through the lobby, con-fident that his newly acquired rubber sandals added to his camouflage. "O Key," he answered in his best John Wayne accent, when a tiny oriental girl sang something to him like a robin then he self-assuredly stepped into an elevator.

Luck was undoubtedly on his side and this lifted his spirits even more. Again he encountered a food tray abandoned in front of a room. But this time, providence gifted him not only food but also what he needed most, weapons. Thrown carelessly on a tray, not even on a plate, were two stainless steel skewers, one still bearing a cube of burnt meat. Kulagin grabbed the implements and smoothly eased the meat into his mouth; he would need all the energy he could master. Then he wiped the steel into a napkin with a cool smile. Now, he was ready.

He approached Faith's room on his tiptoes, stopped and listened, but could not perceive any voices or movement. Just as well, he thought; even if there was no one inside, many things could be learned from a careful search of the room. Then he would wait, safe from any unanticipated encounters. Just like laying in ambush, waiting for a boar rooting through the forest, his weapon at the ready but his body dry and comfortable. He could stay in this place forever, waiting until someone eventually came into his sights.

Did they refill the bar? The thought occurred to him but he resolutely chased it away. There is a time and a place …

He took his card-key out of the pants pocket and quietly inserted it into the lock. The green light went on and he slowly depressed the handle. There was an almost inaudible click and the door moved silently under the pressure of his hand.

Kulagin held his breath because a massive white silhouette appeared behind the crack of the door. He brought his face right to the fissure and saw a very tall and big man in white underwear. The giant was facing away, unaware of Kulagin's invasion, his very pale back bent over a baby-blue shirt spread on the bed.

Where the hell do they find those colossal people? Colonel asked himself. Is there some kind of a farm, perhaps outside Moscow, where they breed these monsters? Or maybe they give them hormones, or special food? Having taken such good care of their agents' size, they surely matched it with training. Faith's feminine skills could only prove his suspicion.

The underwear-clad guy was therefore a very dangerous opponent, although no weapon could be concealed on his semi-nude body. But here was something that this tank commander had learned the hard way: even a heavy tank, like a T-72, will blow up in a fiery explosion if a weapon, even a puny grenade launcher, is stuck point-blank to its side. He had the advantage of surprise attack.

Kulagin invoked the image of his father's malicious face, his toothless mouth moving as though he was mumbling, "Like a rabbit, Boris, like a fucking rabbit." Then he placed the skewers like steel claws, one in each hand, took a deep breath and threw his weight on the door. The momentum carried him over the threshold, right to the white figure still bent over the bed.

Slow like a slug, the colonel made a mental note. And soft like one, he found out with surprise, falling on the big body, which toppled on the bed face first like a big blob of wet putty. Kulagin's ferocious silence was met with the frightened squeal of a farm animal.

What the fuck? He was shocked to find out how low the Russian intelligence services had fallen. Hesitantly, he got off his victim's back and roughly turned him over, using the fallen man's right arm as a handle but still holding one skewer to his neck. His target's long face was marked with wrinkles, but fat flattened them like the leather on an inflated football. The agent was pale, sweaty and displayed long yellow teeth in the grimace of abject terror.

A wave of shame hit Boris Ossipovitch—that's what they think of me! They had sent an old man, some long retired apparatchik to bring me to heel. "*Wstaway stiervo!* Get up, you dead meat!" He roared in fury, grabbing the decrepit agent by his hair, sparse and hardly offering a decent grip, to pull him up.

"What do you want?" he snarled in Russian.

The football face moaned, hands weakly clinging to Kulagin's arm in an effort to save his remaining hair.

"What do you want?" the colonel repeated, letting go of the hair so that he could better look into the pair of small brown eyes blinking in despair. The next bastard pretends not to understand Russian, he thought. Apparently, I have not scared him enough. Again he took both skewers, one in each hand, and raised them slowly aiming the steel points into the man Adam's apple, which started flying up and down his neck like a robin trapped behind a window.

"What the hell you want? And where is Faith?" he said in English, because it occurred to him that perhaps the old agent did not in fact speak Russian. Then he suspended his voice in the most threatening manner and took a deep noisy inspiration.

Before he could go on with his interrogation, the old man dropped his jaw and yelped, "You Boris?"

Now, the memory is coming back, Kulagin smiled

with vicious satisfaction. A paid American hand—that would explain the lack of proper training. "You know who I am," he whispered, as they always do to intimidate a prisoner in spy movies. "And I want you to tell me what you want of me. What am I supposed to do?"

He was shocked and—frankly—scared by the transformation in his opponent. The big soft blob gathered himself into a knot of angry energy, his body trembling with rage, as he pushed Kulagin away and jumped to his feet. "You don't know what to do?" he bellowed with hate. "You spent a night with Faith and you're asking me what I want of you?"

It was clear to Kulagin that the suddenly energized giant, who sprang to his feet with a speed completely inconsistent with his initial performance, would charge him in a second like a bull or a rogue wave on the way to crash a ship. His face disclosed so much ferocious fury, so much hateful aggression poured from his eyes, that no man could be expected to control it, no matter how well trained in his profession.

But the Russian was not scared. "Don't be a rabbit, Boris," he heard his father's voice. "Remember the snare!"

If his adversary were a rogue wave, he would be the rock to meet this deadly force with his own hard and cold determination gathered in his core like a thousand tons of basalt. He stepped back and lowered his head, the steel skewer talons extended on both sides, ready to plunge into the flanks of the challenger.

This scene, portrayed in a thousand bullfight depictions, seemed to freeze in its frame when the door opened, banging against the stopper. Both men threw a quick side look to check on the commotion and noticed the big young woman with platinum hair, a red purse in her hands. Faith was back.

Boris Ossipovitch suddenly realized he was nothing but a fool, imagining himself to be an equal player in this deadly game prepared by professionals to trap him. Like a recent graduate of an officer's school, still green behind the ears, he had charged head first into the big fat bait only to be outflanked and easily defeated. They were *so* right to discharge him from his tank brigade, the simpleton. He was ready to die now, cut down by a bullet shot from the gun about to emerge from the red purse.

His life—but only in small fragments—was rushing by as time stopped.

His mother came as a young girl—before he was even born, but he had seen this picture many times—tall, slim and blond like a white-and-silver birch. "I'm sorry, Boris," she whined. "I told you to learn English and look what it brought upon you."

And she kept sniffling, blowing her nose, and whimpering, "Oy-oy-oy," until it finally got Kulagin angry. Because, although it was true that she nagged him for years to learn English, she would never have succeeded if Irina was not getting her kicks from him yelling in English, when he was ripping the panties off her.

"I'll get your ass, you beeech," he would huff in his gruff voice of a commanding officer, and she would go, "Ayayayayay, my co-lo-nel," jumping on him up and down like the driver of a cheap tractor on a bumpy road. So he kindly but firmly pushed the mother out of his mind. She could do her crying on her own time.

His father came next, as he should in a moment like

this. He just looked at Boris with his sunken eyes, all red—so he was crying after all—the old tough son of a bitch.

"So, you jumped the fence and there was a land mine on the other side. Fuck, you can never know, man. I'll tell ya, though … It's still better than the wire noose. And I'll be waiting for you here. Maybe we will start again, from scratch. There is surely enough time here …" And he waved Boris, who was stretching out his arms, away. "Lots of time," he mumbled again with his gums. No new teeth had grown in heaven, Boris realized. But again, maybe he was not in Paradise.

He saw Irina lining up for the good-bye visitation but the frozen frame suddenly moved. The underwear-clad mountain of a man in front twitched and Kulagin's body braced to meet him head on. He would rather finish this before Irina had a chance to materialize with her laundry list of complaints: about his apartment that she should really get after him, and about the five-hundred rubles that he still owed her, and that she might tell everyone about the time when he got drunk and couldn't get it up. … No, definitely, he would rather end all this in one quick moment, with a bullet fired from Faith's hand.

But time proved its non-linearity that day because it slowed again when Faith's hysterical cry filled the room, "Papa, Boris, NOOOO!"

"Papa?" Kulagin froze in the middle of the charge. They *did* look alike! He stepped back and relaxed his wound up body, while Faith immediately took the opportunity to interpose her bountiful body between the fighting males.

"Daddy, this is Boris. Boris, this is my daddy. Why

179

Alex Modzelewski

don't we dress and have lunch together?"

And the fighting men easily agreed because no scheme is worth scheming, and life itself is hardly worth living if an empty stomach growls. The brunch buffet in the restaurant downstairs had enough star attractions—succulent corned beef in particular—to calm down the most ruffled feathers, at least temporarily.

Chapter 24

The thin blade soared through the air with a reassuring whisper and cut off an inch-wide slice, releasing a burst of red fluid followed by a quick procession of big drops falling into the bowl with loud tinkle. Nakamoto shuddered with pleasure, inhaling the sharp sweet smell then sent the sword flying again. Another thin piece of watermelon fell into the bowl.

Enough. It's a crime to indulge one's body when duty goes unfulfilled, he reminded himself, picking up a smoothly severed chunk of the fruit. Slicing a head off would be just as easy … and immeasurably more satisfying. He bowed low and wiped his *katana* with a piece of wet cloth. Yes, indeed—the excitement and delight of service was lifting his spirit higher and higher, even as the cool calculation of facts was telling him that his chances for success were rapidly diminishing.

He was sure now, Max Bonner, the Honolulu FBI chief had gone *uragiru*, turned a traitor. Even though he never liked his boss, Nakamoto was deeply saddened by his conclusion. What samurai would rather not turn into a burning stick than see a fellow warrior betray his lord? Unthinkable.

Yet the truth had to be faced; hadn't he cut Special

Alex Modzelewski

Agent Nakamoto off the FBI resources as soon as he came back from his vacation? Hadn't he tried his best to obstruct Nakamoto's noble work by taking away his badge? His service weapon already missing, unfortunately sunk under the waters of Keehi Lagoon, the agent was left unarmed because the traitor would not allow him another piece. And finally, who but a double agent would order the only faithful samurai to stay home, while the world was on fire?

Yes, a thousand times, yes! There was only one way left, a road so hard it seemed impossible, but he, Benjamin Nakamoto, would take it. He would take this burden on his humble back and deliver it to the emperor himself. This thought caused him pleasure so intense that the warrior found it embarrassing. He felt like running in the streets, dancing, yelling like a sailor who had had too much sake. And he felt that no one could stop him, because he was faster and stronger than any other human being.

The second slice of the melon fell into a basket, rejected with a dismissive gesture. No need to eat. Hunger—he was above such a base sensation. His soul was soaring into the sky, hardly waiting for the body to perform its physiologic obligations. Nakamoto was determined to focus on the duties awaiting his sacrifice and nothing else.

The traitors had to be punished and the enemies dispatched. Baby, her Texan father and the Russian to start with, but—if possible—the insignificant yet disgusting scoundrels like Gorny and Kamekona Aku should be razed off the earth's surface as well. To have them confess first would be best, of course, but … if not possible, the swift justice from his *katana* would do. He would throw the bloody heads in front of the imperial throne, touch the floor with his forehead and humbly await supreme justice.

"Special Service?" Nakamoto seemed to hear and his face, hovering an inch over the floor, could hardly mask the ecstasy hiding beyond warrior's fierce expression.

"If that pleases ... what? 'Your Heavenly Majesty?'"

What would be the right way to address the emperor? Intolerable pain shot through his heart for negligently not having learnt proper Japanese, but in a moment, relief spread over the aching wound. Of course, when the moment comes, he *will* know what to say. Even now, he *almost* knew how to say it. One thing was sure—he would bow to the floor.

Since he had stopped taking his tablets, he actually felt better and better, even the need to eat and sleep had mysteriously disappeared. He should have stopped this nonsense treatment a long time ago, despite Doctor Kirkpatrick's admonishing. The old Irish doc was nice enough but had no idea what a samurai's spirit could accomplish just out of the sense of duty and pride. And bringing those tablets from Canada— so that nobody in the FBI could catch the wind of his so-called "illness"—was a constant aggravation. But it was just an unimportant straw flying in the wind of his exuberant mind now, when the moment for his greatness had finally arrived.

He bowed again in front of his katana then wrapped it carefully in a long beach mat. Then he took off his kimono and pulled on the gray slacks and an Aloha shirt. The baseball cap and dark glasses completed his disguise; he was a simple Honolulu passer-by now.

Casually, Nakamoto walked out of his apartment building and discretely looked around. Bonner could have his agents posted there but none were present—one more proof of how incompetent the traitor was. Just in case, he walked to the Kuhio Internet café. There he weaved his path through a few different establishments of the building to emerge on Kalakaua Avenue side. The Royal Hawaiian Hotel was across the street.

His headless chicken-like runs around Oahu left him completely empty-handed, therefore Nakamoto decided to change his tactics. Bonner could keep his service car in the darkest part of his rectum. Would it make any sense to chase a deer, bow in hand? Ben reflected sadly on his previous poor decisions. Of course not! One needs to wait for the prey in hiding, and so would he.

Despite lack of any new useful information, Ben Nakamoto had the quiet unshakable confidence that the moment of triumph was close. His heart, rather than his mind, told him that all his suspicions have been confirmed and that the celestial bodies were lining up to deliver him into greatness.

He humbly suffered insolent people, treacherous superiors and even his bad luck— that's the samurai's life—but at this point, he knew everything there was to be known. And he would act on this information as swiftly and decidedly as a swish of his sword.

Chapter 25

I took Lala, Mele and Shark for an afternoon of sailing on *Magic Carpet*. Considering the cost and trouble of maintaining the boat, I should do it more often but something always gets in the way. Still, the enjoyment of those nights when Keehi is a magic place rather than a postindustrial cemetery was fair value for my money, I thought.

But now, relieved from the tyranny of employment due to Doctor Chiu's verdict, I could play a gracious host to Lala. Shark and his woman decided to join us for a brief sailing excursion, as they never saw Honolulu from the perspective of a few miles offshore.

Kamekona was enjoying a bout of extra warm feelings from Mele, as expected after a traumatic event, but he realized that her goodwill would wear thin pretty fast without a substantial follow-up effort on his part. Hence, a romantic cruise suited him very well.

After our frank discussion of the side effects of anabolic steroids, in particular the inverse relationship between the size of his chest and the dimension of his family jewels, Shark foreswore the drugs. Since he tended to take them on a schedule similar to his work pattern, which is to say in a rather haphazard fashion,

I hoped he wouldn't suffer frank depression, a fairly common consequence of the hormone withdrawal. I was not so much concerned about any chemical consequences of the drug withdrawal. It was the psychic pain of seeing his fabulous muscles returning to the range of human proportions that worried me. Could he adapt to life in his still imposing but disappointingly human shape?

"What you're not using, you're losing," I shared with him the ancient medical truth, sending him on a course of intense exercise designed to work out the organs threatened with shrinkage. His muscles would bear the biggest burden of my treatment, but we looked beyond them; the image of lima beans testicles never left Shark's head.

For that I received some extra brownie points from Mele, who enjoyed her honeymoon and matched my friend a benevolent move for each of his loving actions. Such was their mutual fascination that I saw them less frequently now. I had a moment of abject envy, as well as a dose of philosophical self-incrimination, when I swung my dinghy by *Watery Whisper* one late afternoon, just before the sunset.

I heard faint sounds of ukulele behind the mangrove, barely rising over my dinghy's clatter. When I rounded the corner, a picture confronted me that jerked a whole handful of strings in my heart. The golden-red setting sun transformed Shark's dilapidated boat into a magical palace on the water, its master gracefully spread out on the deck. His head was comfortably resting on Mele's lap, while she was leaning against the cabin wall, glittering in the sun. Kamekona had a ukulele in his hands and was plucking on its strings lazily, producing a slow pleasant and romantic tune.

Guru! I wanted to yell. You've got it all! You've figured it out, just as Lala said. Teach me how to reach this nirvana! But I kept quiet, turned my boat and motored away, keeping my RPM's low, trying to make as little noise as I could. That moment was just too beautiful to be destroyed by my interruption; not so often could I see people in such agreement with their nature. I removed myself from the picture, enviously looking back at the golden boat, fast darkening on the brocade of glittering water.

This image stuck in my mind, big, peaceful and beautiful like a harvest moon over the Mokolua Islands, and I made a firm resolution to work harder toward the goal Shark showed me to be achievable. Our roads might be different, but I *would* have my head gently tended on the lap of a white-haired beauty, while I was indulging in something that I had always wanted to do ... even if I was still not quite sure what that might be.

Magic Carpet would have to start working harder to earn its keep, I decided. I was temporarily free and Lala, away from her atoll seal colony, was lost in the world of people. When not on some isolated Pacific island, Lala felt more at home on a boat than in any other place. Even the Kailua house was her parent's residence, not hers. She was still a free-ranging seal.

It was my job to make my catamaran the central and immutable point of her world. I figured that since Lala was cut off from her seals in the Northwestern Islands by lack of suitable assignment, she would jump on the opportunity to patrol the shores and beaches of Oahu. We would explore them from as close to the ocean creature's perspective as possible—from the low deck of my boat.

It worked like a charm. She moved onto the *Magic Carpet* and we made our way around Oahu clockwise. Taking advantage of my catamaran's low draft, we inspected secluded coves unapproachable from the land, slept on sand next to the boat beached by a low tide, and made love under the starry sky, rocking on an anchor. And yes, I had my head on her lap, even though I haven't learned to play the ukulele yet.

For the last leg of our circumnavigation, from the Ala Wai Marina to Keehi Lagoon, we picked up Kamekona and Mele. Big, powerful and graceful like a pair of ali'i, Hawaiian nobility, they stepped on board at Magic Island, accompanied by a sizable pot of *kalua* pig and a cooler of beer.

Shark decided to try his hand at fishing and unrolled a long line from the stern. It dragged through the blue water undisturbed, making no promises despite Kamekona's enticing tugs, softly spoken magic words and other tricks of trade inherited from his ocean-savvy Polynesian ancestors.

Sailing straight out into the ocean, we could soon see the whole shoreline of Honolulu—from the bold outline of Diamond Head to the hazy-white fuel containers in Keehi, against the backdrop of the brown hills of Waianae.

From that distance, animal forms appeared to have been drawn on the steep hills of Hawaii Kai by the streets, convoluted like pigs' tails. Shark, amused, identified the beasts one by one. He wondered whether they were arranged like that on purpose or was it the human mind seeing patterns in chaos, like in a starry sky? I had to confess—I had no idea.

Mele was amazed and delighted to see the deep-green virgin valleys of her island, so difficult to appreciate from the land, and now firmly framed by severe gray ridges. She was definitely losing her hard edges under Shark's tender stewardship.

We admired the gleaming futuristic towers of Honolulu's downtown, and waved to a barge chugging at a stately pace to the Honolulu port. As we were taking in these wonderful pictures, we noticed a motorboat leaving the Ala Wai Channel, her white trail sharply set against the blue water and the colorful rectangle of a skyscraper on the waterfront.

A few minutes later, we were sure that the boat was aiming towards us. She was closing fast. Shark looked at me with the unspoken question and I slumped at the wheel. Who could be pursuing us but Nakamoto? The last time I checked, the scheduling clerk at the Queen's didn't have a boat.

But we were wrong. The fast approaching vessel was a Zodiac, a large rubber boat, not unlike a big dinghy but propelled by two huge outboard motors churning cascades of white water. I had seen boats like that before, usually carrying Coast Guard markings but the approaching vessel had no logos or labels to identify it by. Soon, we could clearly see three men onboard. They were wearing civilian clothes, and to our relief, none of them was Nakamoto.

They pulled along *Magic Carpet*, no more than three feet separating their black rubber side from my white portside hull, and slowed down to match our speed.

"Captain," a middle aged man in a dark-blue windbreaker waved at me with a friendly smile, 'could I come aboard? I need to talk to you.' "

"And who are you?" I opened my arms in a gesture of enquiry. This was not a common request during an afternoon sail.

"Bonner is my name," he shouted, and he waved at us a badge that looked like the identification piece Nakamoto enjoyed so much.

The cheerful atmosphere we had worked up for this trip shattered like a precious sculpture falling from its stand onto the museum floor. Bonner slipped clumsily on his butt from the height of Zodiac onto my hull then proceeded to join us in the cockpit, nervously clinging to the railing. Obviously, he was not a sailing aficionado.

"Took me a while to find you," he addressed me with a slight, good-natured complaint.

"Should I report to Nakamoto every time I leave my condo now?" I was piqued because these guys were pushing their *national emergency!* a bit too far.

"Oh, no, no," he rushed to reassure. "But in fact, I have to ask for your help in connection with Special Agent Nakamoto. I wonder ..." He looked around as though he was counting our heads. "Maybe it would be better if we talked more privately, only you and Mister Aku. Would you mind stepping onto my boat?"

"Not a chance!" I blew up. These people with badges not only considered themselves owners of the city, in the name of national security of course, but also the masters of the ocean. "You can't make me abandon my boat with people on it. You have something to say, say it here."

"OK," he sighed. "Just remember, I wanted to be

discreet." He waved his Zodiac away and it slowly dropped off to trail us, hanging a hundred feet behind my stern. Bonner unzipped his windbreaker and turned to face me with a thin smile. "The reason why I have to ask for your assistance is Mr. Nakamoto. Ben exceeded his authority and has been relieved from any operational responsibilities. In fact, he might be unwell and that worries us because he has disappeared."

The FBI man looked sad and emotional like a father grieving over his son's misfortune. "For some reason, which I don't quite understand, he sought out your company over the past few days. In some ways, you almost might be considered partners in his enterprise." His face hardened like a soft hand curling into a fist. He let us consider for a moment the implications of working for the disgraced agent.

"He looked like his screw was getting loose, somewhat," I said with a shrug. "But his FBI badge looked authentic. Are you saying it was a fake?"

"Alas," Bonner was again a warm-hearted friend. "It was real. I can see why you might expect us to share responsibility for his antics. But, so far no major damage has been done." He averted his eyes from Shark's lip, still showing a sizable sore and looked to me. I showed him my excoriated arms so he turned to Lala.

"But we have to catch up with him before someone gets seriously injured."

"Good luck," I said. "We are done with our brief careers of contractors for national security matters." I became aware of Shark's toe jabbing my foot under the cockpit table. Was he still thinking of getting something out of the FBI? Was this unfortunate rap list still on his mind? I did not think Bonner would be an easy target for his scheme.

But Kamekona reached for his tired wallet, pulled out a piece of paper folded four times and produced the document bearing Nakamoto's signature. "Could you look at this before we go into any further discussions?" Kamekona's English had improved by about five grades. His SAT score would get him into college now, I thought.

Bonner read the paper with the mixture of disgust and irritation then folded it back and put it into his shirt pocket. "I'll see what we can do," he said noncommittally.

"Oh, you can keep it," I remarked. "This is a photocopy. We have a few more copies and the original is in Honolulu." Which was true, because the document, no matter how badly written, was signed by the FBI agent and it could have some legal value; who could tell? With our unsettled behavior and frequent falling into water or rolling down hills, we wouldn't dream of keeping any irreplaceable documents in our pockets.

The agent gave me a very unkind eye and snarled, "For a sexual pervert, you are pretty insightful, Doctor. I wonder what the Medical Board would think about your checkered past. Conviction or no conviction, they would love to hear about a sexual predator in their midst. And a nun for a victim! I really have no idea how you got out of it without a conviction, just kicked out of school. ... But maybe it's not too late to make amends."

Magic Carpet catapulted from the subtropical warmth of the Hawaiian Islands into the climate of the North Pole. Even the wind seemed to freeze in a crystal block, holding everything in the icy stillness. I felt

Lala pressing her body against my back and that was the only warm point in whole universe.

Bonner was enjoying the effect of his verbal assault. Now he had us completely under his thumb. He allowed a small forgiving smile on his face. "Now, this was your second year at school, so you were … what, sixteen?"

No one else made a sound, only heavy breathing.

"I might try to forget about your youthful indiscretion, Doctor, but I would expect some grateful cooperation from you."

Then he nodded toward Lala and Mele, timidly peeking from behind us. "I really didn't mean to spoil the party, but you wouldn't speak with me privately, Doc." He smiled in a jocular fashion. "I will be in touch very soon. Meantime, I expect you to call me immediately if Nakamoto comes anywhere near you." He handed me his card and waved to his Zodiac. He was gone three minutes later like a nightmare that disappeared as soon as the eyes opened.

Bonner gone, the temperature raised a few degrees but remained solidly below the freezing point. "Well, I owe you a story," I said, and they made halfhearted gestures meaning, 'No, no, not at all!'

"What Agent Bonner described actually happened," I admitted. I heard a low moan behind but the warm spot did not shrink away from my back.

"It is just that he got a bit confused with facts. First, I was in the second year of my *primary* school, which made me a few months short of eight."

A collective sigh sounded on the boat as the air was released from the three semi-paralyzed chests.

"Then, nasty and mindless as it was, it was more an

193

enquiry into the nature of human anatomy and habits than a crime committed for the sake of sexual pleasure. I was the youngest boy in my second grade of a catholic school in Chicago. I was a bit precocious, but on par with my peers, preoccupied with questions regarding the female anatomy. Honestly, we were too young to get any proper erotic excitement out of this topic, but we obsessed about the general knowledge questions, like—why is it so much fun to lie on a girl? Or, is it true that a guy puts his winnie between a girl's legs? We saw it depicted in certain magazines, but how does a baby come out of this business?

"We desperately needed to know answers to these and the many other puzzles stuck in our minds like chewing gum on a shoe, even if we were in no position to put the knowledge to any practical use. Still, the enigma of it drove us nuts—the madness of a scientist, you might say.

"There was no question of simply asking anyone at school. As you remember it was run by nuns. Our parents were also quite useless, as they probably presumed they still had soooo much time to talk about the birds and the bees.

"Older boys had their theories, some supported by pictures from 'Hustler', but we had to consider them very unreliable sources because of their contradictions. No one who personally knew Sister Joanna, our teacher and reputedly a woman, could accept those porno pics as a true representation of female nature. Nasty, aggressive crows just do not sing; you know it even when you are eight.

"Then, in the middle of the school year, a new nun joined the school to teach us art and singing. Now, we had to reconsider our prejudice toward pornographic materials. Sister Maria bore important resemblance to Hefner's bunnies. She was young, pretty and friendly. She was an instant hit with us, which was of course not good news for her. The older boys started ruminating about her underwear; what kind of panties a young nun might be wearing under this black cloak?

"I won't bore you with the whole story," I declared, while my friends clamored to hear every last detail of it. Even the wind picked up and the catamaran started splitting the water with its two hulls.

"Come on, Horny," Lala pleaded, "Now we are just getting to the very core of you personality."

"Long story short," I continued. "A scheme had been plotted by the group of fifth-graders to have a direct look at the object in question. As always in June, before we were dismissed for a summer vacation, a school trip was planned into the country, to someone's private property on the shore of a nice quiet lake. The teacher appointed to lead such an expedition was usually the youngest one; Sister Maria was a good bet.

"We were not allowed to swim in the lake, but boys being boys, we always sneaked out through a broken fence to take a dip. The scoundrels' hopeful thinking was that a simulated drowning would force the poor nun to throw herself into the water for the rescue. Could anyone swim in those voluminous sacred robes? We thought not, and I still don't have an answer to this question, because Sister Maria, bless her brave soul, pulled off her black cape or whatever you call it, and plunged herself into the lake, even though she was still wrapped in multiple layers of white fabric.

"You guessed by now that I was the appointed victim, a fate to be anticipated by the youngest sucker in a group. She reached me easily in a good strong crawl and returned ashore carrying me in her arms. And this was the moment when things really got out of hand. Those long white skirts—soaked now and nicely outlining her feminine body—still kept her panties out of view. The gang leader, one Casimir Poplanski, let the success of his operation go to his head and dove under the shirts to find the answer once and for all."

I perceived a low vibration coming from Mele's direction, like a buzz of an agitated beehive.

"My unfortunate contribution to this assault was that, having me in her arms, the nun could not fend him off." I was aware of the hum's growing loudness and increasingly aggressive tone. "And I was clinging to her hands, because she was just going over this old barbed wire fence; if she had dropped me, I would have really got hurt."

I was expecting some sympathy, but instead Mele blew up. "If it was me, I would have brained you … and I would chase down this son-of-a-bitch, your friend … and hold his head under the water until he stopped moving." Lala didn't say anything but I felt anger glowing from both females like from a burnt down forest, flames gone but cinders still hot and emitting poisonous fumes. Only Shark was hiding a happy grin behind his both hands.

"If it might help to absolve me of my sins," I added, "I received Sister Mary's forgiveness. I never returned to that school. Not that they expelled me, I just did not dare go back. I knew that Sister Joanna would crucify me after an obligatory flogging, as the Book said. But I met Sister Mary about ten years later on a bus. Still a very attractive woman, she was wearing a civilian summer dress and had two young kids with her.

'Sister Mary,' I whispered behind her and she turned around, but she did not recognize me. 'You saved my life in a lake,' I added.

"Her face turned red. A moment later she regained her composure and said, 'I should really smack you now." She hesitated for a moment, as though considering the action, then said, "But then … if not for that … I might not have these two.' She pointed to the kids. She gave me a wink like a tomboy and they pushed their way out of the bus."

"So how come you didn't tell all this to that nasty man?" Lala waved toward the Zodiac disappearing in the Ala Wai Channel.

"Because he would come with some other way to twist my arm. Besides, he did a very sloppy investigation. He called someone in Chicago who called someone else and they came up with this old rumor, seriously distorted but good enough to blackmail me, or so he thought. Cops and doctors who do sloppy work must be punished; otherwise they continue in their slipshod ways, hurting people. I will comply with his request until it blows up in his face. And Shark is still not quite finished with the FBI"

"Yeah." Kamekona gave his two thumbs up sign with relish.

Chapter 26

The heaps of delicious food stunned Kulagin's senses. The fresh green of lettuce clashed with the steaming, glistening brown-and-red slices falling off the huge chunk of meat with barely a touch of the knife. The coldness of lobster tails ripped into the moist and hot substance of a cobbler … the sensual orgy of the twenty-meter-long buffet dazed him, though—he noticed with certain satisfaction—there was no caviar, not even the cheap kind that could be commonly found in a Russian officers' club.

Encouraged by Faith, who tore into the rich landscape of the buffet like a wolf released into a corral full of sheep, the colonel started his own journey of discovery. Valiantly but methodically, he worked his way up the lineup of pots, trays and bowls. No dish had been spared on grounds of unfamiliarity; contrarily, the exotic and fancy foods suffered extra heavily due his uncompromising curiosity.

Regrettably, after his third trip, Kulagin realized that his enthusiasm to discover all the wonderful secrets of the long table was just silly. Like those fools who tried to cram into their heads all the grandeur of trigonometry in one night, he was setting himself up for defeat. This research project could not be completed in one sitting and there was no place for self-recriminations.

He discreetly released the buckle of his belt and opened a button of his pants underneath the Aloha shirt Mr. Kruger had lent him for lunch. How clever, he thought, taking a deep and comfortable breath in Kruger's XXX size garment, his waist overflowing. Judged from outside, his décor did not suffer any degradation.

He concentrated now on the glass of brandy that Faith's father suggested, while she was still patrolling the buffet in case something escaped her attention.

From the way Faith was clinging to Kulagin, the old man assumed he was getting himself a son-in-law. A short courtship, he thought, but apparently very successful. Even though as a father he would rather not delve into the details, he knew for some time that very few young men remained in his daughter's good graces after her first "sleepover at her friend's home." And now she was all over the Russian like a greedy bee sniffing and tasting the rim of a Coke bottle. The kids looked very pretty together and he felt his heart melting; so perhaps he would be a grandpa, after all.

"So, Boris … Just in case you would like to move to Texas," he looked at Faith who had just returned with a plate of pastries. She blushed and nodded. "I might use you in one of my corporations," he continued. "You should really start at the bottom, in a mail room, as I did—"

"Daddy," Faith whined. "You don't even have a mailroom!"

"I know, I know," the old man agreed easily. "I

might start you as a management trainee in my pipe-line maintenance division. Lots of hardware, quite appropriate for a tank commander, ha ha."

He kept talking, animated and cracking jokes, while Kulagin felt depression slipping under his skin. Boris stopped listening. The big meal and a few glasses of brandy had put a suffocating blanket over his alertness. But instead of calming him down, his thinking processes suppressed by the demands of the digestive tract, the ensuing daze caused the colonel increasing discomfort. The big clump of white dough across the table was sickeningly happy with himself and was already putting his presumed son-in-law in the corner of his office like a potted palm tree.

Exasperated, Boris watched Faith, giggling at her papa's wise cracks, glowing with the happiness of getting her pony. He was the pony, Kulagin realized.

I liked her better as a K.G.B. bitch, he thought with bitterness. At least her dedication to fuck my brains out could not be questioned. Now, it's like she is ready to get a stable hand to groom her new pet while she drops in for a ride once in a while. With her daddy, they will drive me into impotence.

Boris was reflecting on this developing situation with increasing desperation, seeing his outrageous Internet romance changing into a disheartening més-alliance in front of his eyes. The bold jump over the fence landed him not in the open steppe, to prance around like a free-range stallion, but in a big trough full of pig slop.

"I have to go out," he rudely interrupted Kruger's monolog and pushed his chair back noisily. He turned to the door and went out into the hot Hawaiian noon, closely followed by Faith, still chattering excitedly. Blinded by the sun, he walked a few steps without purpose but his ear caught an interesting sound and he turned sideways, where a huge muscular Hawaiian lay on a cool marble floor, his head resting on a beach basket, a small *balalaika* in his hands. He played, indifferent to the world around him, a simple but sweet tune, not unlike a little song that a fisherman might play on a bank of Lake Baikal.

Boris Ossipovitch felt a tag of nostalgia and approached the musician. He stopped a few feet away, amidst a small group of tourists observing this quintessential Hawaiian scene. He listened to the music, so easy and plain but strangely soothing to his aching soul. Not wishing to crowd the player, Kulagin kept his distance but he did not realize that his fingers had started moving in the air as though he held the instrument and tried to catch the cords. That's why he was startled when the big arm stretched out with a ukulele in it.

"You play? Want to try, bro?"

Without a moment wasted on thinking, he sat down by the Hawaiian musician and accepted the instrument humbly, with two hands. It was quite similar to a *balalaika* and he let it sing the songs of the Volga fishermen and Siberian hunters and peasants plowing the black soil of Krasnoyarsk. He lost himself in this music, as the big Hawaiian nodded his dark head with a smile.

Faith, following a step behind, noticed Shark as soon as Kulagin did and her heart stopped for a moment. The Russian colonel and the Hawaiian prince, the gold medalist in the sexual marathon and the god of masculine beauty—was she dreaming, or was it one of those TV moments when you are shown two great prizes? You can grab only one and if you hesitate for a shortest instant, they both disappear in a flash of garish light and the jarring sound of a discordant buzzer. Faith gripped Kulagin's arm with the speed of a cheetah, but he was already sitting down, oblivious to her touch.

Twenty minutes and four *balalaika* tunes later, they were back in their hotel room. Kulagin, pacified by the enchanting music, lay down, his body requesting rest and time to digest the mountain of food he had ingested for lunch. Old Kruger had already removed himself discreetly to another suite and Faith tenderly tucked in her catch to sleep. She loosened his belt even more and removed his shoes while Boris was already drifting away. He had an urgent appointment.

He knew beyond doubt that his father would have something to say about this new twist in his Hawaiian adventure. To his own surprise, Boris was looking forward to hearing the impertinent observations of the old badger. Unpleasant as he was, Ossip Kulagin had a unique point of view on his son's life. A lesser man would try to avoid the discomfort of hearing the acerbic comments, but Lieutenant Colonel Kulagin was a frontline officer; he would gladly pay the price of personal hurt to ensure the success of this daring operation.

Chapter 27

The orders were brief, concrete and delivered from on high by a low-ranking employee of the Honolulu FBI division. I was almost missing Nakamoto's impassioned style of management.

Bonner assumed, rightly in my opinion, that Ben's disappearance meant he had refused to give up his investigation but, disappointed with Bonner's orders, had gone off the grid. Probably, he would be hanging somewhere around the Royal Hawaiian Hotel, at least as long as Baby and Kulagin stayed there.

Having lost all the FBI's resources, Nakamoto was likely to look for support wherever he could find it, which meant that Shark and I could expect to receive his "national emergency" call for duty. As unenthusiastic in our service commitment as we were, we could be the last instruments of spy craft available to him.

Therefore, by the orders of our betters, we had been stationed at the entrance of the Royal Hawaiian Hotel as bait. Bonner instructed us to be as conspicuous as possible, so that even a deranged man could find us out. One of his men, concealed in the crowd of tourists, would swoop on Nakamoto as soon as he approached us.

It was a simple plot and it should work, as long as people caught up in paranoid mania—as I suspected Ben was—could be that predictable. The second element that seemed to escape our new boss—who certainly had many other and more important problems clamoring for his attention— was that unpaid agents, especially the ones previously pissed off by his clumsy blackmail, might have their own designs and not necessarily in his favor.

We had established our post in a place so exposed that nobody spending his day in Waikiki could miss us, the shady corner next to the Royal Hawaiian Hotel entrance, quite close to the Sheraton. To make it doubly foolproof, we agreed for Kamekona to play his ukulele. He would cut a nice romantic figure of a colossal nostalgia-stricken Hawaiian sinking in his music. If Nakamoto missed that, he was not only crazy but also blind and deaf, therefore not a danger to anyone but himself.

I sat ten feet away on a street bench, less comfortable than Shark because the concrete seat was hard on my butt, but the location submerged me into the pedestrian traffic flowing along Kalakaua Avenue. By design, I was an easy target accessible to anyone who might wish to chat with me without drawing undue attention. Somewhere in the crowd was an FBI agent, or possibly agents, keeping an eye on us, ready to grab Nakamoto the moment he appeared anywhere close to me.

What neither Bonner nor his agents knew, was that there was one more layer of deception in this operation. Lala, wearing a long black wig to cover her very characteristic white mop and dressed like a pretentious

European rich bitch, was patrolling the street around me with the bored-to-death facial expression of a baroness stranded in a tourist trap. Her task was to spot Nakamoto in the crowd before he could approach me. She would intercept Ben before I embraced him like Judas Iscariot, delivering the victim into the callous hands of the authorities.

She was confident that her eagle eyes, trained to discern individual goonie birds in a thousand-strong flock on the Midway Atoll, would detect Nakamoto long before Bonner's agent—focused on my squirming on the bench figure—could detect his presence. Since Ben Nakamoto knew Lala and realized she was close to me, he would be eager to speak with her. And since he was paranoid, he would take her warning of the trap seriously. She should have no problems persuading him to meet me in a more private place.

My car in the underground garage should appear to him a logical choice, and that's where he would be sent. I planned to meet him there, having left my street post under the pretense of bathroom trip. Kamekona would remain in front of the hotel to entertain the agent waiting in his duck blind.

At this point, our actions would acquire certain legal gravity that might exceed the definition of a prank. With the circumstances spun properly, we could be seen as committing the crimes of abduction, misleading authorities and who knows what else. The punishment for those could be a few steps beyond a wrist slap. We could almost sniff the faint but distinct musty odor of a federal penitentiary.

That night after our ruined sailing trip, we engaged in some serious deliberation over a bottle of rum in the privacy afforded by the exterritorial location of *Water Whisper*.

The easiest thing to do would be to play the roles assigned to us. But what would be the outcome of this game? As soon as the FBI grabbed Nakamoto, we would have lost any value for Bonner. Just as an afterthought, he would throw Shark into the wheels of a justice system; his attempt to twist an FBI agent's arm, even the crazy one, would not go unpunished. Kamekona would face a judge for thumping a cop, and probably see the inside of a penal institution for a number of years.

Secondly, we considered Nakamoto's fate. He still was not our favorite man, but out of his cartoonish ineptitude and the comical sense of self-importance, a picture of a sick man started emerging. More and more, I perceived Nakamoto as a bipolar patient with a major paranoia component. To make things worse, clearly, he was deteriorating fast and by now he could be in full mania, a danger to others and a grave peril to himself. Bonner could neutralize the danger to others, but could he be trusted to take care of his troublesome agent?

I had no idea how these things worked in his organization, but Bonner did not strike me as a compassionate person likely to dot over his disease-stricken comrade. I could easily see him throwing Nakamoto into a place without windows until the dust settled down. The treatment could wait.

"So what would be a better place for this acutely sick patient than a hospital?" I posed a rhetorical question to my co-conspirators. "Bonner may find out about this admission with a slight delay." Carried away by my compassionate reasoning, I even managed to convince myself that Bonner himself would suffer if the operation were executed as he had planned it. Nakamoto in his dungeon, Shark under arrest and me trembling in fear of the Medical Board, the poor man would have missed the many benefits of punishment for his sloppiness. His professional development might be stunted, God forbid.

No way, Jose, we decided. We would play this game according to our own design. Before reporting for our baiting station in front of the Royal Hawaiian, I stopped by the Queens' Emergency Room. My colleague on call thought it was very generous of me to personally deliver this acutely delusional patient I knew. He certainly would be available to assess him in respect of committing him to the psychiatric ward. I was pretty sure Nakamoto would qualify.

This way I would end up as Ben's spy, preventing a national emergency, as well as his doctor, delivering him into the shrink's hands. The legal and ethical implications of this arrangement could be the subject of a major scientific paper, which I had neither the time nor skill to produce, but it boiled down to the simple question. Would Nakamoto be better off jumped like a chicken by a fox, then locked up in some scary place? Or would he rather be a patient at the Queen's, enjoying a clean bed, eating good food and swallowing antipsychotic pills? Objections overruled, I decided, pretending I did not feel the exhilarating tingling of my scalp that I always had before jumping out of a plane with a parachute strapped to my back.

As soon as Kamekona assumed his artistic pose in front of the hotel, he attracted a lot of attention. There was not a moment when he was not surrounded by a bunch of admiring tourists. Even before breakfast tables were abandoned, a messenger arrived from Big Joe at the surfing lessons kiosk, enquiring if Shark had lost his mind. The lady clients were storming his kiosk, requesting instruction from this wonderful teacher with the body of Hercules. But Shark just kept plucking his instrument showing no emotions, sprawled on the nice cool marble like a Leonardo da Vinci's bigger than life sculpture.

Fifteen minutes later, the messenger returned in distress, ordering Kamekona to report for duty and bribing him with an additional ten bucks per session.

Shark looked at me. "Could you cover for me here for an hour or two, Chris? Not every day does this kind of money come my way!"

But I was heartless, even though I knew Mele would not be happy, her motto being, "*A buck is a buck.*"

"We have a bigger fish to fry, Shark!" The twenty or thirty extra dollars harvested that morning could not interfere with our grander designs.

He sighed and started another tune, very sad this time, almost squeezing tears out of the tourists surrounding him in a respectful circle.

We had our big catch of the day as soon as he started strumming out his financial frustration. I had to rub my eyes when I saw Boris Kulagin joining the admiring circle. Baby, in her splendid white dress, reminiscent of an oversized Marilyn Monroe, was right behind him. The colonel was really into Shark's music, subconsciously plucking an imaginary instrument.

I held my breath when Kamekona reached out to him and handed over the ukulele. This was not something we had planned, but he was damn right; engaging the Russian could open a whole new range of possibilities for our ploy.

Kulagin was not a bad musician, for a tank commander. Probably, he would play even better given a familiar instrument and having his fingers loosened with a bit of social lubricant. He performed a few sentimental tunes, exchanged a few words and a handshake with Kamekona then went back into the hotel. Faithful Baby floated around him joyfully like a gigantic Tinkerbell.

From that point on, our spirits took a downturn. No event of any importance occurred and boredom gripped us with vengeance. Like the value of my condo with the ocean view, our morale was flat and getting lower for the rest of the day.

I tried to entertain myself by guessing who our FBI angel was. The test I devised consisted of my make-believe sneezing attacks accompanied by violent body contortions, while I was watching for a guy who would hastily pull out binoculars to check me out. I figured out that the bastards were changing every two hours, while we were doing a daylong shift on Bonner's orders.

The fun of the game was lost after the second change as they invariably hid in the ABC grocery on the other side of the street. It was a good choice of a post, I had to admit. The store was air-conditioned while my concrete bench felt more and more like an instrument of torture.

The low point of our entrapment action occurred in the evening, when a well-meaning lady, wearing a delicate sari over her hippopotamus body, put a dollar

Alex Modzelewski

on the marble next to Shark and asked if she could buy him a drink.

Always a gentleman, Kamekona didn't say a word. He just picked up the dollar and barked to me, "See you inside. Can't play anymore. Nakamoto can find us in the bar as well." Then he proceeded to the bar, but without the admiring lady tourist. I waved to the panicky agent scrambling in the ABC across the street then I followed Shark, but only after having discharged Lala from her duty. She was complaining of sore legs and itchy scalp under her black wig.

Where Nakamoto was that day, we didn't know. I felt like his black eyes were burning a hole in my back, however, he never revealed his presence. But this long and frustrating day was not a loss for us because a fat and unexpected payoff materialized when the second round of beer had just started soothing our frayed patience.

From the darkened corner of the bar, where we had set up our fueling station, we caught sight of Kulagin, barreling toward the watering hole at full speed, leaving behind him an empty trail through the crowd like a snowplow on a Chicago street. The poor man obviously needed some sedation; his thinning blond hair was ruffled and his Aloha shirt was half-opened. He was emerging from some traumatic experience.

Shark grabbed Kulagin as soon as he had a beer glass in his hand, and towed him into our corner. Those musicians surely stick together. We spent the next few hours talking, scheming and laughing. Yes, laughing, since the Russian had fully disclosed the nature of the national emergency we had been drafted to deal with. By the time he left, well past midnight, we

210

had a few ukulele-balalaika duets agreed upon, as well as some very interesting plans drawn for the next day, the one that had already started.

Chapter 28

Having stretched his stomach with an enormous quantity of delicious—and therefore high in fat and protein—food, Boris Kulagin did not rest well. Even though his gut demanded all the body resources for the tremendous work of digesting the victuals, just enough blood remained in his brain to produce a depressingly monothematic and disturbing dream.

Rendered in very poor color, grainy like a 60's Soviet propaganda movie, there was only one object dangling in the darkness. It consisted of a short orange-colored stem with a bunch of sickly-green feathery shoots on top. What the hell? Boris asked himself again and again, tired of this boring apparition, but afraid to lose sight of it because there had to be some significance to it. Otherwise, why would it occur to him at all?

The thing jumped enticingly and shook its greenish top but the colonel was too tired to keep guessing; the apparition was already fading when a loud and clearly enraged voice yelled into his ear, "Carrot, God-damn-it, carrot!"

Kulagin's sleeping body twitched from this auricular assault and a good portion of his blood supply immediately diverted back to his brain, making the picture much better in terms of illumination and film quality. Now Kulagin, the father, appeared, still a bit low on definition, but clearly holding in his hand a fragment of a carrot, a small portion of the edible orange root left and its green top reduced to a short brush of half-rotten thin twigs.

"A carrot, Boris!" He was angrily shaking the vegetable. "You don't even know what a fucking carrot looks like! Thought it was always coming in a jar, eh?" But he calmed down, aware that he had a message to deliver, even if scolding his stupid son would be more satisfying.

"You find a treasure like that, or perhaps steal it, working by God's grace in a kitchen for guards, what do you do? An average fool immediately stuffs it in into his mouth like the delicacy it is. The green part in particular, it could have been months since you have last seen such a gift of nature, never mind tasted it. Full of vitamin C, vibrant with chlorophyll… " The old man closed his eyes in admiration.

The old fool is going to recite an ode to a carrot now, his son concluded with disgust because he had more important things to discuss.

"And believe me, it tastes like the natural miracle it is." The older Kulagin opened his eyes, breaking out of his spell of admiration for the vegetable. "But you don't do it!" he hollered, looking ready to smack his son across the face with the object of his desire. "You control your hunger and use to it to get the bigger prize. Because those few rabbits that were too smart to be scared into your wire snare are as greedy for the fresh vegetable as you are. So it is now down to this—who can control his desire better? You, the top achievement of the evolution, or the stupid critter that never had the benefit of his father's guidance?

"If you can control yourself, you will feast on a rabbit *as well* as on the carrot; the beast might have touched it with its greedy teeth but it certainly would not pass its strangled throat."

Here, Ossip Pavlovitch stopped and checked his son's eyes for comprehension. "I don't have to tell you, Boris, that this story goes both ways. Sometimes you are a hunter and other times you are the hunted, but the moral is the same—if you do what the other side wants you to do, you lose.

"You did pretty good with the attack episode in the room, *tankista*," he noted with appreciation and perhaps some astonishment. "Hell, I thought you were a goner. But no, things turned out all right, just as I told you, didn't I?" He looked for some sign of gratitude, but since Boris was stricken with a coma, he shrugged. "You are welcome.

"So now it's the carrot game. The ass on this Faith of yours is truly amazing, even if I prefer smaller women. *Boris*! Don't you start this tragic song about your mother again! It's between her and me, so back off!

"But the attractive power of this wonderful ass, and her papa's wallet, are nothing compared to the beauty of a carrot after nine months of winter. You can do it! You want them—take them both as if they are already yours, but not before you look around for the wire noose very, very carefully. And if your nose twitches just for a second, you back off and find another way to grab them."

Once he completed his sermon, the old man relaxed, nodded a few times to reaffirm its significance and perhaps waited for a question or two. But the matter was already quite clear in his son's mind, so the elder faded away, whistling between his gums and lips a chirpy song dedicated to the pleasures of duck hunting.

Boris Kulagin opened his eyes with full understanding of his current situation; in particular, why he had this premonition of doom when Mr. Kruger started his monolog. Now, the silvery noose shone in the darkened room like a neon sign over the Pacific Center restaurant down Kalakaua Avenue. Has he escaped the drudgery of his empty life in Vladivostok in order to put a leash on his neck, with the oversized buffoon holding the chain? Hell, he might be better off going back and buying flowers for Irina, who—in view of his ongoing ownership of the apartment—would likely accept his remorse with grace.

But again, Faith had got a hold of his heart. He closed his eyes and the pair of enormous thighs appeared before his eyes, straddling him, and the fantastic pink butt appeared, grinding with the inexorable strength of a power generating station's steam engine.

One lightning bolt after another had surged up his rod, shooting through his overcharged circuits, blinding his brain with white light. But his fuses— naturally suited to endure high currents and hardened by his rich experience—held out until this magnificent power system melted down with a scream, shutter and, finally, a resigned moan.

Where in the world could he find another girl like that? Besides, did his father say: "Back off, Boris?" No, he said: "Back off *and* find another way to get what you want!"

Back out of this ambush, the colonel yelled to his inner driver. Through this brush on the right, we out-flank the bastard and stick the canon up his ugly ass.

Faith was not at his side anymore and—since it was 8p.m.—she had certainly had her dinner already. He could safely presume she was in her father's suite. He jumped off the bed, surprising himself with the verve that his long snooze had filled him with.

A young lieutenant, son-of-a-bitch, a young lieu-tenant, he snickered, smoothing his still blond mous-tache resolutely on his way to Kruger's room.

About the same time, Faith was getting off her fa-ther's knees, her tears already drying because she had got what she wanted. The old man initially held sternly to his plans of starting Kulagin as a manager trainee. He would plant Boris in a standard cubicle, and only when he had proven his value, would he be promoted to a proper position, one that would come with a nice office and a secretary.

Faith wished to seal her bedding rights as soon as possible, but Mr. Kruger proclaimed firmly that the wedding should happen only after sufficient time had elapsed to evaluate the candidate. "Baby, we don't even know if he is a Christian," he exclaimed in frustration, "never mind a Baptist!"

"But I am thirty-five," Faith moaned, soaking her dress and her father's shirt with her tears. "And I know that I will never, *never* meet another man like Boris. I love him, Daddy."

Her father felt the weight of Faith's words because she did not utter them lightly. She had already tested most of eligible bachelors in the southern half of the great state of Texas and none had passed her scrutiny. There had to be something special about this Russian; losing him, just like that, because of his standard hiring practices might prove to be a grave error.

As with a new company acquisition, sometimes you go through a long due diligence process and lose money at the end. And another time, you have your gut telling you: just go ahead. It could be just that you liked the prospective partner's handshake. You take a plunge and—bingo, you've got yourself a winner.

For this entirely unscientific reason, as much as Baby's strong lobbying effort, Mr. Kruger agreed to take Kulagin on as his personal assistant right away. The wedding would be arranged in a few weeks, as soon as the paperwork allowed. All the problems solved, he thought. Chances were excellent that Baby would finally settle down to produce some grandsons for him and baseball players for the junior league.

Colonel Kulagin dove into this happy family moment determined to trample, explode and otherwise destroy any obstacles placed between him and the power plant of his romantic love. But he would not act rashly, like an inexperienced youngster.

"Good evening," he said and gallantly kissed the hand of Faith whose face turned red from happy embarrassment. He extended his hand to Mr. Kruger, who looked at it without understanding for a moment, and then took it with an uncomfortable delay.

"Well, my boy, as my new assistant, you need to learn something about your duties." Unaware of Kulagin's leaden gaze, he rumbled about his wake up call at exactly oh-six-forty-five; about files to be prepared for his perusal—neat and up to date; about a fresh shirt to be kept so he could change at a moment's notice ... He went on and on, splattering saliva, blowing his nose and scratching his bald scalp but paying no attention to his new employee.

Lieutenant Colonel Kulagin stood in the corner, feeling his blood pressure rising well past the red line, but still undecided how to smash this audacious assault on his freedom and personal dignity.

Unlike her father, Faith perceived a destructive tornado approaching and started slowly insinuating herself between Boris and his future father-in-law. But she was too late because Kruger shifted gears from the indirect affront of remaking this officer into his secretary to a direct insult on his honor.

"And you, *sir*," he added casually, looking into Kulagin's eyes with a hint of disrespect, "you will have to wait for the proper paperwork to be completed before the wedding ceremony can be arranged and the work permit issued."

A patrol inching through the enemy territory without the sound of a broken twig, not a molecule of steamy air showing in the frosty morning stillness, and then ... someone steps on a land mine. The tremendous energy pent-up in the nervous system, now triggered by a loud bang, explodes in a fury of violence, angry shouts and the urge to kill. Kruger had stepped on the mine; the mocking word "sir" slipping quietly off his tongue like the click of a detonation mechanism and he suddenly found himself in the middle of a firestorm.

Kulagin's hands grabbed his shirt in an effort to lift the body and slam it against the wall, but even this reasonably fit man could not accomplish it. This would be a task for a crane.

"*Sobaka*, you dog," Boris roared, dancing the offender into the corner like a two-door armoire. "I will show you a wakeup call!" Here, he finally managed to crash Kruger against the wall.

He yelled and cussed and insulted in the language he would have sworn was English, while Kruger heard only Russian. This much he understood, though; he was going to die.

Faith, who tried to interfere with the explosive development of this natural disaster was sent flying onto the bed, where she reasonably stayed, observing the terrible spectacle from a distance. With whom should be my loyalty? she asked herself, and seeing Boris, magnificent in his fury, she answered it promptly—Daddy would like to see me happy! Hope Boris won't get hurt!

Firestorms end like they start, suddenly, in a bout of terrible silence, interrupted only by subdued groans of the wounded. "Stop it!" Kruger whispered hoarsely, when the strong hand grabbed his throat, threatening to stop the flow of his respiration. "I don't want you be my assistant!"

"Daddyyy!" Faith's wail of despair came from the bed but Kulagin's grip relaxed a bit.

"No?"

In this critical moment, like in many other crucial events of his remarkable career, the old billionaire was saved by his instinct and his ability to draw on the experience of many decades of his prolific life. The sensation of a hard hand gripping his throat matched another record in his memory, filed away fifty years ago and waiting patiently like an old-fashioned manila folder in his company's archive.

The indexing miracle of Kruger's mind clicked on the memo preserved in a form of an archived film, a bit faded but still very clear. The movie clip displayed Private First Class Rick Kruger, a six-foot-six tall, thin and noodle-pale young man. Rick was hanging with both hands on the brawny forearm of sergeant Williams, which kept him suspended by the throat like a crane above the dirt of a training field. Kruger instantly recalled the desperate effort to preserve his airways, as his long but completely confused legs could not find ground.

"You do this once more, flatworm," Williams was breathing into his face, scattering a fine spray of saliva, "and I'll rip this pinhead of yours and throw it into a latrine." He said some other unpleasant things, impossible to repeat exactly after all those years, but the general meaning of the sergeant's sermon was stuck in his mind forever.

One thing Kruger would never deny, even if he hated Williams for this and his many other educational efforts. People with such a force of persuasion are rare. And outside the armed forces, they simply cannot be found. The task of drilling all the young MBA's into a proper business protocol was taking forever. Coming from their B-schools, full of highfalutin theories, those pencil-necks had no understanding of the real world or sense of teamwork. More than once he had reminisced about Sergeant Williams' tutoring method with the shade of sentimentality.

And now ... the same hard hand on his throat ... Colonel Kulagin had the same quality! You bet, he had! "School" he rasped, as soon as he caught a breath of fresh air. "You give teamwork development courses for my executives." He escaped the dangerous corner and maneuvered behind a heavy mahogany table in the middle of the room.

Kulagin let his hands drop, listening with great attention.

"Colonel," Kruger addressed Kulagin properly, regaining his composition, "you might open a training center based on your army experience. You could call it … "First Texas Tank Academy," or maybe the … "Houston Red Army Tank Brigade.""

"Oh no, we are done with the Red Army," Boris objected but without the sense of offense because it actually sounded pretty good.

"Your call," Mr. Kruger was on a roll and regaining the momentum. "But I want it to be based on the sound principles of a Russian officers' school!

"You've got it, Pa," Boris Ossipovitch declared. "I need a drink now, though. But I will be back!" And he left the room with a lewd wink toward Faith, who had to sprinkle cold water in her face to suppress the bout of heat rising from below her apple-red belt.

Chapter 29

Someone calling Shark lazy, would … would simply not know him at all, for my friend was obsessed with work. The problem was that nobody could force him into doing something he didn't like. Unfortunately, to Mele's chagrin, most paying jobs fell into his "dislike" category.

The night we celebrated in the bar with our new Russian friend, Kamekona erupted into artistic activity so inspired that at 2 a.m., he had to paddle to *Magic Carpet*, where I was sleeping. Mele chased him out of *Water Whisper* on the pretext that she might fall asleep at her cash register the next day if she didn't get a few hours of sleep. Rest was not coming to her while Shark kept plucking his ukulele in the throes of composing.

As I was rather heavily sedated by our celebrations, and didn't need to work the next day anyway, Kamekona chose to carry on with his work on my boat rather than push his luck with Mele. Time was short; he had promised a new and original love song for Kulagin and Faith's wedding.

Since—despite papa Kruger's sentiment—we had planned the ceremony for the coming Sunday, less than forty-eight hours from our leaving the bar, Kamekona felt the responsibility weighing on his shoulders, especially because his would be the only music gracing the event.

The timing of the wedding was Kulagin's idea. "A follow up strike before the enemy can regroup," he explained in simple tactical terms.

"*Za pobiedu*, for the victory!" we answered raising our glasses. The only problem he anticipated—since the bride would be enthusiastically on the side of a quick conquest, and her father still had not recovered from Kulagin's first strike—was the issue of who could marry them off at two days' notice.

"Hawaii ain't Nevada, you know ..." Shark counseled.

He might be right, this friend of mine, so full of practical knowledge about his islands. In the first place, there is no ocean in Nevada, making it quite a different place, but there were few other things I could throw into the differential diagnosis. However, none of those were relevant in my opinion. Three miles out of Honolulu there was no state of Hawaii. In fact, there was no state whatsoever, just the open Pacific Ocean— blue, friendly and free of the silly laws and regulations governing the land to the north. An hour of sailing out, just to make sure we were out of the territorial waters, and we would be governed by the rules of the sea.

Once there, Captain Christopher Gorny, the Master of a fine sailing ship *Magic Carpet*, would bless the young couple and allow the groom to kiss his bride, while a ukulele in Mr. Aku's artistic hands sang a romantic backdrop. Then I would sign a previously prepared document declaring that the marriage has been completed. On our sail back to Honolulu, Colonel and

Mrs. Boris Kulagin would enjoy all the legal trappings of a married couple.

Upon dissolution of our meeting in the bar, Boris went upstairs to explain the arrangements to his fiancée while Shark and I, responsible citizens, went to Keehi by taxi. Kamekona threw himself into the work of composing while I fell into the fitful sleep of someone who, unaccustomed to substantial drinking, had allowed himself to be caught up in the enthusiasm of serious celebration.

I was still at the deep level of unconsciousness when an obnoxious and persistent ringing dragged me up to the surface. I was about to throw the offending noise-maker overboard when I recognized it at as Shark's cell phone. Kamekona was resting at the cockpit table, his head rolling gently sideways with the boat's movements, but reliably holding down a stuck of paper pages covered with musical notes. The sun was hitting us, heavy like a ton of grain falling into an elevator, and I was in no mood to chitchat. "We're asleep!" I growled into the phone.

But the voice persevered. I listened a moment longer only because I could hardly understand the message. Soon, despite my headache, a wide smile spread across my face. Boris was telling me that Mr. Charles Dougal, Faith's godfather, who also happened to be a high ranking official at the Homeland Security Office, would fly in for her wedding.

"How romantic!" He had reportedly commented on our boat wedding plans.

And how *useful* his presence might turn out to be, I thought. In my vinegarish set of mind, I vaguely perceived certain opportunity in having Bonner's superior on my boat. While I wished all the nice and sweet things for Faith and Boris's union, I would just as much hate to see Mele and Kamekona's companionship end due to Shark being sent to jail. The golden scene where Kamekona had his head on Mele's lap had left a permanent mark on my psyche.

An extra bit of clever scheming was required, even though my head still resonated with pain every time the drill started its whine in the boatyard.

Free of any obsessions, including a fanatical adherence to man-made commandments, I needed to find the way for two bad deeds; Shark's slugging a policeman and Bonner's lousy investigation, to produce one positive outcome, Kamekona's freedom. And if that required a bit of arm-twisting, or even a tiny bit of morally gray persuasion … heck, nobody would get hurt, and my conscience was not that snow-white in the first place.

Saturday late morning is a busy time in Keehi. All the boat owners, gainfully employed during weekdays, show up in force, ready to work on their yachts. This moment in a boater's life when he has nothing to do because everything is already in the best possible condition is a myth at best. It never happens and anybody who owned a boat for 24 hours knows it. So plainly, it is a lie, a prevarication used either for self-deception or more often to mollify a spouse.

"You see, darling, as soon as I finish … (add your own lie here, like, disassembling and lubricating winches, or changing filters in a diesel, or fixing the wind vane etc.)…we will have time to do shopping for some really fine garden furniture."

For this reason, faced with the impossibility of ever

completing their tasks, hordes of middle-aged men appear in the marina to do a bit of work, but without a fanatical drive to the finish. There is always some time left to catch up with one's social life and perhaps grab a taste of brew.

But that Saturday, Kamekona and I were working like dogs on *Magic Carpet*, trying to make it not only navigable but also presentable.

My personal sailing philosophy favored diverting my limited resources of time and money toward the practical things like sails, a motor and steering system, which left mere crumbs for the inconsequential things, like cockpit seats, berth covers and grime on the windows. I could get away with it because Lala shared my preference for the starry sky, which meant that she rarely ventured into the cramped cabin, where my laissez-faire might offend her senses.

With the wedding planned for the next day, all this neglect had to be overcome in record time. With Lala's outbursts of outrage resonating from the cabin and Mele's sonorous grumbling radiating from the windows she was cleaning, I positioned myself as far from the trouble as possible, on the mast top, where the main sail's halyard had the bad habit of getting stuck whenever the conditions required its smooth operation.

Shark had an epiphany that instilled him with the sudden knowledge of internal combustion engines and he offered to check the motor, thus recusing himself from any janitorial work. I let him get away with it because he had a secret mission to Waimanalo planned for the afternoon.

Just as we settled into productive work, a phone call

from Lala's mother threw a wrench into our well-oiled organization. "You have no idea what you are talking about," she yelled over Lala's phone. "A captain can tolerate illicit sex on his boat, if this is his idea of helping friends, but cannot legalize it." Masters of boats big and small have no power to solemnize a marriage, she implied, suggesting I was an incompetent imposter.

The word *incompetent* makes me always very angry, but she cited the example of one Captain Heikki Tuukkanen who has to decline officiating marriages between visiting biologists a few times a year, and instead counsels them to go ahead and fornicate.

But Kasia Tuukkanen was not a person to be frightened by difficulties. This being only Saturday morning, she advised me, we still had half of a day to properly constitute a new church, if I would offer myself to be its founding Father.

The congregation met in the shade of the same public utility wall where I had had my first pastoral meeting with Brother Kamekona a few months ago. We signed the documents of incorporation and I registered myself with the State of Hawaii as a new bishop with an hour to spare, while the newlyweds obtained a marriage license.

The side benefit of this distraction was that, as I was printing documents with the letterhead of the Church of Pacific Blessings, I also had a marriage certificate prepared, ready for my signature a moment after the ceremony.

Somehow, we forgot about Nakamoto. We came to believe that the silly idea of national security threatened by Agent Baby and a Russian colonel had exploded in a shower of confetti, and the man would be found one of these days, one way or another.

The wedding plans proceeding smoothly, I extended an invitation to the Kruger family for a pleasure sail on Sunday morning. A half-day diversion on the water would relax the participants and contribute to the wedding's success. Mr. Dougal, the godfather, was supposed to fly in at 3p.m. and the ceremony was scheduled at 6 that evening; there was a lot of time to kill.

We brought the old girl, *Magic Carpet*, to the best condition that her thirty-year-old hull could manage by sundown Saturday. Sprawled on her deck, Lala, Mele and I were catching up with our body fluid imbalances by means of a cold Heineken, when Shark pulled up in Mele's station wagon. He unloaded a crate full of wine bottles, some yummy looking canned food and then—after casting a sharp eye around—he casually removed from the car a three foot long package wrapped in oil-stained burlap sacks. Unlike other bags and packages, it went directly into the front cabin. The hidden objects, now filling the tiny cabin with the crisp smell of greased metal, were not easy to obtain. But we got them anyway, because I needed something that could divert Kruger's attention without failure; the operation's success depended on it. The toys in the burlap bag held this power. I knew that no American male could resist them, especially when challenged by a foreign rival.

We broke the reunion soon after, tired enough to go to sleep as soon as our heads touched the pillows. The next day would be full of excitement, even fuller than Faith and her father might suspect.

Chapter 30

Sunday started like any other day in Waikiki; a pleasant warm breeze spreading aromas of delightful food wafting out of open restaurants under perfectly blue sky. Faith knocked on her father's door at nine, tightly clinging to her fiancé, whose pink cheeks and confident smile told Mr. Kruger that this man was indeed a rare find, an inexhaustible product of some mystical Siberian mutation.

A three-story aquarium stocked with big fish, including a couple of sharks, in the restaurant a short walk away caught Boris's imagination. Why not have breakfast there?

Walking anywhere, in particular to a restaurant, seemed like a wild idea to the Texan but on a fine day like this, why not? The story of Kulagin's night at the Ala Moana Park was hilarious, especially as it turned into a "guess the proper word" game for all the participants. Breakfast was not bad, even if the portions of waffles were rather disappointing in comparison with Texan eatery standards.

Another short walk toward the park ended in front of the memorable big black pipe. As Boris was showing his night rest spot to his truly amused father-in-law to be, a light-brown Honda Accord stopped at the curb and its driver shouted greetings from inside. I was this driver. I had to make three rounds through the surrounding streets, waiting for the party to appear at the agreed place, worrying that something stopped them, ruining our plans. But Kulagin's word was as good as gold; they traipsed in, late but beaming good spirits.

"As good a time as ever to go sailing. No need to go back to the hotel," I suggested, and Colonel Kulagin agreed with me wholeheartedly. Everyone was overdressed anyway. Faith was wearing her splendid snow-white Marilyn Monroe outfit, and her father cut a fine figure as a colonial gentleman in an off-white, three-piece suit. Kulagin was a bit less formal, but he still managed to find clean pants in his suitcase, complemented by Kruger's Aloha shirt and a pair of real leather shoes, fortuitously purchased at the last moment in Vladivostok.

My sailing companions squeezed their bodies into Honda, a wild adventure in itself, and we took off for a twenty-minute ride over the picturesque Pali Highway to Kailua Beach. There, having sailed from her Keehi slip overnight, *Magic Carpet* danced romantically on the small waves right by Flat Island.

Laughing excitedly like kids going for a summer camp, we boarded the catamaran, weighed the anchor and took off faster than a water taxi, straight out into the ocean. Propelled by the steady trade wind, we swiftly passed the twin mountains of the Mokulua Islands and glided across the cobalt plane of the ocean to where it met the cerulean sky.

Soon Oahu looked like a prop from an adventure movie. A thin yellow line of sand, interrupted by small sticks of palm trees, separated the light-blue coastal water from the dark green and brown curtain of the vertical Koolau Mountains in the background. People could not be seen on the beach anymore, the island seemed to return to its primary state of wilderness.

This optical illusion worked both ways; we were disappearing from the islanders' view just as fast. Our vanishing act was played not only for the benefit of beach goers but also for whoever was keeping his boredom-droopy eyes on a radar screen. My radar reflector had somehow fallen off the mast on Saturday afternoon and we were quickly becoming invisible.

From the steering wheel, I joined my guests in conversation. Kulagin discovered that his future father-in-law was an Army man at one point, and they had a great time holding a friendly squabble over military matters. Faith, her platinum hair flowing in the wind, was glowing with happiness, seeing her barefoot males bonding and engaging in a friendly manner.

Some time later, Boris excused himself and disappeared into the cabin below while I was entertaining the Texans with stories about King Kamehameha, who had won the big prize of Oahu in the battle of the Pali, not far from the highway we had motored through.

Kulagin returned on deck twenty minutes later, giving me a meaningful pat on the back as he moved back into his seat next to Faith. The big game had started. He had sent the last signal to Shark over my VHF radio and set up the electronic jamming. How he did it, I didn't know, but I believed his claim that screwing things up is way easier than making them work. He used to do it for a living, blowing up bridges with explosives, crashing mud huts with tank tracks and jamming communications with his tank radios. If he was right, no cell phones or radios would work on my boat.

We would know very soon how successful he was, because minutes after his last message, a few TV stations in Honolulu would receive an anonymous tip. A Texas billionaire and his daughter had disappeared without a trace from the Royal Hawaiian Hotel. Last seen on Kalakaua Avenue, they seemed to have vanished into thin air and all attempts to contact them by phone had failed. The possibility of a kidnapping had to be considered, even if no ransom had been demanded so far. The exciting news of a wrongdoing of this proportion happening in the placid criminal landscape of Waikiki, where pickpocket thieves get to be featured on a "Wanted" list, had to stir the media in a major frenzy.

I feared a ring coming from Faith's or her father's pocket any moment, but nothing interrupted the heated discussion about the relative effectiveness of a well-concealed bazooka-armed infantryman against a battle tank. Phones remained silent and my VHF was mute. Not a shred of stray conversation bouncing through the ether made it through *Magic Carpet's* speakers. Indeed, we were in a radio silence mode.

Kalugin would not hear a word about the superiority of M16 rifle over AK 47, causing Mr. Kruger's blood pressure to jump dangerously. Time flew as we drank beer and skimmed the waves like a big shearwater, Oahu remaining a faint outline over the horizon.

Eventually, Faith—who had lost her diamond encrusted watch somewhere in her hotel room—started gently enquiring if the time would not be right to head back. After all, it would be only decent to greet Uncle Charlie at the airport, at three.

This problem had been anticipated and we counterattacked with Lala appearing in the companionway with a tray of splendid looking, tiny sandwiches. As a tribute to Kulagin, we managed to find some caviar in Honolulu and it became an instant hit with the Kruger family. Presented on a bed of Gorgonzola cheese, the small black and shiny pearls lounged seductively on crackers, surrounded by tiny pieces of red marinated paprika. They smiled at Faith like a diamond necklace; now, she loved *everything* Russian.

I brought up a few bottles of wine, whose vintage and parentage had no meaning to me but I knew were good because I'd paid 110 dollars a bottle in Foodland, where Mele promised to take back any unopened bottles.

Faith succumbed to her appetite and forgot her time concerns for a while. I watched the precious wine disappearing at the speed of hundred-and-ten dollars—more or less an hour's worth of my night shift, taxes not included—every twenty minutes. For a good cause, I resigned myself, while Boris gave me a hooligan's greeting with his bent elbow, pouring down his throat another precious glass outside his turn.

Lala kept making trips to the galley and I kept pouring the juice of forgetfulness but eventually the company's enthusiasm started to wilt and their attention wander. Before Faith had a chance to ask about time again, I rolled out my next diversion.

"There is only one way to establish which weapon is superior," I reignited the M 16 versus Kalashnikov discussion, as it was already dying slowly between burps and hiccups. "You must shoot it side by side. I happen to have both arms on my boat; whoever kills more floating bottles, he—and his rifle—wins."

"You have assault rifles on your boat?" The Texan's eyes became round like two quarters. "Why?"

"Pirates," I confessed, visibly disturbed. "It's not entirely legal, I know, but I never take them out in the territorial waters. But once outside, I am prepared to defend myself. Isn't it what you would do in Texas?"

"Do you know what pirates do to the women?" Lala almost wept into Faith's ear, her eyes full of terror and her eyes getting misty.

"Were you…?" Faith, seeing Lala's distress, almost choked on the last sandwich.

""No, but I know this girl …" Lala started whispering in her ear, shuddering and choking from her hardly controlled emotions.

The other woman's expression quickly changed from appalled excitement to disgust and, finally, pure fear. "Daddy," she whimpered, inching closer to his lap, "I really like it that Chris has guns on his boat!"

"I would never set my foot on *Magic Carpet* if he didn't," Lala declared.

The mood on the boat changed radically when I brought up two well-oiled rifles and a few boxes of ammo. The two warriors grabbed their respective weapons and started sending empty bottles to the ocean floor exploded into tiny shards. Considering the boat's rolling, heaving and pitching, they were both doing pretty well. Clearly, we were well protected from pirates. Even Faith got sucked into the competition, cheering alternatively the Texan rifleman and the Russian *tankista*.

I was the person who had the least fun. At one-forty five, Kulagin undid his jamming arrangement, as I was waiting for a message from Shark regarding the success of our land operation. But minutes passed and the radio remained silent. It was dead and I had no idea how to proceed in this information blackout.

I kept turning it off and on. I played with all the controls I could access without ripping my radio apart, but all my ministrations produced not a squeak of reception. Seriously worried, I called down Boris on the pretense of sharing with him the beauty of my GPS plotter.

He turned the radio off and on again. Swearing in the long smooth phrases of Russian profanities, he carried the exploration of my VHF's bowels somewhat further but without any better result. "It's much easier to screw something up than make it work." Those were Boris's own words and he couldn't bring my radio back to life. We remained in radio silence.

Blinded by the fog of war of our own making, I didn't know what should be our next step to take. At the very least, I thought, we would be better off in some very private place. I decided to show my guests a big sea cave off Mokapu rock. It could be approached stealthily from the open ocean side, and the cave was tall enough to swallow my catamaran without de-stepping the mast. And the mountain above was solid enough to protect us even from an F-16, if Bonner got very pissed.

Chapter 31

The first news of kidnapping reached Agent Bonner at ten-thirty, when a news flash interrupted the Animal Planet he was watching, while having his late Sunday breakfast. The Texan billionaire and his daughter … His jaw stopped moving momentarily because an alarm sounded somewhere at the back of his mind then he moaned, "Operation Baby!" Exactly the people he was asked to look after on behalf of some big wig in the Homeland Security. A few seconds later, he learnt from the same TV news that this disappearance coincided with a mysterious Russian colonel vanishing as well.

He didn't even make it to his home phone before it rang. His office was calling to report "a friendly heads-up message" from headquarters. Mr. Dougal, the deputy chairman of the Homeland Security was on the way to Honolulu, apparently on private business but … Bonner better be forewarned and prepared.

A quick check confirmed to a terrified Bonner that the Homeland Security Deputy on his way to Hawaii was the same highly placed official who had asked for a bit of extra care for Baby.

Had Max Bonner ever believed in coincidences, he

would be either dead, wasted as a young agent whose livelihood depended on daily dives into the scum pool of criminality, or relegated to the archives department, where being paranoid was not a prerequisite for the job. He certainly would not be an up-and-coming field operations chief.

The concurrence of the kidnapping and the visit by the Homeland Security official was as likely to be an innocent happenstance as finding a copy of the *Times* — opened on an ad for an Audi TT Coupe—on his desk, two weeks before his twentieth wedding anniversary. If he wished to remain in his professional position, and he did, he needed to guess who was pulling the strings driving this puppet theatre and why. And, probably, it needed to be done within a timeframe defined by the official's arrival to Honolulu.

Nakamoto! Crazy Nakamoto was still on the run, doing God-knows-what while cunningly escaping the FBI net thrown over Oahu. But how could a single man pull this off? Without his service weapon and the all-door-opening badge … with his car taken away… just staying undetected on the island for a few days was no mean feat. Could he grab two men and a woman without a major commotion?

Bonner retrieved photographs on his laptop. Mr. Kruger was an older man, but had to be close to three hundred pounds, and his daughter … well, Baby looked like she could throw Nakamoto out of a sumo ring in two seconds.

Conclusion—he could not do it alone and therefore he had helpers. A conspiracy then … Now a Russian colonel goes missing in the same moment.

The agent's mind soared to get the bird's view at this

conflicted situation. Even the nature of this presumably criminal event was not clear. They were missing from the hotel ... perhaps. But to call it kidnapping ... it was a pretty long leap. Who had made this bold assertion, and why? Now, what was the significance of the Homeland Security's deputy arriving here at the exactly such an inopportune time?

The smell of a foul ruse seemed to emanate from the TV set now. A very influential hand was arranging figures on the chessboard called Honolulu, his home territory. Despite a large fan blowing air from the room's corner, Bonner felt sweat leaking over his forehead and neck. The affair might be *way* above his head and clearance level, but the unknown schemer wanted it this way and there was no way this mess could be sidestepped.

He recalled Nakamoto's crazy ravings and suddenly experienced pangs of empathy. Now *he* was in the same impossible predicament. He would have to pursue some outrageous clues leading into the stratosphere of the power structure or he could pretend to be deaf and dumb. His career was dangerously close to a cliff's edge either way.

Bonner shook off his fatalistic premonitions. First things first. Who could be helping Nakamoto? The FBI newcomers that his wayward agent had used during Bonner's vacation had been already transferred out of Hawaii. Their lack of common sense was now upsetting some other chiefs. That would leave as suspects Kamekona Aku, the man sought by the local police and Christopher Gorny, the emergency room doctor. Were those two idiots helping Nakamoto, even after his personal intervention and orders to help in his apprehension? Hard to believe but worth checking.

Twenty minutes later, Agent Bonner learned that Doctor Gorny was on sick leave. Another coincidence, he smiled. A few minutes later he found out that Gorny's boat in Keehi Lagoon was missing from her slip. He was just about to call the Coast Guard in order to arrange search for *Magic Carpet* when another message came in; his agent dispatched to Keehi Port had Mr. Aku in custody.

The investigation was moving ahead efficiently. Pretty soon, he was going to know much more about this affair. He felt it in his stomach, which started to relax. The only problem was time, as Mr. Dougal would be landing at three, three hours from now. But Kamekona Aku—even if he was not the brain of this operation—was likely to lead him much closer to the mischief maker, and he was sitting handcuffed a mere fifteen minutes' drive away.

Shark was sitting calmly in the back seat of a gray Buick. He kept his head uncomfortably bent forward, as he was too tall to fit on a backbench of a regular sedan. The handcuffs restraining his hands behind his back added to this awkward position but he was watching pigeons on the shore with a placid half-smile of an idiot. Which one is Caudillo? he wondered. Must be that arrogant bastard walking like a cop in a Kamehameha Day parade.

"Where are they?" Bonner asked louder, as though the prisoner might have missed the question due to hearing problems.

"Sir?" Shark asked stupidly, but signaling his overpowering desire to cooperate.

Alex Modzelewski

"Gorny, your friend Gorny, where is he?" His phone rang just as the agent was fighting the temptation to smack the man across the face. It could be done without too much risk, as Aku was properly cuffed and there were no witnesses around. But as he was listening to the phone message, the color drained from his face and his dry constricted throat could hardly utter, "Thank you."

His office just advised the boss that Mr. Dougal had found out about Kruger's kidnapping from the TV news flash on his in-flight entertainment center. A second later, the dignitary placed a call through his in-flight telephone and, just to make sure, he also instructed the pilot to call the control tower in Honolulu. The Honolulu FBI office received both messages: the chief had been requested to meet Mr. Dougal at the gate, fifteen hundred, sharp.

"Water boarding," the words flashed through Bonner's mind, as he looked into Kamekona's eyes with hatred. But the logistics of this otherwise simple procedure exceeded the time available before his professional life would be executed at the gate of American Airlines.

Dick Cheney, where are you when your country needs you? he wanted to cry, but—thanks to many years of training in his unforgiving trade—his eyes remained cold like Arctic glaciers.

"Kamekona," he started again, this time in his warm sympathetic voice, hiding the frozen chunks of blue ice behind his eyelids, "You will go to prison for assaulting the police officer, for years. Let me help you … I might make recommendations to the court on your behalf."

"I've already resigned myself to die in a cold underground cell," Shark answered, matching the agent's emotional appeal a tear for a tear. He bent his neck some more, lowering his face to his knees.

"You think it's a joke, Aku?" Bonner screamed. "If you don't cooperate, I will have you locked up with sex abusers and rapists!"

Kamekona's shoulders shook promisingly, as if in an uncontrollable sob but when he raised his face, the bastard was laughing. "Ah, never too much love!"

A moment of strong emotions passed. Agent Bonner was drawn in turns to the temptation of shooting the recalcitrant scoundrel during an 'attempt-to-flee' and then overcoming the desire to throw himself to his knees, begging for help.

A resolution to this difficult scene came when Shark declared, "I don't know where Doctor Gorny and Mr. Kruger are, but I might try to guess."

Despite his poker-polished negotiating posture, Kamekona was also worried because the operation was running behind the established schedule. By two o'clock, he was supposed to call *Magic Carpet's* crew with the news, hopefully reporting that his charges were dropped and the wedding was free to proceed.

"Please, guess!" Bonner choked in gratitude.

"First, these …" Kamekona turned his back, showing his big hands imprisoned in steel manacles. The handcuffs fell off with a low metallic clink. "Now, I want you to make the charges for this cop's broken jaw go away." He was looking sternly into the agent's eyes, rubbing his wrists.

"It can't be done, Aku," Bonner exploded in frustration. "It's in the court's hands!"

"Nakamoto said he would do it! Even if he had to kidnap the cop." Kamekona looked at the agent accusingly. "Unless *you* don't want to cooperate." He turned his back to Bonner and placed his hands behind, ready for cuffing.

"Wait!" The FBI man ground his teeth. "Maybe he will drop the charges, withdraw his report. I can try to call him."

The procedure of calling the officer injured during his stint in Hawaii was a business much more complicated than anyone could expect because, taking advantage of his Sunday off, he had gone bass fishing on a small lake not far from Springfield, Oregon, where he was a part of the municipal police force.

The local office in Portland had to send a helicopter to reach the poor chap on his bass boat. But the measure was not a complete loss because the policeman could not ask for a better proof that the phone call from the chief of the Honolulu FBI office was not a cruel hoax by his colleagues, who never forgave him for looking for greener pastures in tropical islands.

He was putty in Bonner's hands. Yes, he would withdraw the old incident report, which still brought him more scorn and ribbing than bedwetting during a summer camp, and he would be happy to join the Honolulu force in consideration of his good will.

Unfortunately, all this activity pushed the minute count on Bonner's watch to the number forty-five, the arrival time minus fifteen.

" Done!" Bonner hollered enthusiastically. "Now, where are they?"

"Now, you write it down. Nakamoto did! It only takes two minutes." Kamekona was methodical and thorough.

Bonner ripped a page from his yellow pad, wrote a full page of report recommendations and signed in a nervous overwrought hand. "Here," he handed it to Kamekona, who read it carefully.

"Terrible handwriting," he noted. "Now we have it signed by a witness. The driver will do."

"Aku," Bonner wheezed, "we have to go to the airport! We have a deal, man! Where are they?"

"Everything will be just fine, Mr. Bonner," Shark assured him respectfully. "Just one more signature and we can go to the airport. And I'll make Mr. Dougal so happy that you will get a promotion for sure."

The unmarked car spun its wheels, shot the parking lot gravel and catapulted out of the Keehi Small Boat Harbor toward the airport a moment later. The engine's roar masked the words rolling out of Special Agent Bonner's mouth again and again, "I hope you are right. I hope you are right."

"Just pass me your phone, Mr. Bonner," Kamekona's voice was assuring and calm but his heart was racing because too much time had gone by without any coordination with the boat's crew.

Chapter 32

The dividend on the four hundred and forty dollars I had invested in the Bordeaux started rolling in over the next thirty minutes, once the precious wine made it from my guests' throats to their brains. First, Faith put her head down on a pillow, just to rest a little. Soon she was snoring softly and sweetly, despite the ongoing cannonade produced by her men with the AK 47 and M-16.

The warriors ran out of ammunition soon after and put away their weapons, still without a clear consensus on which one performed better. They produced much harsher and discordant sounds once their eyes closed, the kind one might expect in overcrowded barracks. Four bottles of wine for the three of them, as neither Lala nor I touched the liquid gold, proved to be enough to induce a light coma, especially on top of the beer imbibed at the beginning of our trip. I still had two bottles in reserve, in case they opened their eyes.

I turned the bow toward Oahu and we glided in the nice easterly wind as swiftly and smoothly as only a catamaran can. I'd taken us four miles into the open ocean to ensure that concerned authorities would not interrupt our shooting competition. On our way back, we flew through this distance in about thirty minutes, watching houses in Kailua grow, palm trees reappearing and finally people swarming on the beach.

I dropped my sails in the narrow isthmus between the big brown mountain of Mokapu Peninsula and a black craggy island-rock, Moku Manu, where the sea cave was. The ocean calmed down in the protected cove, white caps disappeared and we motored through the smooth cobalt water toward the huge black hole, gaping in the mountain like a cathedral gate. Wide open, the cave invited any comer but also threatened with intimidating unspoken menace. Seen from the sun-drenched outside, the cavern seemed flooded with black ink, which blotted every detail behind the rough dark-gray granite of its entry.

But—having been there many times in a kayak—I knew that one could actually see his way around, once inside. Spacious like a jetliner's hangar, the cave was tall enough to accommodate a sailing boat and it was sufficiently large to hide a small flotilla in its belly. But my sailor's heart was filled with the instinctive fear of its irregular basalt walls; this was not a right place for the creature meant to fly in the sun like *Magic Carpet*.

I just put my nose inside the cave and stopped there, right past the entrance, barely deep enough to hide from overflying planes. There was no good reason to go any further; my tourists were still unconscious and completely insensitive to the wonders of nature. I kept the motor idling, making small adjustments from time to time to keep *Magic Carpet* in one spot.

"Hope you know what you are doing." Lala slid on the bench behind me and draped herself on my back. It felt good. The air in the cave was cool and my mood was chilling fast, as I was considering the implications of losing control over our precisely planned operation. Lala's arms around my neck and her front plastered over my bare back were helping. "Not much could be pinned on me for making those sandwiches," she thought loudly. "Kulagin might be simply kicked out of the country, but you ... for you, they certainly could find some law to smack you with."

"You can't win a prize without making a bet," I shrugged gently, trying not to dislodge her cheek from my back. "I'm just a nice guy taking these nice tourists on an exciting ocean adventure. I don't have a license for that, true, but I am not charging any money either. Maybe they could slap me with a fine, that's all."

"Guns," Lala reminded. "I have picked up all the casings I could find, and you could just dump the hardware into the ocean, but the powder residue must be all over the place. No need for a gas chromatograph, the whole boat stinks. If Kruger opens his mouth, you sink like a stone. And you can kiss your medical license good-bye."

"Why should he blabber? He did more shooting than anybody else." I tried to reassure Lala but she was right, this *was* a concern. "You might also add a fine from the Coast Guard if they catch me without a radar reflector; yeah, that's a possibility. But if you weigh it against the almost certainty that Kamekona goes to the slammer, somewhere far away on the mainland, I'll take the bet."

I shrugged nonchalantly, trying to make things look light, but I knew the gun business could become a thorny issue. No question; I have overdone the Sunday entertainment.

"You know, Horny, you're pretty naïve … but so is Shark, so maybe it's fair." Lala's hand reached for my hair. "I like it … I'm thinking … if that's what you would do for your friend, who knows what you might do for someone you actually loved."

We just sat there, listening to the snoring, the soft purr of the motor and the low-pitched grumble of the waves echoing a thousand times against the cave walls.

"Now, outlaw, I will share with you *my* family criminal history, so you don't feel like you are the only noble lawbreaker around." Lala brightened up.

"Told you how my parents met, but it's not even the best part of their story. They were on the atoll, I was on the way, and their legal situation was far from regular. In fact, the only reason they were left alone was that there was no immigration office on Midway.

"My mother already had a green card. It was quite easy for her to get it. There was martial law in Poland then and Communists were arresting people left and right. Almost anyone could get refugee status. But my father was a Finn; he could not claim any sort of persecution. He should have been gone from America a long time before. Overstaying his welcome, he would be deported when caught without a chance of coming back, ever.

"They worried and worried; finally my mother said to him, 'You look pretty Polish to me … as long as you don't open your mouth. We go to Guam. What do they know about the differences between Poland and Finland? They are probably shorthanded, anyway, and won't pay too much attention to your case.

"'We go to the Immigration together and I say you are my husband. You've jumped a Polish ship to join me, a green card holder. But you've been so trauma-tized that you can hardly talk in your native Polish, never mind English. Obviously, you have no papers except for a birth certificate you'd stuffed in your pocket before the move. As might be expected, your captain, a bloody Commie, kept your passport in his safe.

" 'I'll do a little job on your birth certificate. You know, change Helsinki for Helsinko, that's one small letter, and Finland for Poland, that's two letters. Then I'll do the translation into English; won't even charge you a penny. The public notary's stamp is in the har-bormaster's desk; that's your desk, the second drawer on right side.'

"They worked for a few weeks to teach my father a bit of Polish, just in case the immigration guy had a Polish neighbor or grandmother. After chatting with my father in English, you know he doesn't have a great knack for languages. Eventually, he mastered three phrases to perfection, two simple ones and one com-plicated. He can still render them so well that nobody would turn his head in the middle of Catholic mass in Warsaw if he spoke.

"*Tak* for yes; *nie* for no; and the difficult one: *Mat-ko Boska!* for everything else. This phrase, meaning "Mother of God!" had to be accompanied by him pulling his hair and other signs of terrible distress. The idea was to stop his interrogator from pursuing this line of questioning, if he had any decency; not a sure thing among immigration officials. My mother could fill in all the required information without torturing the poor man."

I started laughing loudly, imagining the distinguished Captain Tuukkanen pulling his hair to the hysterical cries of *Matko Boska,* the phrase I knew from my childhood.

"So you are a bastard, Lala," I croaked, wiping my eyes.

"I prefer a love child," Lala answered with dignity.

My hilarity caused some commotion on the boat and Faith opened her eyes. "What time is it?"

It was three-fifteen. At this point, our outing would start looking like a real kidnapping if we did not turn toward the shore. I could not hide in the cave anymore. We had to emerge and face the real world. By now, Shark had either managed to get his account dry-cleaned or the operation had failed and we all needed some serious legal counsel.

True to her mother's deviant ways, Lala told Faith that Kamekona would greet her godfather at the airport and bring him to meet us. A poor lie but it kept grumbling Faith off my back for now. The mood on my boat had definitely turned sour. Kulagin went downstairs to tinker with my radio again but it refused to be resurrected. He returned to the cockpit with the angry expression primarily invented for Chechen guerillas. Faith was silent-mad, nursing her father who appeared to have a colossal headache and a touch of upset stomach.

Sailing now straight into the face of the easterly wind, it took us well over an hour to cover a couple of miles separating the Mokapu rock from Kailua Beach. Not a word was uttered during this time; only Mr. Kruger's moans resonated pitifully whenever the boat heaved.

I passed Bird Shit Rock on my starboard and sailed

outside the reef, aiming at the reef break by the Flat Island. On the other side of the passage, the world of regulations, legal concepts and armed servants of the state would take us in. Whatever fate had prepared for me, the burden of uncertainty would be off my shoulders, but handcuffs might be applied to my wrists.

I was deliberating the question of disposing of the illegal arms, carelessly thrown on the V-berth. In strictly rational terms, Lala was right. I should throw them overboard while we were still on the deep ocean, but I knew Shark would be mad like hell. He had borrowed them from his brother and they were to be returned in mint condition. And then, the powder residue was probably enough evidence to convict me anyway. Whichever way I looked at it now, it was a stupid idea to take them in the first place. But at this point, the luxury of self-flagellation was just a plain waste of time.

"There!" a mumbled word fell out of Kruger's drooling mouth. He was kneeling on deck, vomiting my precious Bordeaux over the port railing, but he stopped and jabbed his index into the air, pointing ahead of the boat. Parallel to the beach, just outside the line of surf marking the reef, two long boats raced toward us with a clear intention of cutting us off.

I had missed them, staring into the ocean and looking for a good break in the reef, but they were already pretty close, no more than a hundred yards, closing fast. They looked surreal. The two long narrow objects, no more than a foot wide but over forty foot long, were gliding over the ocean like two needles aiming their sharp points at us. On each, a black head was nodding at us every second in unison with yellow flashes on the boats' sides. Hidden behind the first paddler was a row of more heads bobbing in the same rhythm, as though they belonged to the same multi-headed monster.

Two six-man outriggers bore at us at racing speed. Those guys were no recreational paddlers; they moved like the well-oiled parts of two powerful six-cylinder motors.

"You have some ammo left, Chris?" Kruger moaned as he climbed up the railing to his full height, looking around for his M16. Faith, as white as her outfit, could not decide if she should hide from the pirates behind her father or Kulagin. In effect, she was making nervous short trips from one to another, slowing for a moment at the companionway, as though she considered hiding under the berth as well.

Kulagin grabbed the binoculars hanging by the steering wheel and stared at the boats for a moment. A wide smile spread on his face and his teeth came into full view under the blond mustache. "Shark," he said, winking at me. Then he turned around toward Faith, who was trying to disappear behind his back. "Your Hawaiian Prince."

She snatched the binoculars from his hand, but by now, we all could see that the first paddler was our friend, his big chest glistening from sweat. He wore no shirt but was decked out like a groom. The maile, a Hawaiian green leaf crown, adorned his head. Behind his big body, I noticed a happily smiling, middle-aged *haole,* also wearing a green wreath on his gray head, and paddling with enthusiasm.

"Uncle Charlie," Faith squealed and grabbed Lala for a hug.

The outriggers were close now but did not slow

down. They just kept racing, overtaken by the instinct to be first, no matter what was the reason for the trip. I understood their motivation better when a huge individual came into view in the other boat. He looked practically identical with Kamekona, like a carbon copy. This had to be Palani, his twin brother.

As the boats were closing on us, we could hear something like a rhythmic song or a war cry. Every ten or fifteen seconds, the lead paddler was emitting an explosive "Hut" which was answered by a low, thunderous "Ho" bellowed from the five big chests behind. The call kept coming like a locomotive chug, driving six bodies in a perfect synchronization.

They zipped by us side by side like an express train. Apparently, Kamekona and his brother never gave up their competition. Only then, after they had swished by my boat separated by barely a few feet of water, did I notice Special Agent Bonner in position three of Palani's canoe. I bitterly regretted my indecision, but it was too late to send the lethal playthings to the bottom now. The outriggers separated, made tight U-turns and pulled up to *Magic Carpet*, one on each side.

Chapter 33

With all the interested parties on board—
even if not dressed in their best wedding out-
fits—there was no particular reason why the
wedding would have to wait till six. Without
even giving a thought to the cultural impact
of this momentous occasion, we were introducing a
new trend to the upper echelons of American soci-
ety—a marriage pirate-style. Faith pointed it out to us,
peasants unaware of the ceremonial and perhaps commercial value of our undertaking. She and her father
experienced tremendous kicks from this new twist on
the ancient ceremony, so refreshing in their formal social circle.

The bride easily persuaded her father that my Pacific Blessings Church was very much like Baptists …
only of the Pacific islands variety. Mr. Kruger turned
out to be a very open-minded gentleman and happily
joined the game of guessing, what will her friends in
Texas say? The bride was dying to tell the world the
incredible story of her wild courtship and outrageous
barefoot wedding. And then she would show the pictures! Faith looked over the semi-naked paddlers, glistening in the setting sun like bronze statues of Greek
heroes, and she was sure that first-class tickets from

Houston to Honolulu would be hard to get for the next few months.

Fortunately, I had a camera on board and Lala busied herself with the photographic documentation of this avant-garde event. Quite surely, Bonner would have some pictures as well, even if he didn't seem to carry a camera. The blue sky above might not be as empty as it looked.

This was a very fortuitous finale to our somewhat undercooked plot, but a big weight was still pressing on my heart in the shape of two assault rifles smelling in the front cabin like Honolulu during New Year celebrations. I resolved that no partier would be allowed below *Magic Carpet's* deck until the problem has been solved.

Lala assumed a defensive position at the bottom of a companionway. Her performance against Nakamoto invading my apartment in Honolulu gave me a glimmer of hope that we could still get away with our trespasses. If someone *really* had to go to the bathroom, I was ready to invent a new tradition. The attending pirates could throw a wedding guest, secured with a sturdy rope, into the ocean. But no one would be allowed past Lala to snoop and smell down below.

I felt Bonner's viper eyes scrutinizing the boat and people casually. Was it his professional habit or was he looking for something with which to hook me like a tuna? I was sure he had a heart-felt desire to bring me under his professional authority, at least to play with a bit, if I was lucky. To start with, all he needed was a half-decent probable cause. The rest could be worked out later, at leisure.

There was no need to rush things. If he could pick

up just a small tasty piece of incriminating information now, he could haul me out later, when Charlie Dougal—living through this adventure like Peter Pan on the pirate's ship— left Honolulu for his faraway home. Once the high priest of the Homeland Security was gone to his temple, Bonner, the master of the Hawaiian Islands, would exact the payment for the trouble and humiliation I had caused him. This cobra was not defanged and remained in the hunt. I would swear he tasted the air with tongue flicks, too fast to be observed.

The canoe paddlers stayed in their outriggers; there simply was not enough space on my boat for such a crowd. Once Dougal and Bonner climbed aboard, the bulging shiny bodies in outriggers looked like extras on a movie set. Lala valiantly hung out from the boat's lines in an attempt to place them in the wedding's photographic compositions.

As the excited celebrants were making merry and the camera was clicking, Shark pulled me aside. All done, he winked with a grin. Then he introduced me to his brother, an individual almost indistinguishable from Kamekona but decidedly less friendly.

"My guns …" Palani started curtly without bothering to finish the sentence.

"Good thing you've come along," I sighed. "I was thinking of dumping them."

"Wat!" He instinctively lifted his paddle and I, as instinctively, stepped back behind the shrouds, the steel lines holding up the mast. "Dump my pu's! Beach boy no tell you?" He gave his brother a malignant look. "They for *hui*. You lose them you buy new ones!"

Shark was very busy observing the Koolau Mountains, making sure his eyes would not catch Palani's angry stare. The Hawaiians took possession of their burlap bag with visible relief, but their joy was nowhere close to the ecstatic release I experienced. The heavy oil-stained package crossed over the railing into the outrigger, giving away a characteristic metallic clunk.

Bonner's disinterested eyes were upon us as soon as he heard the soft noise, but Palani met them with a hard stare, murmuring under his breath, "Come and get them, *lana*." He slid into his outrigger, gently placing the bag in front of his legs. Bonner was looking past him with the studied expression of disinterest on his face. The predator picked the scent, but did he guess what was hiding in the burlap?

I turned the bow into the full ocean, leaving the paddlers behind. We had a mission to accomplish and the wedding guests were enthusiastically in its favor. The enchanted Texans, including Charlie Dougal, were ready to submit to any new adventure our imaginations could come up with. Bonner, an individual much harder to impress, went along, smiling benignly and chatting up the Homeland official.

I relaxed at the steering wheel, happy to see my responsibilities reduced to running the boat and performing pastoral duty. Relived from guarding the illicit cargo, Lala emerged from the cabin to sit by my side. Suddenly, the whole affair turned romantic and entertaining, the legally hazardous background quickly dissipating. We caught the mood of enthusiasm from elated Faith.

In the midst of laughter and excitement, silent Kulagin was sitting alone by the mast, sending Faith perfunctory smiles from time to time, but watching the activities with the air of detachment. Probably, he was still trying to establish if:

A. He was still in Vladivostok, sleeping off too much moonshine, which turned out to be contaminated and hallucinogenic.

B. The events of the past two days were a wild dream, a continuation of the vision brought on by the medication-spiked whisky. He had to consider the possibility that he was still reclining next to the shit pipe in the Ala Moana Park, while the need to re-enter the real world was looming.

C. The whole affair *was* real, the possibility unlikely but not negated by any clear contrarian evidence so far.

Whichever was the case, what could be gained by not playing along? Kulagin moved to the starboard, where Faith was sitting by her father's side. He squeezed his bottom next to hers and swept his bride in a powerful embrace. As she purred with pleasure, Boris engaged his prospective father-in-law in friendly conversation.

However, even at this warm instant, right before his marital bliss was to begin, he could not shake off his uneasiness. He needed the approval of his cantankerous but wise father because he trusted the old man to smack him over the head with any flaw hiding in his life's plan.

Ossip Pavlovitch had proven to have a fresh and unconventional look on his life. And just importantly, he was not shy to share it with his son, despite being dead for a number of years. Convicts are known to have ways of transcending barbed wire fences, barred windows and—apparently—boundaries of life and death.

A wire snare, a rotten carrot, a rabbit stew ... the old jailbird was a veritable treasure store of enlightening parables. Boris could hardly wait for the night when he could close his eyes and draw on his father's gulag education. An insult or two, he wouldn't mind, as long as dear Papa wouldn't find a way to rub his nose into some *real* problem. Then he would feel safe.

It was the first wedding ceremony I had ever officiated in my capacity of bishop and, honestly, I did a fantastic job. I dropped the sails, donned my captain's hat, acquired this very morning at a party shop, and lined up the bride, groom and other wedding participants in front of the mast. They were swaying like a bunch of drunks in front of a bar because the boat started dancing in increasing wind, but I kept the young couple waiting for their "kiss the bride" moment. This experience would make them appreciate the dangers and uncertainties facing their new family, I hoped.

I made personal courage the theme of my sermon. Were they not a great example of this admirable quality, overcoming the great distance separating Texas and Vladivostok? Haven't their bold love bridged the cultural abyss gaping between a Texan heiress and a Russian *tankista*?

Kept in check by Lala's concerned look, I managed to hold back my musings about their love having won over the perils of common sense. Lala had her own family story to support the sentiment of respect for miracles. After all, they don't happen too often. Finally, Faith and Boris were allowed to embrace. Mr. Kruger wiped his eyes and even Charlie Dougal's eyes had the misty look.

The wedding party dismissed from *Magic Carpet's* deck, I hauled up the sails and turned my bow south. As the guests were finishing my supply of the damn expensive wine—fortunately Kruger and both Kulagins were abstaining now—*Magic Carpet* flew across the ocean like her namesake, hardly touching the foamy seas. With the trade wind blowing a solid twenty knots from the northeast now, we would be in Keehi in two or three hours. I was sure Kamekona would be there with a proper welcome for the pirate-wed couple.

Chapter 34

A three-stringed *shamisen* played sweetly in Nakamoto's ears as he was lying in the dark hot metal pipe, waiting patiently for the inevitable climax of his toil. He felt no need to know what the source of his confidence was. His very soul told him to wait here, in the culvert, which—semi-buried in the gravel of the Keehi Small Boat Harbor parking lot—offered a clear view of the port entrance. No one could come or leave unnoticed because, fearful of missing his target, he never rested his eyes even for a moment. He had not eaten or drunk for the past twenty-four hours, patiently waiting in ambush. Oh yes, the ninja's life is made of self-sacrifice, but he would not change it for any other.

To question such a direct order did not even pass his mind. The exhilaration of waiting for the traitors—his *katana* ready for the judgment day—like a righteous demon *Oni*... oh, it was more than a fair payment for the last few days he had spent like a rat. In fact, his self-sacrificial lack of interest in food and water amazed him. His body seemed to have only one need, to knock his foot against the metal of the culvert. The regular, strong beat of a drum— he went to see *taiko* drumming shows on a few occasions in

Honolulu—punctuated the time slowly winding past him, releasing the tension permeating his body.

Knock, tsuku, tsuku … the metronome-like throb helped to overcome his desire to run and yell and hack the traitors with his sword. Now, thanks to his *taiko* foot, those crazy desires were already things of the past; he was a new and self-possessed person.

Mu … Nakamoto was sorry to have wasted all those years without learning about his heritage, but this much he had read: if you make your ego disappear, a new world opens to you. Or perhaps it's the old world, just perceived another way. Confusing, for sure, he should have taken a proper training … but now he knew that he, Special Agent Ben Nakamoto, ceased to exist. All that was left of him was his duty to serve the emperor. Where was the emperor? Tokyo? Washington? He was not sure and it did not bother him.

Do your sacred duty and kill the traitors … then the sweet rest will come until the master demands your sword again. His world had become beautifully simple, like a Zen garden.

Baby, Kulagin, the big Texan and that traitor coming straight from the emperor's court had to die, not because Nakamoto hated them—he did not any more—but because the celestial ruler needed them dead. And he would do his work gladly, the faithful samurai, no matter what might happen to his worthless body.

Chapter 35

Even the Metropolitan Opera's chief chore-
ographer could not have arranged this happening better. By luck rather than skill, the
elements of the wedding event were falling
into place like acts of a theatrical production,
each closure opening a new dramatic scene after a
brief intermission. As soon as fatigue had started setting in after the emotional wedding and the celebrants
had slumped in the cockpit, the next act started, her-
alded by the change of lighting.

The red, iron-hot sun dunked into the water behind
the lonely light shining on the chimney at Barber's
Point and darkness started falling rapidly. Halogen
lights broke the sky above Honolulu Port just as we
were passing it, but as soon as we escaped from their
harsh glare, the new glow caught everyone's attention
down the coast. Orange and flickering, it arose past
the fuel storage tanks at the Keehi Small Boat Harbor.

As we were closing, the glow separated into many
moving points of fire concentrated around the harbor's
loading dock. Kulagin looked to me questioningly but
I had no knowledge of this phenomenon.

Faith raised herself from the deck on her elbows,
her excitement overriding fatigue. "Look, Daddy.

What else they are coming up with?" Like a child in a candy story, she *knew* it was another salvo in her honor. And she was right. As I motored through the lagoon in the darkness, we saw the loading dock lit by torches held by Hawaiian gods and princesses, each decked in fabulous lei or maili. It was King Kamekona's royal welcome, prepared according to the best examples of the cruise industry.

As soon as *Magic Carpet*'s ropes looped over the bollards, two lines of torch-bearing Hawaiians formed on the landing and Kamekona appeared at the head of the double file. Still adorned with his spiky crown of green leaves, he wore a ceremonial white loincloth, which looked suspiciously similar to my newly acquired bath towels. He held a ukulele in his hand, the instrument ridiculously small against his big body.

As he serenaded the young couple with his newest composition, I ushered Mr. Kruger, Special Agent Bonner and the godfather, Mr. Dougal, off of my boat. They gathered on the dock in a small group, clearly moved, while I approached Faith. Kulagin jumped out and from the loading dock, extended his arms to the bride.

She took his hands with trust, but anyone looking at the almost two feet difference in level between the deck of Magic Carpet and the loading dock had to worry how she would climb it. Short of a miraculous levitation, her ascent was unlikely. For a confirmed agnostic, I had seen enough miracles that day not to dare to hope for another.

I gathered all my courage and took the position directly behind her, a place inherently dangerous should she slip. Kulagin set his feet firmly on the concrete

and bent low. One, two, three! We all gave a heave-
ho, him pulling, Faith groaning and me pushing her
buttocks upwards. The big girl overcame gravity and
landed firmly on her two feet on the dock, her happy
yelp masked by the noisy crowd on land.

The procession formed, led by Shark who was still
plucking his ukulele and singing in falsetto. Faith and
Boris paraded right behind him, barefoot but with the
poise of royalty. Then the two gentlemen from Texas
marched splendidly, tall and large like two whales,
closely trailed by Agent Bonner, who suddenly felt
completely out of place. The procession was getting
longer as it proceeded, because those of the torchbearers who had been passed joined the parade at its tail.

This well-ordained march came to a sudden stop
when it encountered another force, up till now held
back beyond the security line Kamekona had arranged. A mob of reporters, who got wind of the spectacular end to the kidnapping scare, was waiting with
their cameras and microphones. As if on command,
a salvo of flashes and TV lights went off, triggering a
general melee. The security line broke down and the
two groups mixed into a disorganized whirl of people,
lei, torches and cameras. The excited dint of questions
shouted by the reporters, declarations made by the
wedding guests and sounds of ukulele enveloped the
loading deck, robbing the ceremony of its dignified
pomp.

Then, in the most unanticipated manner, an un-
worldly cry cut through the noise like an archangel's
trumpet announcing the moment of judgment. From
my spot, still on the boat, I could see the panicked
crowd parting in the middle to reveal the small, skin-

ny figure bursting out from the ground like a blood-thirsty ghost in a scary fairytale. He took off, sprinting toward the head of the parade and swinging a shiny sword high in the air.

His clothes ragged and face darkened with soot, I had no inkling who it might be, but he clearly had murder on his mind. It's only when he made another terrifying cry that I recognized Special Agent Naka-moto.

He streaked past Shark and the Kulagins to stop in front of Mr. Dougal. His sword shone high above as he took a swing at the Homeland Security Secretary, who remained frozen like a pillar of salt. Kamekona took a step forward and lashed out at Nakamoto's head with his puny ukulele. The path of the *katana* changed mid-flight and the musical instrument fell to the ground in two pieces, connected only by metal strings.

Now enraged, Nakamoto turned upon Kamekona. But before he could split my friend into two parts as well, another figure, exactly like Shark, appeared be-fore him.

I think I can recreate what went in Nakamoto's brain at that point. The object of his attack multiplied into two identical parts; everybody knows that de-mons can do that. He could slash the left one or the right one; in either case, the remaining ghoul could take him down, leaving his sacred duty pathetically unfinished. In a split second, Ben had chosen to cut through the vital link uniting them, eliminating the demonic pair once and for all. He let his weapon fly in between the two big devils.

At the same time, a bottle, still filled with expensive wine, flew out of Mele's hand and struck Nakamoto's head. Instead of connecting with it in a hard blow, however, it only glanced off his baseball cap. He suffered a moment of confusion but remained upright, if momentarily stunned.

That brief moment of disability dramatically compounded Nakamoto's first mistake, giving Kamekona time to lunge forward with a demolishing stomach jab. The poor samurai crumbled on the ground among bright lights and flashes, while Mele went to recover the bottle, still unbroken, from the hands of the lucky catcher. It could still be returned to Foodland for credit. Even though the credit card was mine, her heart bled over the price of the wine, and she would make damn sure that my financial ruin would not be complete. This is what friends do for friends in Hawaii.

Chapter 36

The genuine and violent end to our simulated and velvet-gloved kidnapping was witnessed by almost every Oahu-based journalist and recorded by a dozen TV cameras. The event's illumination was a little off, as the torchbearers fled to the sides in panic, followed by the marginally slower TV lighting technicians. Consequently, the main stage, where sword-wielding Nakamoto confronted the wedding procession, was left somewhat underexposed. However, a bit of postproduction video tinkering resulted in video clips so dramatic, so fantastic in their imagery, that the scene would be a credit to a billion dollar action movie.

The sudden change of mood from the joyous, innocent-native, fairy tale wedding to the brutal terrifying attack could shake the most cold-hearted audience. The murderous gnome emerging from his underground lair—the *real* evil goblin—shattered the nerves of even the most jaded public worldwide.

Then one must consider the visual effects: The two identical semi-naked giants of Kamekona and Palani—dark, glistening with sweat and threatening—standing firmly and nobly like Roman Praetorian guards against the devilish figure of crazed Nakamoto and his shiny sword. The attacker, jumping with great agility and swishing around his *katana*, must have sent a chill down the spine of every man and woman watching the TV report, as he was closing in on his victim with the speed and shrill sound of a Tomahawk missile.

And who was the object of his attack? Charles Dougal, a pillar of the most patriotic of all the federal agencies. Talk about a political message gushing from this ten-second clip! No money could buy the unforgettable impression of the crazed assassin charging the political soul of America with a deadly instrument in hand, only to be defeated by the heroic patriots.

Ben Nakamoto produced this great image so easily because nothing can beat the truth, if only a cameraman presses his *record* button in time. Professional propagandists of both parties must have dropped their heads in shame; they could not produce such a jewel, no matter how big their budget.

Even a moment of hilarity squeezed itself in the puny few seconds of recording, when Shark engaged Nakamoto's shiny sword with his ridiculously flimsy ukulele.

The next video take had less of a big Hollywood action movie quality; it decidedly switched genre toward a political drama. As soon as the rogue agent slumped onto the ground, deflated by Kamekona's jab, Mr. Bonner, his chief, sprang into action. With a great sense of timing, he shot from the background as soon as his ex-agent was unconscious, and put his foot on the naked weapon, symbolically de-fanging the forces of evil.

He placed Nakamoto, now weakly squirming on the ground, under arrest and called for backup. He reassured his Homeland Security boss and calmed down the stunned Texans. In other words, Bonner did everything right to ensure that he appeared to be in charge of the situation. Indeed, one could not resist the impression that he was the real hero behind the great rescue.

Even Charlie Dougal in his first row seat, had to be totally confused as to who was who in this brief drama. The only clearly bad guy, regrettably an FBI special agent, ended up unconscious on the ground. The rest of the characters appeared to be marionettes controlled by the strings of the savvy puppet master, Honolulu chief Max Bonner. Barely a minute later, after the puppeteer's great public relations performance, that impression was the only reasonable explanation of events.

One had to admire Bonner for his lively mind and ability to improvise. I was sure at this point that he had a great future assured in his organization. Quite possibly, the Keehi event would be the inflection point on his hockey stick trajectory of advancement.

I could not, however, wish him all the success with my heart light and mind relieved of the burden. Although our adventure ended with his great victory, I had the gnawing suspicion that Bonner was harboring some ill feelings toward me. Had I allowed myself a pessimistic point of view, I could have seen Bonner's increasing status and power as the increased likelihood of me getting my well-deserved rewards.

I considered it my good luck that the cameras missed me completely because I was still on *Magic Carpet* when the dramatic sword assault was taking place on the dock. Over the next days, I studiously kept my profile low, doing my best to avoid crossing paths with any journalistic types. Whatever I said, Agent Bonner could and probably would use against me.

To hope for his forgiveness would probably be too much to hope for, but couldn't he simply forget me? The man had to be very busy in the whirlwind of his media success and—I sincerely hoped—he could be promoted out of the Hawaiian Islands, leaving the memory of me behind like a well-used and tattered welcome mat.

This hope was dashed a few days later, when a friendly lady from the hospital's Human Resources office let me discreetly know that certain government agency had requested a copy of my employment records. Apparently, Bonner was not *that* busy.

Lala nodded her white head in the darkness melancholically, when I disclosed the news about the FBI's newly rekindled interest in my person. She thought for a moment and declared, "You know, Horny, I have to pull you out of here. We do it occasionally, when the environment becomes too toxic for our animals. You are an endangered species now. Left in here, you are not going to survive much longer.

"Someday, someone is going to plant a small package of white powder on your boat. They will lock you up and I will have to arrange a jailbreak. My mother, who would be my first associate in this crime, is not getting any younger. It will be so much easier if you go with me voluntarily now, when we still can sail away."

Theoretically, she was right. Every hospital needs an emergency doc and I could make my living wherever I go. But I liked Honolulu! I liked the Queen's and I enjoyed my apartment shared with Caudillo. Best of all, I liked the informal, funny, easygoing folks rambling between Ewa Beach and Waimanalo. Where else could I find a friend like Shark?

Would it be reasonable to count on Bonner's magnanimity and capacity to forgive, the features so characteristic of great leaders? After all, Sister Maria had forgiven my sins.

No, I had to admit with a sigh. Scorpions should not be trusted to respect a bare foot. Lala was right. I should disappear from Bonner's sight. We spent that night poring over maps and searching the Internet. When the sky over the Diamond Head turned pink, we already knew our next address; Guam, a pretty island in the middle of the warm ocean. The important man in Honolulu, or perhaps even on the mainland, would not pay too much attention to Guam and its emergency department.

Lala could check on seals in the Mariana Islands, and I was pretty sure that kids put beads into their noses on Guam as much as in Honolulu or New York. Diabetics get confused with their insulin injections there and cars still crash. They needed me, even if they had not yet heard about Doctor Gorny.

I dragged my feet for a few days, getting goose bumps at the thought of starting the drudgery of paperwork when Lala weighed in again. "I will make it worthwhile for you," she promised with a bawdy wink and suggestive hip grind, seeing the terminal apathy in my eyes. Were I still hesitant, this wink would do it.

We sealed the deal immediately on my couch and I handed in my resignation letter two days later, when Lala moved in on *Magic Carpet* full time.

For sake of complete disclosure, I have to add that in her drive to pull me out of Honolulu, she received support from the least expected direction. While I was still haggling with Lala over dates and the exact meaning of her lascivious wink, I went to visit Agent Nakamoto in his psychiatric ward.

I wouldn't call him my friend, but he had played quite a prominent role in my life recently, therefore I considered it only decent to drop in and see how he was doing. Ben was much better—a bit sedated but clean, well hydrated, smiling, and friendly. He did not invoke a national security even once, but—truth to be known—it was not his concern anymore, as he had lost his job at the FBI

I thought it would upset a dedicated agent like him, but he confided with a joyful glint in his eyes, "You know, Doctor Gorny, I figured out an even better job." He twitched his black brush of a mustache and kept me in suspense for a long moment, while I was trying to imagine him making sushi, driving a taxi or even opening a school of martial arts.

" … Politics! A nurse told me that with my name I would be a shoo-in in state politics." He enjoyed my shock for a moment, his eyes glistening with pride. Then he added thoughtfully, "There is so much mess to straighten up! First, I will run for mayor of Honolulu."

At that point, I became firmly committed to starting the implementation of our moving plans as soon as possible, thinking, what if he wins?

My consolation prize for parting ways with Honolulu was seeing Kamekona thrive. His biggest crime had been purged from the judicial system due to Mr. Bonner's good services, and he had received a wholesale pardon for the rest of other, small-time, misdemeanors filling the two pages of his rap sheet. How else could the grateful nation treat this hero? His true character could be seen by millions, revealed in a short moment of drama on Keehi's loading dock.

He was not worried about Bonner's vengeance. Shark felt that his *Water Whispers* offered a lot of protection against any underhanded actions and, if thing turned really tight, he could always move under his brother's wings in Waimanalo, where they felt somewhat exterritorial to any current *haole* administration.

After every TV station on the planet had played his Bruce Lee performance at the Keehi sword scene at least three times, Shark received many offers of a Hollywood career. Seriously, any entertainment executive who did not immediately approach Kamekona with a serious offer should be fired on spot. The man's physique was complemented by a charm many female tourists would love to testify about, and millions more would gladly cough up ten bucks to spend two hours in his photogenic presence.

A few serious propositions to join this or that political movement came as well, though not with the speed characteristic of a private industry.

Shark turned down all the offers without even reading the attached contracts. His life was already arranged in a perfect fashion and all those proposals could only disrupt the finely arranged balance of his days and nights. Surfing and music remained his priorities. Besides, he decided not to take "this chemical shit" that was at least partly responsible for his Herculean body. He would hate to disappoint his fans, as his awesome physique would inevitably be declining toward the proportions more usual among the human race.

Mele was also strongly in favor of staying in the world she knew. She had a good job at the Foodland and intended to keep it. There was even some loose talk about her being promoted into the ranks of junior management, once she had sorted out her educational shortcomings. Mele made every effort to ensure that the moment of fame didn't go to Shark's head. Whatever her arguments and debating techniques were, she emerged as a force powerful enough to anchor Shark firmly on the shores of Oahu.

However, they did advance in life. Shark's sudden fame and the steady trickle of money from Mele's retail career generated the financial conditions necessary to allow them to move *Water Whisper* into a slip in the Keehi Marina.

How did they manage to navigate the three hundred yards of deep water in their leaky bucket? For years, it had rested its unworthy bottom on the sand surrounding the mangrove island that Shark and Male called home. In my opinion, the sand's precious support was the only reason *Water Whisper* did not quietly submerge under the waves, and now this successful leap across the deep water ... This miraculous journey was as much a mystery as the inexplicable results of the boat inspection that *Water Whisper* had to undergo in order to be admitted to the marina.

I knew for the fact that her motor was not quite right as it was missing an engine block, because that's what Shark occasionally used as an anchor for his dinghy. And her sails could be used to catch baitfish ... yet a certificate of seaworthiness had been issued. Both those fortuitous events can be only credited to this uniquely Hawaiian magic that makes life so good in the Islands. As an emergency doc, I had to admit my imperfect judgment on more than one occasion and, once again, I bowed my head in humility when confronted with these marvels.

Whichever way they made it into the slip, their lifestyle has improved tremendously. The undignified morning dinghy runs to the public toilet gave way to stately strolls, and Mele's commute time to the Foodland store had been cut by twenty minutes. She started taking classes at a community college, the position of assistant manager firmly in her sights.

Shark, after his brief brush with fame, holds a court once a week on Olelo, a Hawaii community access TV. He plays his newest ukulele hits and sings his songs that, he claims, are in the noble language of King Kamehameha and Queen Liliuokalani. I don't know anyone with a Hawaiian vocabulary exceeding twenty words so we cannot verify his claim, but we all agree that his creations sound very authentic and are strangely moving.

He fell out with Big Joe after that famous stint we had in front of the Royal Hawaiian Hotel, but he takes occasional surfing students on individual basis. Mele does the recruitment, collects his instructor's fees and provides the security, sitting in a folding chair at the water's edge with a pair of binoculars in her hands. Shark understands well that any of his finger slippages will be noted and properly dealt with.

Chapter 37

Faith Kruger and Boris Kulagin. … Without them, Shark's and my story would be empty and insignificant like an empty can of Heineken, crushed and abandoned under a bus stop bench. They swooped into Honolulu from opposite parts of the world like big ravenous birds, innocent in their intentions but threatening like elephants because of their size and ambition. When these two supercharged bodies fused, a major energy release was bound to happen. Kamekona and I got caught up in this dangerous phenomenon, and when we emerged—amazingly unharmed—we felt enriched by getting to know those two bigger than life characters.

Before a shiny Learjet carried them away—it was not a submarine that had brought "Baby" to Honolulu, after all—we had resolved to cultivate our unusual friendship. Was there any other group of buddies in the world made of a Texan billionaire heiress, a Russian tank commander, a Hawaiian beach boy who actually might be a prince, and a Chicago-born emergency doc? Not likely. We were a unique band and we decided to celebrate it at least once a year.

Our first reunion took place in Honolulu, about a

year after the pirate wedding, when Lala and I had relaxed a bit from our worries of Bonner's retribution.
For many months, nobody saw the man in Honolulu
and we thought he had been promoted somewhere far
away, hopefully as far as Washington D.C.

Faith and Boris flew in from Texas in her papa's
personal jet. Kulagin immediately invited Shark for
a jamming session—ukulele, balalaika and a lot of
beer. I could not participate in the opening of this important event. I abstained not only due to lack of any
musical talent, but also because the airline had mis-
placed Lala's luggage. Her folks picked her up while
I waited at the airport for the investigations to con-
clude. Having nothing better to do, I looked over the
shiny bird that had brought the Kulagins. There were
no Russian markings on it.

"What's wrong with you?" I asked Boris, once I
caught my friends relaxing their artistic fingers in the
hotel's bar, before they could start some serious work.
"You can't afford your own jet?"

"Maybe the next time, comrade," Boris told me.
"I agree. It's kinda embarrassing to fly in this boring
limo. It's bad for my image. A Cold War warrior like
me should be swooping into Honolulu in a 'tank bust-
er' like Sukhoi *shturmovik*. But parts for Suhhoi could
be hard to come by in Houston, so I might have to settle for something like a ground-assault Mustang P-51."

His business was doing great. Boris had purchased
a T-72 heavy tank, his favorite, from a certain sergeant
in Vladivostok who had gotten himself into card debts.
"That's Faith's dowry," he slapped his wife on the butt
and she blushed, overtaken by a surge of happiness.

Boris decided to call his tank school "The Houston

Tank Brigade." He admitted that his heart was aching for the "Red Army School of Tank Warfare," but he had to compromise for political reasons. "Some idiots are still not quite aware that the Cold War has been over for a while," he grumbled. The Red Army name might delay his school's license on grounds of national security.

"The truth is, my friends," Boris was looking at us seriously, his sobriety incompatible with the number of vodka glasses he had emptied, "there will never be a better tank training than the Red Army used to provide. The surviving students would do anything not to be retained for remedial education."

Boris could personally recall a colleague of his, a poor student admittedly, who upon failing his final exams, wrote an application to fly into space as a subject of biological experimentation. But they failed him on this front too. Too big, they said. A dog will do.

Young and ambitious Texan executives had to sign up six months ahead for the privilege of getting sworn at and insulted in English and Russian. He could buy another tank and open an extra class for enrollment, as the Vladivostok sergeant's luck did not turn for the better, but doubling the number of graduates might rob the school of its image of exclusivity.

The colonel grasped the concepts of marketing with great speed and ease. His natural talents, augmented by years of studious perusal of tank warfare field manuals, allowed him to quickly uncover the uncomplicated nature of capitalism. "Why, you do what they are willing to pay you for, that simple!"

But this is not to say he didn't experience a culture shock. In fact, he was still struggling to adjust to his students' outlook at life. "They eat rotten potatoes three times a day ... and they riot if the food gets too good," Boris complained. "It makes the training less authentic, they say. I have to keep the stinky slop for three days outside in the sun, before it gets bad enough for them. It just drives up the costs," Kulagin sighed, "but what can you do? They pay for it."

So he kicks—literally and metaphorically—their asses as they crawl through the hot, red dust, just as he would his recruits' in Russia. No more, no less; fair is fair. However, unlike his Soviet conscripts, the young Texan gentlemen do not have the common sense to hide in shade whenever they can get away with it. And faking exercises is below their ethical standards.

In effect, in addition to being their tormentor, Boris has to be their nanny as well. "Have you drunk your fucking water, *proclataya sobaka*, you damn dog?" Colonel Kulagin has to roar at some beetroot-faced, pencil-neck every day. A man of his experience knows that seeing a student tripping over his shoelaces is a bad sign; the damn fool is a minute away from having heat stroke. The school will have to pay for an expensive ambulance ride.

"Sometimes, I feel I work harder than in Mother Russia," he confessed with a tinge of nostalgia. "They still have not discovered how to malinger injuries in order to get into the comfort of nurse's air-conditioned office." He hung his head low, overcome by depression and possibly feeling the early effects of the booze.

Then his head jerked up and he looked at me brightly, struck by a new idea. "Listen, Doc, how about you joining me? I'll stop worrying about the damned recruits and, together, we might offer a new line of training. A new profit center ..." Kulagin's business vocabulary kept pace with his understanding of the capitalist economy.

"How would you like to be a professor, teach something like ... say ... battlefield health care. No, no, it sounds so wimpy ... completely not fitting into the school's hard ass image. How about a course titled: *Wounded Warrior Care*? You could start making some real money!"

He looked at me with high hopes then almost immediately waved his hand dismissively. "You and your liberty ideas! You just don't understand what the smell of diesel and dirt in one's mouth does to a man's soul. You have no idea how it elevates the male ego to a completely new level. We make the world a better place!"

For their efforts, the graduates of the Houston Tank Brigade receive a diploma bearing a big picture of a dangerous-looking gun turret. This document, along with the battlefield camaraderie of other scions of the Texan elite, is fast becoming an entry ticket into Houston's corridors of power.

Tough school and damn expensive, but overall it's a fabulous deal, everyone agrees. Boris is warming up to the idea of buying a proper ground-assault aircraft for himself. Grudgingly, he might take a Mustang P-51, not bad on technical grounds, but a pilot ... Frankly, Kulagin would not put his life into hands other than ones trained to fly a MIG or Sukhoi.

The only concern, my friend confessed, even if it was a bit embarrassing, was old Kruger's impatient attitude to procreation. The old bastard got it into his head that for all those billions he was going to leave, and pretty soon, he had a right for a grandson, *now*.

Just like having an option on stock.

His kind enquiries about the condition of Boris's prostate, his stupid faces whenever the question of childcare in his business empire arose, these were easy enough to ignore. What penetrated Kulagin's psychological armor were the dumb jokes about a tank firing blank rounds.

"Let me tell you, Chris," inflamed, Boris threw back another shot of vodka, "Nikita Semionovitch Rostovskij, may he rest in peace, the old drunk, was my first instructor in the officer's school. He drove his T 34 all the way from Stalingrad to Berlin. If you wanted to find out any obscure fact about tanks, you just needed to ask him, but loudly, because he was deaf like most *tankistas*.

"He told us what you would not find in any history book; they had a lot of duds in their ammunition. Every time a gunner fired his cannon, he never knew if the bloody thing was going to explode on target, as it should, or was it going to bounce of a German panzer like a rubber ball or perhaps would blow up before leaving the barrel, ending the war for this particular crew. It gave the whole new meaning to the term Russian roulette."

He looked at me with the intensity announcing that the point of his anecdote was arriving. "So I am asking you—did they make it to Berlin? Yes, they did! Because, as Nikita Semionovitch used to say, 'Blank or no blank, you keep shooting until you get your target or your barrel bursts!'"

He looked down below his now slightly paunchy belly. "My barrel is still quite all right."

I did not have many one-on-one conversations

Alex Modzelewski

with "Baby", but Lala told me that she was very much in love with her husband and happily participating in the cannonade. I can only admire the old soldier's spirit and wish him one lucky shot.

Separated by thousands of miles, we all live our own lives, but we do exchange e-mails between out re-unions. "Chris," Boris Ossipovitch wrote me recently, "I'll never understand you people. Those executives never seem to have enough abuse. Now, they demand to have a regular Red Army hazing. I will charge a few hundred dollars extra, no problem there. I have already hired some local hooligans to do the face slap-ping for me, but tell me, is this something about your American mothers that makes you people enjoy mis-treatment so much?"

"You are cheap, Boris," I answered. "A thousand, not a dollar less. And don't worry about the ethics of abuse. We love to get slapped around, kicked and lied to, as long as it is patriotic and manly. Ura!"

He thanked me; the thousand-dollar fee has been swallowed without any resistance. Then he returned to his old idea— if he branched out and opened the Pa-cific Submarine Warfare Center in San Diego, would I sign up as a professor? There would be none of the red dust I had objected to. The school would be right on the oceanfront and maybe I could finally afford a real boat.

Chapter 38

The world is not that big after all, Lala and I discovered. It still takes a while to sail from Guam to Palau and even more to Japan or Thailand, but wherever we go, the same landscape emerges after the first few days, when everything is so new and exotic.

Orders and restriction—all backed up with stern penalties—fill most of the free time left in the lives of our new friends, leaving the exhausted subjects little time and energy for reflection. Often, they feel as if they are standing at the edge of abyss, saved only at the last moment by a mysterious and not quite legal favor. Is there method in this madness?

As an emergency room physician, I meet the folks who harass our friends. Big and small officials land in my emergency room, some having crashed that big Mercedes Benz that came as a job perk, others having fallen into a pothole while raiding a farmer's market.

They are good patients, I must say. Well fed, clean and—unlike our friends—they are always covered with excellent government-provided health insurance. Moreover, they often have favors to offer and dispense them generously with an understanding wink. A special parking permit, a hidden express pathway through the labyrinth of government red tape, a nullification of a speeding ticket ... those small perks certainly make one's life easier.

I accept those tips with an uncomfortable smile, even if Lala calls me a graft-seeking scum, because they are the second currency in circulation, the informal part of my remuneration. Personal favors, debts of gratitude and old obligations are remembered, stored and exchanged when necessary. They are the saving grace that rescues our friends now and then. The guys who issue this second currency wield as much power as cash paying employers, even if their payroll is less conspicuous.

Is this way of life our future or a thing of our past? I keep asking myself. The naughty kid inside me, who grew up in Chicago, just shrugs. "It's just the way things are, always have been and how they will continue. Ask Sister Joanna, you moron; there might be a special tense in English grammar for this kind of *forever* situation." And then he wisecracks, "You don't like it, go somewhere else!"

Actually, this is what Lala and I have been doing. We still hope to find the place where making enough money is all one needs to live. I would really like it because I know how to earn my living, while I am hopelessly clumsy in those wink-and-favor situations.

Until then, I appreciate the benefits of being a migratory bird. For example, we sailed into Suva port in Fiji archipelago, where I was to do a six-month stint in the city hospital's emergency room.

A six-and-a-half foot tall, uniformed officer, by his size somewhat similar to Kamekona, boarded my boat. He looked us over, with great difficulty restrained himself from touching Lala's white top, glanced indifferently upon my work permit and smashed his stamp into our passports. "Watch those Indians," he growled over his fearsome black moustache and stomped outside.

A few hours later, a soft-handed Indian hospital administrator kept my papers five inches from his myopic eyes, lingered over them a few minutes, then sighed. "You must be very careful with those Fijians, Doctor. Completely unpredictable."

During the next six months, I saw them both in action, joyfully harassing their compatriots, but they did not waste any of their valuable time on me. I belonged to the outside world. I was the resource to be used when necessary but not the subject of their rule. I was not their peasant.

I like it this way. Being somebody's serf was never my ambition, no matter how benevolent my master might be. I don't mind being ignored by authorities. Lala understands my feelings, she says, but honestly, she is more attuned to the seal and dolphin politics and way of life. They are very reasonable in their uncivilized ways, she assures me. They eat, make love and live their lives rather peacefully. Occasionally, they do beat on their families and neighbors, but hardly ever without a good reason.

But I miss my brotherly evenings with Kamekona who instinctively shared my attitude toward higher powers. We would sit at Keehi, or at the Ala Moana Park, sipping our beer, saying nothing. Then out of the blue, Shark would say something deep, like: "They want my soul, butt fuckers." Nothing more.

No need for him to elaborate because I would know

exactly his sentiment. Someone demanded money from him, or threatened him with court, or did something else that could be fixed only if Kamekona sold his soul, abandoning his surfing and his music. Mele would go into a tizzy, scrambling feverishly to comply with the demands, but it's not so easy to shake down a guy like Shark, the individual willing to overlook the pathetic little problems of daily life in order to satisfy his spiritual needs.

I would say nothing, contemplating the conflict between one's need to hold on his values and the predicament of satisfying the desire to eat, have shelter and buy pretty things. This contradiction is irresolvable, like squaring a circle. The best one can do is to achieve a painful compromise, a temporary and unsatisfactory solution.

"We are all whores, my friend, swapping our souls for money," I would say ten minutes later, and he would understand immediately that the nature of work we happen to do is irrelevant. It is the act of exchanging one's non-renewable resource of time for the soon-to- be-spent money. This is what places us in the same category as ladies of the night.

We enjoyed each other's company, because our minds had been stitched from the same kind of fabric, the kind of material that wears well, is easy to maintain but does not look too glamorous.

"Jeans?" Kamekona would read my mind, and I would nod, without saying a word. He knew instinctively that the fabric of our souls was not only tough but, in addition, did not cling to any shape it was stretched on. No political formation or official icon—that people like Bonner promote—can invoke our blind adherence. His own man, they used to say about people like us, and once it was a term of respect. No one owns us, and if we grant the ownership rights to our lives, the recipients are people we love, no one else. But we are tolerated and welcome because we are useful like blue canvas trousers and our services are needed. It's just we won't stick to any butt.

Lala and I swing by Oahu once a year—still on *Magic Carpet*, since I decided not to offer my services to the Pacific Submarine Warfare Center—to visit her parents. A few weeks of sailing together on a small boat puts a couple in the most intimate circumstance possible. A hundred little things that escape notice in a suburban marriage become the shared knowledge, especially if one partner has a supersensitive nose, as I do.

Somewhere between Guam and Oahu, I was confronted with the view of Lala sniffling over her family album. The brave girl was rubbing her eyes red in an effort to hide her emotional imbalance. A strange thing it was, as Lala is an emotional athlete.

I went out to check on the sails and started considering possible causes of her distress. I would not like to sound sexist here, but when a young woman presents with a new and unexplained symptom, especially if she lives with a man, an emergency doc has an instinctive suspicion of pregnancy. That would be the first thing to investigate. On further reflection, I recalled, we might have missed a period. My nose would know.

But Lala did not declare her condition and I did not prod. We were only a day away from Oahu.

Once we checked into her folks' home, Lala and

Alex Modzelewski

her mother immediately went to a pharmacy after a short private conference, while the old white-haired captain, wrapped in his beach towel, took me behind his tool shed, where he was experimenting with photovoltaic panels.

"Wanted to tell you something, Chris," he said. "Before ... I didn't bother ... you screw up, you suffer the consequences. My Layne could have whoever she wanted, like that ..." He snapped his fingers, and it occurred to me that he was not such a nice man as I had assumed.

"But now things are changing, I am being advised by my wife." He looked at me with suspicion. "You know what I am talking about?"

I grimaced, meaning: yes and no, I know, but will not admit until officially notified.

"Those Slavic women ..." He started tentatively, without further introductory remarks, as he was cleaning the gecko droppings from the panel with a corner of his towel. "I did well ... and Lala is just like her mother. Though she looks more like me, don't you think so?" He looked at me hopefully, rubbing his white scalp.

"Strong like a tugboat and stubborn ... like a mule they say here in America, but any Finn will tell you, there is nothing more persistent than a bear trying to get to the kitchen scraps a lazy cook left in a garbage bucket outside.

"Speaking of a bear, these women are very loyal, but the other side of this admirable quality is, they have an almost hysterical attachment to the concept of monogamy." He looked at me meaningfully.

"Having grown up in the liberal Scandinavian tradi-

288

tion," Captain Tuukkanen started soldering his panel wires in a parallel circuit, "my wife's ferocious reaction to my being friendly to another young woman shook me in my boots early in our marriage."

He looked at me with the distress twisting his face even now, many years later. "And for what? For giving friendly advice to a nice French lady about some Finnish delicatessen, herring in oil."

"Chris," he gave me a sorrowful look, "Kasia saved me from more troubles than I can remember, and Lala will pull you out from the bottom floor of a sinking ship ... but if she catches you doing another woman on the side. ... You just jump out of the boat and swim, man. And pray she is not standing on deck with a harpoon in her hand."

At this point, I decided to never joke about herring in oil; some things carry meaning far beyond their utilitarian character. They should be left respected and undisturbed.

"On the other hand," the old Finn cheered himself up, "they are such a handful that even a horny bastard like you might not have that much energy left over."

I had almost forgotten to mention Agents Bonner and Nakamoto in these last words, probably because my mother told me once not to say bad things about people.

For his expert management of the sensational rescue of a certain Texas billionaire and his daughter in Honolulu, Bonner was promoted into a position that was not divulged to the public for the sake of national security. I think he is far away from Hawaii and that's good enough for me; though if I had any say in this matter, I might suggest Ulan Bator, Mongolia, as his next station.

Ben Nakamoto, a civilian now—and still looking for a nice Japanese girl—is crazy no more, although he skips his medications on most days, as they interfere with his creativeness. Nowadays, he is well regarded as an unconventional out-of-the box thinker. He didn't make it into the Mayor's armchair yet, but he heads a major sub-committee in the State Senate.

More and more I am persuaded by Lala's argument that seals figured out the happy way of living long time ago—come to a beach to socialize and rest, but the rest of life is best spent in or on the water. For us humans, I would also add: we need to land from time to time to fill the tanks and stock the pantry. We may have to whore away a bit of our time to pay for the supplies, making sure we do not get too greedy. But for the rest of life, there is no place like the wild ocean. Sharks and barracudas hunt there but the Bonners and Nakamotos of this world would rather stick to the firm land.

This story is closed but I cannot leave at that because a new and wonderful development has come to my attention. After all, I have found out, one doesn't have to be a hermit to enjoy the freedom offered by the big open water. People started migrating out of the land-based jurisdictions to make floating communities, which are subject to no one's rule. They call it seasteading. I like the name and the idea. I will have a closer look. They must suffer broken bones and heart attacks like everybody else; they will need an emergency doc.